A Five Fates
Prequel

BROKEN THINGS

LINDSEY BROUNSTEIN

Cover design by MiblArt

Map by Cartographybird Maps

Editing by Between the Lines Editorial

First edition 2025

ISBN 978-1-964237-07-7 (paperback)

ISBN 978-1-964237-08-4 (hardcover)

ISBN 978-1-964237-06-0 (ebook)

www.lindseybrounstein.com

CONTENT WARNINGS

Thank you for your interest in *Broken Things*, a Five Fates prequel. This is a fantasy novel intended for readers 18 years and older. It contains strong language, mild sexual situations, and violence. Specific content warnings are listed below. If you'd rather not see the content warnings, you can skip this page.

This story includes themes and descriptions of events that may not be suitable for everyone. These include:

- physical violence and murder

- mild sexual situations (fade-to-black; no graphic descriptions)

- emotional abuse (by a parent) and emotional manipulation

- mentions of amputation

- ableism

- alcohol abuse

- depression and PTSD

- suicidal thoughts and ideation

- surviving a natural disaster (flash flood)

If at any point—including right now—you need to put the book down (whether for a little while or forever), please do so. Take care of yourself, friend.

THE KNOWN WORLD
MAPPED IN THE PRESENT AGE
CAPITAL CITIES
MINOR CITIES
NOTABLE TOWNS
SNOWFELD
THE WILDS
LOSTWARD
ARMATHAIN
WHITEHOLLOW
VALDA
CLOUD BAY
AETHERANN'S REACH
PORT MERRICK
THE CRESCENT MOUNTAINS
AETHIR
WESTHOLD
GOETH
THE MISTVALE MOUNTAINS
WERYN
FORDRYN
THE SOUTHERN ISLES
NEOMA

PYRRAH
EMBER DEPTHS
EMBERCLIFF
KIREKWALL
THE MOONTIDE SEA
KYLERIA
BREMMARAN
RAVENSPORT
FALLWOOD
BROOKSHIRE
THE RED FOREST
DRAHKONIA
FINNEGAN'S FORDE
SOUTHREACH
TAERNFANE
SOUTHPORT

Pronunciation Guide

Aetherann: AY-ther-ahn
Aethir: AY-theer
Aethirian: ay-THEER-ee-an
Ainam: EYE-num
Bremmaran: BREM-mer-ahn
Cora Sylus: KOR-uh SY-lis
Drystan Kalon: DRIS-ten KAL-en
Kyleria: ky-LEER-ee-ah
Lanara: lah-NAH-rah
Noel Torin: NOLE TOR-in
Pyrannis: pie-RAH-nis
Taerna: TARE-nah
Valda: VAHL-dah
Verity Corallan: VAIR-i-tee KOR-uh-lahn
Vire: VY-er
Weryn: WARE-in

A NOTE FROM THE AUTHOR

Broken Things is a prequel to the Five Fates series. While the events in this story take place prior to the main series, it is recommended that you read *Fire's Hand, Fate's Heart* first. If you choose to read *Broken Things* as your introduction to the Five Fates series, please note that some elements of the story are written with the assumption that readers will already have some familiarity with the world.

This story includes mentions of amputation, as well as characters living with physical injuries and disabilities. As a person without disabilities, I have worked with a sensitivity reader with the intention of making these depictions as thoughtful as possible. Drystan's and Verity's journeys are uniquely theirs, and are not intended to be representative of the lived experiences of people with disabilities.

For those on their own journey of self-discovery and healing.
May this book be a comforting hand on your shoulder.

Keep going.

CHAPTER 1

"Hey, dipshit! Get your ass out here!"

Drystan Kalon shook his blond hair out of his eyes as he raised his head from where he'd been hunched over documents for the last two hours. He stretched his ink-stained fingers as his older brother, Gray, stuck his head through the doorway.

"Time for your lessons." Gray was tying his brown hair out of his face. He was Drystan's oldest half brother, although their shared father, Phillip Kalon, had always insisted the boys think of themselves as full brothers.

There's nothing more important than family, their father always said. *And you boys are all family.*

"What're you working on?" Gray craned his neck. "Forging travel papers?" His rough face screwed up in disgust. "That can wait."

"No, it can't." Drystan nodded toward the paperwork on the desk. "Dad's gonna kick my ass if I don't finish this by dinner."

"Dad wants me to start training you so you can go on jobs with him," Gray said. "Your forgeries suck anyway."

"They do not." Drystan sat up a little straighter as Gray's words clicked into place. "Wait, go on jobs? With Dad?"

"Did I fucking stutter?" Gray headed down the hall. "Come on."

Drystan scrambled out from behind the desk, his mind reeling. "What training?" he called after his brother. "What kind of jobs?"

Drystan had always known that their father's business—the family business—wasn't exactly typical. He'd been helping in small ways since he was little. He was running messages and deliveries at six, and helping forge papers by the time he was twelve. But any kid in town could run deliveries for a couple of copper pennies and a pat on the head. Drystan wasn't a kid anymore! He was fifteen years old, and he wanted more. He saw the pride on his father's face whenever one of the crew pulled a big score. He wanted that. He wanted to be a part of the family business with his brothers.

He wanted his father to be proud of him.

Drystan followed Gray downstairs, through the kitchen, and outside. The midwinter sun was climbing toward midday, and Gray hadn't even bothered to grab his coat, despite the layer of snow covering the ground.

"Do we have to do this now?" Drystan complained, rubbing his hands along his arms to stave off the chill already creeping in.

"If you didn't spend so much time inside staring at those stupid books, you'd be used to the outdoors by now."

Irritation flickered through Drystan. "What are we even doing out here?"

Gray smiled, slow and wicked, as he cracked his knuckles.

✹

"Don't tuck your thumb in like that or you'll break it."

Drystan corrected the position of his thumb, moving it to the outside of his fist as Gray instructed.

Gray checked Drystan's form and tsked. "Come on, Dris," he said sternly. "Do you want to be the baby forever or what? You've got to know this stuff so you can start pulling your weight around here. You're fourteen years old, for fuck's sake."

Gray was well aware that Drystan was already fifteen. Drystan knew Gray was only doing it to get a rise out of him. He tried to ignore him, but a huff slipped out.

"Come on, this is serious," Gray said. He gave Drystan a shove. "If you want Dad to take you seriously, you need to learn this."

Drystan shook out his shoulders. His father had hardly taken an interest in him, short of irritated glares whenever he caught Drystan lost in a book. But once Drystan's voice had lowered and he'd hit a couple of rapid growth spurts, his father had begun looking at him as though he were some type of problem to be solved.

While his half brothers had taken after their father with their ashy brown hair and rough features, they'd all taken after their mother with their shorter, thinner builds. But Drystan had been the opposite, taking his blond hair and green eyes from his mother, and inheriting Phillip Kalon's height and broad shoulders. At fifteen, Drystan was already taller than all three of his older half brothers.

"Try it again," Gray said, holding his hands up like targets.

Drystan threw another punch, striking Gray's open palm.

"Better. Alright, now that you know how to throw a punch, the fastest way to learn how to fight is by fighting." He rocked back and balled his hands into fists. "Try to hit me."

"What?" Drystan dropped his arms in time for Gray's fist to connect with his jaw. It wasn't anywhere close to Gray's full strength, but it still stung.

"Protect your face."

"What the hells, Gray!" But Drystan's complaint was met with another punch at half strength.

"Don't drop your guard."

Drystan cocked his arm back and threw a wild punch. Gray dodged it with a short sidestep.

"Don't let them know what you're going to do," Gray said. "I saw that coming a mile away."

They tramped circles in the snow for the next hour as Drystan tried to hit Gray, all while the oldest Kalon brother took shot after shot at the youngest. By the time Drystan returned to the house, he was sweat-soaked and fuming.

He rushed past the sitting room where his mother sat near the fireplace in her favorite chair, an embroidery hoop in her hands. He aimed for the stairs.

"Drystan?"

He paused with a foot on the first step. ". . . Yeah?"

His mother cleared her throat softly.

"I mean, yes?"

"Come here, sweetheart."

Drystan turned and trudged into the sitting room. His mother beckoned him over with a graceful wave of her hand, and he crouched in front of her.

She lifted Drystan's chin. "What happened, sweetheart?" she asked. Her thumb brushed across the split in his lip.

Drystan winced. "Gray was teaching me how to fight." His hands clenched into fists. "I was pretty shit at it," he admitted.

His mother tutted at him gently as her hand moved to stroke his hair. "You'll get better with practice, if that's something you want."

"I do! Gray said Dad'll take me on jobs if I learn."

His mother's hand paused for only a moment. "Are you certain that's what you still want?"

"Of course!" It was all he'd ever wanted. "There's nothing more important than family," Drystan repeated dutifully.

"You're right," his mother said, ruffling his hair. She smiled, but it didn't reach her eyes.

Drystan pushed forward. "I'm sick of being left behind all the time. I want to run grifts like Thomas." His second oldest brother was able to talk anyone into just about anything, it seemed. He was the best looking of the Kalon brothers and everyone loved him. Drystan always admired how his work seemed so effortless.

"If those are the types of jobs you want to go on, you should be learning from Thomas, not Gray."

Drystan sighed, crossing his legs to sit on the floor at his mother's feet. "I know, but Dad told Gray to teach me."

"No one said it has to be formal training. Watch what he does. Watch how he moves through the world. Learn everything you can from him."

She always looked out for him in her way. Always gave him good advice. "Alright, Ma," he said. "I will."

"That's a good lad."

She picked up the embroidery she'd been working on. "Now go do your archery practice."

"My arms are killing me and there's snow on the ground," Drystan groaned. He just wanted to curl up with a book and pretend nothing else existed for a little while.

"Archery first," she repeated. "Settle your mind. Then you can read."

She knew him too well.

Drystan stood and grabbed his coat before plodding back outside and heading toward the small outbuilding in the back where he kept his bow.

Half an hour later, the straw target had a cluster of arrows in the center. A couple outliers stuck out of the snow a short distance away. His mother was right, as she often was. The slow, methodical motions always quieted his mind, even though his arms burned with each draw.

Most of what Drystan learned was at the order of his father, but archery had been at his mother's behest. She wanted something that would teach him discipline, but would also give him somewhere to focus his energy. It was something that belonged only to them—to Drystan and his mother.

"That's a tight grouping," a deep voice boomed across the yard.

Drystan turned as his father strode toward him, his long wool coat billowing as he moved. He was dressed in his finest business attire, a dark suit with gold buttons at the collar and the cuff. Gold and jeweled rings glittered on his fingers in the waning sunlight. He must have just come back from an important meeting in town.

"You've gotten pretty good with that thing," his father said as he came to stand beside his son.

A swell of pride filled Drystan's chest, even as he stood in his father's shadow. "Thank you, sir."

Phillip Kalon's dark eyes darted to the swollen, scabbed-over split in Drystan's lip, then out across the yard. He waved a hand toward the target. "Don't let me interrupt."

His father had never watched him practice before, and the pressure to impress him settled over Drystan as he raised the bow. He was suddenly acutely aware of every movement, every hesitation.

"Do you see that knot in the yew tree on the far side of the yard?" his father asked before Drystan could loose his next arrow.

Drystan kept the bowstring taut. "Yes, sir." The knot was huge and easily visible from this distance, although it was twice as far as his current target.

His father muttered a quiet *hmm* before interrupting again. "Could you hit it from here?"

Drystan hesitated only a moment before he switched targets, angled the bow to account for the increased distance, and fired. The arrow sailed over the straw target and struck the yew tree's knot dead in the center. Drystan's smile stretched from ear to ear as he turned to face his father.

Phillip Kalon nodded solemnly. Not a hint of approval. "Again," he said.

Drystan shrugged out of his coat, not willing to take a chance on the fabric impeding his range of motion. When his next shot struck the knot again, his father selected a new target. And another, and another, until the yard was littered with arrows embedded into various objects. Drystan had just collected the handful of arrows from his original straw target and returned to his father's side when a hawk landed on one of the heavy branches of the old yew tree.

His father pointed. "Now, there," he said. "The bird."

Drystan fumbled the arrow as he drew it from the quiver. "What?"

"The bird is your next target."

Drystan swallowed hard. He'd never aimed at a living thing before. His fingers tightened around the arrow, eyes never leaving the hawk as he nocked and drew back the bowstring. He needed to impress his father. He wanted the chance to be more than just the errand boy who sometimes scribbled forgeries in the back room. If he could be part of his father's crew, he would finally feel like part of the family.

He took aim, the hawk's body the smallest target his father had given him so far. The bird's head twitched. Drystan held his breath.

A branch snapped somewhere in the underbrush and the hawk took flight. Drystan moved his bow, leading the bird as it flew.

The arrow loosed. The hawk fell.

Drystan stood in the circle of packed snow and released the breath he'd been holding. He stared at the space in the distance where the hawk had been.

Phillip Kalon clapped his son on the back. "Ha! Outstanding!" he cried. He started across the snow-covered yard.

Drystan followed, the bow clutched in his hand. His chest tightened. Excitement was part of it—excitement at his father's praise—but there was something else there too, though he didn't let himself examine it too closely. It was probably just nerves, in any case.

"You'll continue training with Gray daily," his father said, not even checking to make sure Drystan was behind him. "And I will be taking over your archery instruction. Any free time will be spent socializing with your brothers or the rest of the crew. You want to be a part of the crew, you're damn well going to act like it. No more hiding in your room with your nose in a book, understand?"

Drystan jogged after his father. "Yeah, alright," he mumbled, his thoughts still focused on how the hawk had dropped from the sky.

His father spun and Drystan nearly barreled into him. "What did you say?" he barked.

"Y-yes, sir."

"Good." Phillip Kalon continued across the field in silence.

Drystan found the hawk near the raspberry bushes. His arrow had pierced straight through its chest. He stared down at the tiny, unmoving body. It didn't look real, the way its wings had splayed out when it fell. But it *was* real. It had been alive only a few minutes ago. It had been beautiful as it soared through the sky.

Until Drystan killed it.

His stomach twisted, bile rising in his throat.

"That was a hell of a shot," his father said, coming up beside him. "A hell of a shot." He clapped Drystan on the back again. "Who knew my son would have such a talent?"

A talent? Drystan's stomach roiled.

More nerves.

His father turned toward the house. "Grab your arrow and let's head back," he called over his shoulder. "We have work to do."

Drystan stared down at the dead hawk. At the arrow sticking out of it. He wanted to just leave it there, but he was responsible for all his arrows. Any that were broken or lost, he had to replace with his own meager savings. He couldn't afford to leave it behind.

Swallowing hard, Drystan grabbed the shaft of the arrow and set his boot over the hawk's body. He pulled.

Drystan turned and was sick into the raspberry bushes. Then he hurried across the yard to the house where his father was waiting.

CHAPTER 2

THREE YEARS LATER

DRYSTAN TRUDGED DOWN THE streets of Alton, the nearest town to his family's home. The tavern he liked—Simon's—was just ahead. His right hand still stung, the cuts along his first two knuckles red and angry. He shook his hand out again. It was nothing that a couple pints wouldn't dull. Besides, it hurt a lot less than the man's face he'd punched in.

Drystan had practically begged the man to pay the money he owed Phillip, but he'd refused, saying he needed that coin to feed his family. Drystan had no choice but to enforce his father's rules. That was his job now, and had been for the last three years. Phillip Kalon was not a man to be trifled with or stolen from, and anyone failing to pay the money owed received a visit from his youngest son, either up close or at the end of an expertly fired arrow.

It was his *talent*.

Simon's was busy, as it usually was in the early evening. A small group at the bar saw Drystan enter and quickly vacated their seats. Drystan slid onto one of the stools without a word.

He was working his way through his second pint when Gray hopped onto the empty stool next to him. "I heard you taught old Morton a lesson," he said cheerfully as he flagged Simon down for his own drink. "Heard he'll be lucky if he can open either of his eyes tomorrow. Nice work, brother." Gray laughed and jostled Drystan's arm with his elbow.

Drystan's ale sloshed up and over the side of his mug. "Dammit, Gray," he muttered. He took another long swallow of his ale, draining what was left. "What're you doing here?"

Gray leaned against the bar, surveying the room. "Dad's got a line on a big score. The crew's meeting at the house tonight to go over the details."

Drystan sighed over his empty mug. "And?"

"And he wants you there," Gray said casually.

Drystan spun to face his brother. "He wants me there?" He couldn't have heard Gray right, could he? Their father never let Drystan in on these meetings.

"He specifically told me to make sure you didn't miss it." Gray ruffled Drystan's hair. "Congratulations, Dris. You made it."

Drystan blew out a long breath as Simon returned with Gray's drink and a new ale for Drystan.

Three years. Three years of being his father's enforcer, his father's sniper. Three years of trying to prove himself—prove that he was worth being a real part of the crew. Part of the family.

Finally.

Gray held out his mug to Drystan. "Here's to the family business, eh?"

Drystan tapped his own mug against Gray's.

"Fuck Phillip Kalon!"

The tavern went silent. Drystan angled himself away from the bar, as did Gray. A man stood alone in the center of the room. All eyes were on him as he glared at Drystan and his brother.

Gray slammed his mug down on the bar. "What did you just say?"

The whole room held its breath.

The man stood taller, puffing out his chest. "I said, *fuck Phillip Kalon.*" A brave friend tried to shush the man, but he shook them off, wobbling a little as he moved closer to the bar. "And fuck you two bastards. You think you're so fucking special, just 'cause your father thinks he owns half of fucking Alton. Well he *don't.* He's nothing but a lying, backstabbing, sonofabitch."

Gray stood and Drystan stood with him. A few people closer to the drunkard scurried away.

"Say that again." Gray's face twisted in rage as he moved toward the man.

"He's a sonofa—"

Drystan's heavy tankard collided with the man's nose, sending him stumbling into another table. Drinks and plates crashed to the floor and chairs toppled as people scrambled back.

Gray shot a look over his shoulder to where Drystan hadn't moved from the bar. "Show-off."

Drystan let a cruel grin slide across his face. If they wouldn't let him lose himself in a drink, then he'd lose himself in a fight instead.

❋

The tangle of bodies, the sting when his fist connected with his target, the bite of pain when someone else landed a blow. It was easy for Drystan to let go amid the chaos.

By the time the fight was over, the two Kalon brothers had an assortment of cuts and bruises—Drystan more so than Gray—but they walked out of the bar, each on their own two feet, which was more than a lot of the other patrons were able to say that night.

Along their way home, Gray laughed as he stretched to ruffle his younger brother's hair again. "Nice work in there, Dris," he said.

Drystan swatted uselessly at Gray's hand. "Fuck off," he muttered. It was Gray's fault his night of drinking had been ruined. Drystan doubted that drunkard would've bothered with him if he'd been the only one at the bar. Drystan had been keeping to himself. He hadn't wanted to start anything.

But he sure as Vire's hells was going to finish it.

A sharp sting pulled Drystan's attention as Gray poked one of the cuts on Drystan's cheek.

"Ow! What the hells, Gray!"

"You're getting sloppy. You keep dropping your hands."

Despite the years of lessons with Gray, Drystan wasn't a great fighter. But he was big and he was strong. His fist connecting with someone's nose was going to do some damage, regardless of his form. If he took a few hits in the process, then fine. That was part of the job.

"I said fuck off," Drystan complained again.

"No need to be so pissy," Gray said. "What's your problem?"

"I'm not pissy."

"Well, you sure as shit better pull that stick out of your ass before we get home, or Dad's gonna change his mind about letting you in on this score."

Drystan inhaled deeply and followed his brother the rest of the way home.

By the time they arrived at the house, Drystan's father and his primary team—including Drystan's other brothers, Thomas and Elias—were gathered in the spacious kitchen. Maps, building layouts, and floorplans were spread across the table, with everyone in various states of examining the documents. No one looked up when Gray and Drystan entered.

"The manor grounds will be open for the event," their father was saying. "We'll have no trouble getting in with some invitations." He glanced up at Gray, as though he and Drystan had been there all along. "That's where you'll come in."

Gray leaned over Elias's shoulder, taking in the plans splayed out. "A wedding? That's the job?" He let out a small laugh that made Drystan tense in anticipation. No one got away with questioning Phillip Kalon like that. Except his eldest son.

Phillip looked down his nose at Gray. "The *job* is Baron Miles Venbarra's vault. The wedding is the time we move in. It's in six months." He slid some papers around on the table. "Thomas will take point on distracting the guards while Elias and I empty the vault."

"What about me?" Drystan asked. Everyone turned to stare at him as though a dog had just spoken up. He stood a little straighter under the weight of their collective stares. "What do you need me to do?"

His father was undeterred. "I need you to do what you do best," he said. "You'll be our sniper on the manor's roof. You'll make sure our path is clear for our escape."

Drystan's lips tightened into a line. Why had he expected some new opportunity? As his father had grown fond of pointing out, his talents were in hurting people.

"I'll need a real invitation to work from," Gray interjected.

"And we'll get you one." Phillip's eyes lingered on Drystan for a moment more before he turned to Gray. "In three weeks, the baron is having another event. The engagement party for his second youngest daughter in the form of a masquerade ball. However, word is he's also using it as a match-making party for his youngest daughter. He's looking for a suitor." Phillip gestured to his second oldest son. "Thomas will attend the party and court the baron's daughter long enough to secure an invitation to the wedding."

Drystan couldn't stop the scoff that came out of his mouth.

Thomas shot a look at Drystan. "Hey, fuck you."

"You have something to add, Drystan?" his father asked. His tone suggested that the answer had better be *no*.

"Only that Thomas is almost ten years older than Lady Venbarra," Drystan said, indicating the paper his father had passed around. Apparently, Drystan had had just enough alcohol at Simon's to loosen his tongue.

Thomas fumed. "Baron Venbarra won't care about—"

"No, but you're not trying to court Baron Venbarra. You're trying to court his youngest daughter, who just turned eighteen. You're going to need her to be interested in you for this to go on long enough to secure an invitation to her sister's wedding."

Phillip Kalon crossed his arms, going stone still. It was a dangerous pose, like a cobra rearing back to strike. Drystan had seen what happened to people caught on the wrong side of that stare. "Thomas is the best grifter on the crew. You think someone else would do better?"

Did he? Did he really think someone else could do it better than Thomas? Than *Thomas*, who brought in coin for the family just in gifts from the four ladies he was courting in secret? Who'd convinced more people of more lies and tricks than Drystan could count? But Drystan had taken his mother's advice. He'd been watching his brother, watching the way he talked to people. This might be his only chance for something more than halfway decent forgeries, sloppy brawls, and sniping from rooftops.

Drystan stepped toward the table. "I could do it."

Laughter erupted around him as Gray clapped him on the shoulder. "You can't be serious."

But he was serious, so Drystan spun them a story. He told them how he'd swung by another one of his father's debtors after visiting old Morton and had convinced him to give an extra ten percent on top of the money owed, all without having to resort to violence—Drystan would find the money later. He mentioned a few other smaller scores and one longer game that would be coming to fruition soon with some extra money for the family.

The table fell to silent, furtive glances. Phillip Kalon studied his youngest son. "Very well."

Drystan had to school his face from giving away his shock. Had he actually managed to convince—?

"You'll both attend the masquerade ball. One of you ought to succeed." Phillip eyed the two of them. "No undermining each other, understand? This score is too big to risk blowing it before it even starts. So unless it's for wooing the girl, keep your dicks in your pants, got it?"

They reviewed the plan again before everyone dispersed for the night. Thomas glared at Drystan on his way by.

"Don't get in my way at that party," he sneered.

Drystan kept silent, though he drew his shoulders back and pulled himself to his full height. Thomas would never dare challenge him to any sort of physical altercation and they both knew it.

When the others had left, Gray perched on the table, studying Drystan. "This isn't a game, Dris. Baron Venbarra's nearly as ruthless as Dad. You really think you're good enough to convince this girl to fall in love with you and not get caught?"

"I don't need her to fall in love with me," Drystan grumbled. "I just need her to like me enough to keep me around for a while."

"And you think you're good enough for that? You think that experience of yours is enough to pull this off? Against *Thomas*?"

Drystan let a grin slide into place. "I convinced you and Dad that I had any experience at all, didn't I?" He turned and walked out of the kitchen, leaving Gray with his mouth hanging open.

As Drystan passed the sitting room, his mother's voice reached him. "Drystan?" she called. "May I speak with you?"

He stepped into the room, though he lingered in the open archway. "Yeah?" She raised her brows.

"Sorry," Drystan mumbled. "Yes?"

His mother beckoned him closer until he was crouching in front of her, like he always used to. He hadn't done that in years. She surveyed his face, her eyes lingering on the cuts and bruises from the tavern brawl. Her lips thinned.

"Drystan, I heard what your father's planning." She hesitated, glancing toward the hall behind him. "This job . . . Is this still what you want, sweetheart? Are you certain?"

"I-I am," he said, a tightness moving into his chest as he spoke. "I've been working toward this chance my whole life."

Her face changed, something unreadable flashing across it. She took his hand in hers. "I know. I know you have. But I never—" She froze.

Something behind Drystan had caught his mother's attention, stopping her in mid-thought. Before he could turn to look, she continued, "Be safe out there, Drystan." She leaned forward and set a gentle kiss on his forehead. "Be smart. Understand?"

"Stop clinging to your mother's skirts," his father said, his voice somehow even more stern than usual. "Vire's fucking hells, you're not a child."

Drystan stood and spun, finding his father leaning against the archway. "Sir, I—"

"Go meet up with your brothers out front. They're going for drinks in town."

He didn't know how to tell his father he didn't want to go back out tonight—that he'd rather have a few minutes to sit and talk with his mother. He didn't expect his father would understand in any case, so instead Drystan said, "Yes, sir," and headed outside.

Chapter 3

Baron Venbarra's estate was just north of Sevrun, a day's hard ride east of Alton. Drystan's father secured a safe house where he and his sons would be staying for the six months between the engagement party and the wedding. That would give Thomas—or Drystan—sufficient time to woo the baron's youngest daughter, and would give the rest of the crew time for reconnaissance of the estate and the comings and goings of the baron's staff.

But until then, Drystan's father worked him harder than ever before. He had him checking in with anyone who owed him money and was approaching their deadline for repayment, collecting the weekly protection payments—that was typically Gray's area—plus running deliveries again like he was a child. His evenings were spent socializing with the crew until he was too drunk to walk straight. And if he was lucky, his nights were spent with one of the fair number of women in Alton who seemed to get a thrill out of bedding one of the notorious Kalon brothers.

The week before the engagement party, Phillip Kalon and most of the crew, including Drystan's brothers, were in the final stages of preparation before leaving Alton.

When he had everything set, Drystan stepped into the sitting room where his mother was waiting. He only had a moment before his brothers would call for him to join them outside at the carriage.

"Take care of yourself, sweetheart," she said.

"I will, Ma." Drystan gave her a quick hug.

She held onto his arms for a moment as he stepped back, and it looked as though there was more she wanted to say.

"Dris!" Elias shouted from outside. "Come on!"

Drystan turned, but his mother's fingers moved to caress his cheek. "My sweet boy," she said quietly. "I'd always hoped—"

"Drystan!" It was his father's bellowing voice this time.

"I have to go," Drystan said, pulling away. "I'll see you soon." He ducked outside, jogging to where his father and brothers were waiting for him.

When Drystan arrived at Baron Venbarra's estate the night of the masked ball, the party was already well underway. The manor was set at the top of a gently sloping hill, with a winding path down the back that led to a sprawling garden larger than any of the green spaces within Alton or Sevrun. Drystan had grown up in relative comfort, but this place . . . The size—the opulence of it—put everything he'd ever known to shame.

To think that some people had so much when others had so little.

Drystan secured his mask in place as he approached the front gates. He had to focus. He couldn't let Thomas get the better of him tonight.

His mark was Lady Genevieve Venbarra, youngest daughter of Baron Miles Venbarra. She was the last of the lord's children to remain unwed, or would be now that the second youngest was engaged. A young man courting Lady Genevieve wouldn't be unusual, as there were bound to be many others attempting the same feat that night, including Thomas. All Drystan had to do was win her over. And maybe if he kept his eyes open and could gather a little additional information about the estate grounds in the process, his father would be even more pleased.

The forged invitation sat heavy in Drystan's pocket. Enough of those had gone out all across the barony that it was easy enough to find one to work from. His father had insisted that both Drystan and Thomas fend for themselves while Gray made the invitations for the others who would be in attendance.

The extra few seconds the guards took to review the invitation had Drystan's heart pounding in his throat, but they soon waved him through. Pyrannis's flames, if they'd thrown him out before he'd even made it inside, he'd never have heard the end of it.

He was in. Now all he had to do was find Lady Genevieve and strike up a conversation. Although he'd never seen her before, and it was a masked ball, he knew who he was looking for. Lady Genevieve Venbarra was short and slim, with flowing blond hair that was so pale it was said to be almost silver. She'd also be the one swarming with men wanting to talk to her. He'd have no trouble spotting her.

The estate was decorated throughout with glittering glass orbs and magical lights. The gardens were, too, and although it was still winter, a warmth hung in the air through the sprawling space, keeping the flowers blooming as though it were spring. Drystan could only wonder at what that kind of magical enchantment must cost in upkeep. And yet it was the most beautiful sight he'd ever seen.

Right up until he turned and collided with a woman in a flowing purple gown. Her dark hair was piled onto her head with elaborate curls all woven through with purple and white blossoms. A delicate mask of gold and violet flowers perched on the bridge of her nose.

Drystan forgot how to breathe.

The gold in her mask highlighted the golden flecks in her striking brown eyes, which dragged over Drystan, appraising him from head to toe. He suddenly felt self-conscious in his dark, finely tailored suit—far finer than anything he was used to wearing. He was even second-guessing having his hair pulled back and twisted into a knot at the back of his neck. It wasn't quite long enough to do it properly though, which left the top half mostly loose around his face.

"E-excuse me," he murmured, regaining some semblance of his composure. He gave a belated bow. "I didn't see you there, Lady . . . ?"

She tsked him, waggling a finger gloved in purple satin. "Now, now, it's a masquerade ball, my lord. No names or formal titles are allowed."

Drystan's cheeks grew hot, and he was grateful for the mask, styled in the manner of a lion, that hid most of his face. "Of course. But I must have something to call you."

A delicate arch of her brow. "Must you?"

He smiled. "I'm afraid I must."

"Hmm." A finger tapped her lips. "In that case, you may call me Jenna." She offered her hand.

Drystan bowed again as he took her gloved hand and kissed it. "A pleasure to meet you, Jenna."

"See, now you have me at a disadvantage, my lord," she said, pulling her hand back. The air was cold against his fingertips where the soft fabric of her glove had been. "I still have nothing to call you."

He mirrored her gesture, tapping his finger to his lips in mock consideration, and was rewarded with a quiet scoff. "In that case, you may call me Drystan." No one here would know him, and his real name was as good as any fake name for the fake noble he was supposed to be tonight. It would keep things simple—fewer lies meant fewer places to slip up. *Tell as many truths as possible*. It was one of his father's rules.

"Drystan?" Beneath her mask was the slightest, most delightful scrunch of her nose. "If you insist."

He should move on; he had to find Lady Venbarra before the evening got too late and Thomas, or some other suitor, pulled her attention, yet he couldn't help the next words that came out of his mouth. "Would you like to dance?"

Her lips twisted into a wry grin that made his heart flutter. "How very bold of you, Lord Drystan."

He extended his hand to her, but she stepped back. "That wasn't a *yes*, my lord."

"It wasn't a *no* either, my lady." he said. "But I would never dream of presuming." He tucked his hands behind his back. "I shall wait for your enthusiastic *yes*."

"*Enthusiastic*?" Was that a blush coloring her cheeks? She twirled her skirts side to side. "My lord, are we still talking about the dance?"

Gods above and below, this girl was going to be the death of him. "Of course," he said. He couldn't help the mischievous smirk that played across his lips. "What else would I be talking about?"

Her eyes wandered over him again, more slowly this time. At last she said, "Will you walk with me?"

How could he say no? Drystan offered his arm and Jenna's hand slid into it like it belonged there.

"Have you been to Baron Venbarra's estate before?" she asked.

"I've never had the good fortune to," he answered honestly.

Jenna gestured ahead of them. "There's a lovely walking path just that way."

Drystan let her lead, though they walked side by side. "Have you come here very many times?"

"I like to wander the gardens when there's a ball happening. Too many people all in one room gets so stifling." She tightened her arm where it was looped through Drystan's, pulling herself a little closer. "Though it's nice to have someone to walk with."

He swallowed hard, his mouth dry.

They walked for a while, Jenna leading him down various twists and turns along the garden paths until they came to a wall of hedges taller than Drystan.

"It's a maze," Jenna said as she pulled away from him and moved a little closer to the entrance. The lantern light caught her eyes, making them glitter like diamonds behind her mask. "Care to join me?"

Drystan's heart was beating so hard, he was certain she must have been able to hear it. He cast a quick glance the way they'd come. They'd left the partygoers behind several turns ago. This part of the garden was clearly a more private area, likely used only during smaller, more intimate gatherings.

Then there was the matter of Lady Venbarra . . . Drystan still needed to find her. "Should we be over here?" he asked, nearly wincing at how awkward he sounded.

Jenna giggled, like music, and his knees weakened. "If they didn't want people to come this way, they would have it blocked off. Besides . . ." Angling toward the maze, she beckoned him with one finger. "You wouldn't let a girl wander in here alone, would you?" She pouted, though Drystan had the distinct impression she was toying with him. "What if I get lost?"

With one last smile, Jenna stepped into the shadows of the maze.

If Drystan followed her, he'd be all but giving Thomas the win when it came to Lady Venbarra's affections. But as he jogged after Jenna, he couldn't have cared less.

Chapter 4

Although the strange, magical warmth still filled this part of the gardens, there were no lanterns or glittering lights in the maze. The only light came from the moon and stars overhead, as well as whatever glow filtered over from the rest of the garden. They'd taken a few turns, and Drystan was doing his best to remember the way back.

"May I ask you a question, Lord Drystan?"

"Of course."

She stopped, turning to face him so quickly that he nearly bumped into her again. "I want you to answer truthfully. No matter what, understand?"

His mouth answered before he had a chance to think. "Alright."

"As a young gentleman who's never been to the baron's estate before, I hope you understand the reason why I must ask." Jenna raised her chin, defiant.

Beautiful. She was so beautiful.

"Are you here to win Lady Venbarra's hand?"

"She's not an object to be obtained," Drystan said.

Jenna rolled her eyes, huffing with impatience. "Are you here to woo her?" she demanded. She was breathing hard, her chest rising and falling quickly. Her pulse fluttered at her throat.

"I was," Drystan said. "Meeting her, hopefully getting to know her a little—that was the reason I came. But . . ."

What was he doing? That was his whole purpose in being here.

When he didn't say anything else, Jenna crossed her arms over her chest. "But *what?*"

Drystan swallowed hard and tried not to stare. He focused on her face, her lips—no, her eyes. It was hard to think straight when all he wanted to do was hold her. "But I think I've changed my mind." He took a tentative step closer.

She didn't move away.

"I'd rather be here," he said, a little breathless. "I'd rather talk with *you*. Maybe get to know *you*."

Jenna's eyes pierced him as she watched his every move, taking the measure of him. "And when I'm through talking with you?"

"Then I'll leave with the hope that we might speak again."

"And if I don't want to speak with you again?"

Drystan shrugged, helpless. Gods above, he was helpless. "Then I'll leave, and you won't see me again."

She arched one eyebrow. "You wouldn't pursue me?"

"Not if you didn't want me to." This was crazy. And maybe he was crazy for not walking away, but . . . "Jenna, I—"

But her lips were on his as she crashed into him, and every other thought in his mind evaporated as he drank her in like she was the finest wine he'd ever had. She was intoxicating, and Drystan's hand slid to the back of her head, pulling her into him. Her arms snaked under his, pressing against his back.

Drystan forgot how to think. How to breathe. His entire world narrowed to this moment as though it were his last, his first, his *only*.

Jenna's hands were roaming now, and Drystan angled his head to kiss along the side of her neck. The soft moan she let out in his ear nearly did him in.

Before he could process what was happening, Jenna was moving, pulling him along with her. Her hands—her mouth—were still on Drystan as she navigated the maze. He followed where she led, no longer caring at all about finding his way back.

The next time that Drystan had the wherewithal to observe his surroundings, Jenna had detached herself from his lips long enough to peer around the corner of a long hallway. They were inside.

Inside the manor.

"Jenna," Drystan whispered, his voice hoarse. "Where—"

She silenced him with another kiss, and Drystan forgot whatever it was that he was worried about. "Quiet," she whispered against his lips. "Just trust me."

Up a small back stairwell and down another hall, Drystan followed. The household staff must have all been dealing with the guests downstairs and outside. They didn't pass another soul.

At last, Jenna opened one of the doors and pulled Drystan inside by the front of his shirt.

Leaning back against the closed door, she grinned wickedly as she slipped the satin gloves from her fingers. Drystan tore his gaze away from her to take in the room—the four-poster bed with sheer drapes pulled back and tied to each post, the plush fur rugs, and roaring fireplace.

Before he could raise the question of whose room they were in, Jenna's bare hands slid along the sides of his neck, cupping his face, and his skin seemed to burn where she touched him. She stood on her toes and guided his mouth back to hers, and he lifted her up, bracing against the door.

They staggered and stumbled their way to the bed, neither able to keep their hands off the other. At some point her mask tumbled to the floor, as did Drystan's. As she pulled him down with her onto the bed, Drystan propped his arms against the pillows, pulling away enough to look at her face.

Gods, she was beautiful. Stunning brown eyes stared back at him.

"Why did you stop?" she asked, breathless.

Drystan sucked in a lungful of air. "Is this alright?" he asked. She'd brought him here, of course, but he needed to make sure he wasn't doing anything she didn't want. "We can stop, i-if you want."

Jenna's brow furrowed. "Does it look like I want to stop?"

His face heated. "No, but I—"

"Do *you* want to stop?"

"No," he said too quickly. "I—"

"Are you looking for an *enthusiastic yes*?" she asked, drawing her thumb across his lips.

He nodded slowly, feeling equal parts embarrassed and a fool.

"I wouldn't have brought you to my room if this wasn't what I wanted." She slid Drystan's jacket off his shoulders. "But, fine, if you must be such a gentleman about it, *yes.*"

Drystan was not naive to women's pleasure, and he was rewarded for his efforts with the most delightful moans and other little noises that sent a thrill through him with each sound. Neither of them went unsatisfied, and when they were both completely and utterly exhausted, Drystan pulled her in close. Jenna rested her head on his chest as his fingers twisted one of the loose curls of her dark hair.

Eventually his wits returned to him, and his mind finally snagged on the words she'd spoken a few hours earlier.

"Did you say this was *your* room?"

Jenna giggled into him and his heart skipped a beat. "I did."

His sluggish thoughts worked to catch up, the mystery slotting into place at last as he mentally swapped one letter for another. "*Genna,*" he said slowly, "That's short for Genevieve, isn't it?"

Genevieve Venbarra laughed again, though this wasn't the innocent giggle of a moment ago. It was a deeper, more sultry sound that raised goosebumps where her breath skittered across his skin.

"Surprise," she murmured.

Drystan's face heated again, and he knew he must be bright red. "I . . . I thought you were supposed to be blond," he said lamely.

"You and everyone else." Genna's expression darkened. "And most days, I am. But tonight . . ." She sighed and turned away from him.

Drystan tilted her face toward his with a finger under her chin. "You knew that all the lords at the ball would be trying to win your hand tonight. You wanted a night where all eyes *wouldn't* be on you."

She nodded. "And I wanted to spend time with people who wanted to be with *me.* Not the idea of me." Her eyes flicked down to his lips and then up again. "I suppose you won me over when you chose me over *Lady Venbarra.*" She propped herself up on her elbow. "But you have me at a disadvantage again. You know my real name, and all I know is your silly fake one."

Drystan's lips quirked to the side as he said, "That's not entirely true."

"You don't expect me to believe that your name really is *Drystan*." When he didn't answer, she laughed again, nuzzling a kiss into his neck. "And here I thought I knew the names of all the local lords and their progeny."

"You likely do," Drystan said, pulling her on top of him.

Genna leaned in and kissed him again. "As much fun as this delightful little distraction was, you should go. I think the ball is likely winding down by now, and it'll be easier for you to leave while there are at least a few guests still wandering about."

Drystan sighed, letting his arms flop down onto the bed. She wasn't wrong. In fact, she was completely right.

With one last kiss, she rose and crossed to an adjoining room. The sound of water splashing into a basin reached him once the door was closed. He stood after a moment and gathered his clothes. He was dressed by the time Genna returned wearing a robe cinched tight around her waist.

She walked him to the door, bidding him goodnight with another deep kiss that nearly had Drystan ignoring the hour and pulling her back into bed.

"Can I see you again?" he asked when he managed to find his breath again.

Genna leaned against the door frame, the shoulder of her robe sliding down slightly as she crossed her arms. "And if I say no?"

"I'll go and you'll never have to see me again," he said. "I don't see why my answer would have changed."

"Then yes, Lord Drystan. I look forward to when next we meet."

"Tomorrow?" What a fool he was, not only asking to see her again, but so soon. And yet he couldn't stop himself. "Can I see you tomorrow?"

Her lips curved gently. "Alright then. Tomorrow. Meet me in the hedge maze at the tenth chime tomorrow night."

"Tenth chime?" he asked. The manor would be closed to guests that late. There was no way he'd be able to talk his way in or—

"If you truly wish to see me again," Genna said, pushing off from the door-jamb, "I trust you'll find a way."

CHAPTER 5

IT WAS NEARLY DAWN by the time Drystan's overstimulated mind calmed enough for sleep, so the meeting his father called at the eighth chime that morning was as unwelcome as it was surprising.

"Get your ass up, Dris," Gray shouted from the hall. "Looks like Thomas failed last night and Dad's pissed. You're not going to want to miss this. Hurry up!"

Drystan hesitated. "What about me?"

Gray pushed the door open and stuck his head inside. "What about you?"

"Is Dad pissed at me, too?"

Gray looked at Drystan like he'd just burst into song. "Why would he be? Come on, let's go!"

It hit him then, like a splash of cold water. They'd *expected* him to fail. They'd known it with such certainty that it was only Thomas's failure that had drawn their father's fury. None of them had thought Drystan would have any chance at all.

Turning this thought over in his mind, Drystan dragged himself out of bed, threw on a questionably clean pair of pants, and slunk downstairs after Gray.

While still large enough for each of the Kalon brothers to have their own room, the safe house was a fair bit smaller than their family home in Alton. Without a proper study, the kitchen had been converted into his father's war room. It served them all just fine, as his father always tended to call meetings around their dining table back home anyway, much to his mother's chagrin.

His father and brothers were gathered around the wide table, along with the other members of the crew who'd come with them to Sevrun. A tea kettle hung over the hearth, and Drystan grabbed a mug and poured himself the dregs from the pot, a few leaves escaping into his cup.

All focus was on Phillip, who was currently berating Drystan's brother. "Explain to me," Phillip said with lethal calm, "how you managed to not only *not* woo Lady Venbarra, but not even *talk* to her for the entirety of the evening."

"I-I-I couldn't find her," Thomas stammered.

"Couldn't *find* her?" Phillip bellowed. A few of the others took an instinctive step back. "She's not a trinket that you set down and forgot where you fucking put it. She's the baron's youngest daughter and, next to her betrothed sister, was the centerpiece of the entire fucking party. And you expect me to believe that you *couldn't find her?*"

Thomas had been helplessly thrown to the wolf that was their father, but not one of those watching the display would step in to defend him. You kept your head down and your mouth shut if you knew what was good for you. And Drystan knew. He'd learned that lesson well over the last eighteen years.

"None of the other suitors could find her either," Thomas said, straightening his shoulders. "It wasn't just me."

"I don't give a fucking rat's ass what the other suitors could or couldn't do! You're *my* son. And when I give you a job, I expect you to do it right."

Thomas's eyes darted through the gathered crew, no doubt looking for corroboration on his story, though none of them would have had their focus on the baron's daughter last night. No one except—

"Drystan!" Thomas thrust a finger toward where he stood near the hearth, his first sip of tea halfway to his lips. "He'll tell you. She wasn't at the party. I can't woo a girl who's not even fucking there!"

Phillip's gaze turned—and everyone else's with it—to regard his youngest son. No one spoke.

"Tell them!" Thomas implored.

Thomas didn't want to face their father's ire alone, so he wanted Drystan to put himself on the hook. Although a part of Drystan had considered keeping his night with Genna a secret, he also knew that he needed this win with his father and brothers. With the crew. He needed them to know he could do more than just hurt people.

"Thomas is telling the truth," Drystan said. "She wasn't at the ball." He took a slow sip of his tea, its bitter flavor a match for his current mood. "At least, not most of it."

"Don't play games with me, boy," Phillip barked. "Was she there, or wasn't she?"

Drystan needed to be careful here if he wanted to get his point across without making things worse for himself. He couldn't lose his nerve. "She wasn't at the ball because she was with me."

No one moved.

"Bullshit!" Thomas shouted. "There's no way she was with you the whole fucking night!"

Drystan arched a brow, doing his best to present a calm exterior, even while his face heated. He didn't want to talk about her like this. He wanted his time with Genna to be something special, but what choice did he have?

"It might not have taken *you* the whole night," Drystan quipped. "But I like to take my time."

Gray snorted a laugh from the other side of the table.

"Bullshit!" Thomas yelled again.

"Oh, shit, it's true," Gray choked out through his laughter. "Look! Little Dris is blushing!"

Dammit! Drystan's face only flushed hotter as everyone laughed. Everyone except Thomas and their father. Drystan willed himself not to hide.

He'd done what they wanted. Wittingly or not, he'd succeeded where they'd all assumed he'd fail. Drystan stood tall, eyes locked on Thomas, who fumed silently.

Phillip only nodded. "Good. Let's discuss how to make sure you remain in her good graces." His voice was devoid of emotion, though he pinched the bridge of his nose like he was vexed with some sudden headache. "We'll need to work with you on this to make certain she wants to see you again."

"I'm seeing her again tonight."

This time his father's eyes widened. "You're . . . seeing her tonight?"

"How the hells did you manage that?" Thomas demanded.

"She invited me," Drystan said, standing up a little straighter, though his nerves caused his voice to crack, which sent the others into another round of boisterous laughter.

Drystan's father clearly didn't find any of it amusing. His posture threatened trouble as he stared at Drystan over the heads of the laughing men. "Don't fuck this up."

★

It was late afternoon when Drystan arrived at the Venbarra estate. The gates were still open, and it would be easier to slip in among the servants and other guests unnoticed. He wore his regular clothes, though he made sure to grab the pants without holes and the cleanest shirt he had—looking like a servant was fine, but he couldn't give the impression that he'd wandered in off the streets.

At the gates, a butcher was unloading some crates of meat wrapped in wax paper. "Here," Drystan said as he held out his arms for a box. "Let me give you a hand with those."

The butcher smiled appreciatively, handing him a crate, and Drystan was in.

Prior to last night's party, Drystan and his brothers had all been made to study the layout of the estate, so finding the kitchen was no trouble at all. He made himself useful there, acting the part of a new scullery boy. No one paid him any mind. So long as you acted like you belonged in a place, Drystan had learned from watching Thomas over the years, and didn't make yourself a nuisance, people often overlooked your presence. Being actively helpful worked even better—Drystan had figured that one out on his own—and the overworked kitchen staff weren't about to turn down a strong back and another set of hands.

It was nearly the tenth chime by the time Drystan ducked outside and headed toward the maze. Thankfully, the enchantment that had kept the gardens temperate during the party was still in effect. Was it always like this? Drystan found the spot where Genna had brought him the previous night and waited. He kept to the shadows to avoid the passing guards and any wandering eyes from the windows overhead.

By the eleventh chime, Drystan was considering whether he should wait longer or cut his losses when a woman stepped into the hedge maze. Her hair was still dark, as it had been the night before, though now she wore a simpler dress of deep blue.

Drystan moved from his hiding spot. "Genna."

The light from the moon shined against her fair skin as she turned. Her beauty nearly sent him to his knees.

"You're here," she said, though it seemed half a question.

"Of course." Drystan stepped closer. "You asked, so I'm here."

"I'll admit, I didn't think you would manage it." She set her hands on her hips, lifting her chin. "So how did you?"

Drystan told her about his afternoon spent helping the kitchen staff.

Genna's gaze raked over him, as though she was taking him in for the first time. "I've never known a lord who would stoop to even dressing like the staff, let alone actually *working* with them."

Drystan gave a helpless shrug. "I suppose you still haven't."

"What do you mean?"

He didn't want to lie to her. Vire's demons, she'd knocked him off his feet the moment he'd laid eyes on her. If he was going to make an honest try at building something for once in his godsdamned life, he wanted it to be built on trust. And he wanted it to be with her. Even if it didn't last, even if she told him to leave right then and there—even if it ruined the job—he wanted to try.

Drystan held his hands out at his sides, inviting her to examine his appearance more closely. "I'm not a lord."

"Of course you are," she said, laughing like wind chimes on a summer breeze.

"I'm not."

She stopped laughing. "Explain," she demanded. "Right now."

"I forged an invitation to the ball."

She watched him carefully as Drystan held his breath. If she were to call the guards on him, who knew what punishment the baron would inflict?

But rather than scream or yell at him, she drew her lower lip between her teeth. "So, you're some kind of scoundrel?"

"You could say that," he admitted.

"Why would you sneak into the ball?"

Guilt tightened his chest. What was he doing? He wanted to be honest with her, but . . . but could he avoid completely betraying his family while staying within the bounds of the truth? Running his mouth about *everything* seemed unwise for only his second meeting with her. He'd already said far more than he should have as it was.

"To meet you," he said.

She reached for him. Drystan braced himself to be slapped, but instead she grabbed the front of his shirt at the collar and pulled him down to her, meeting his lips with her own.

He wrapped his arms around her, his fingers gliding through the soft locks of her hair.

As they had done the night before, Genna and Drystan snuck through the manor halls, all wandering hands and desperate lips, until they reached her chambers. When they finished making love, she snuggled against his shoulder again, though this time, when she spoke, it was not to usher him away.

"Will you stay?" she asked, and the question poured more warmth into him than the magic of the gardens.

He wanted nothing more than to lie there with Genna for the rest of his days, but he managed to say softly, "Only if you want me to."

Genna curled more tightly into him. "Stay," she said.

So Drystan stayed.

Chapter 6

In the months that followed, Drystan spent many nights with Genna, sneaking into the manor in one way or another, and sneaking out again before dawn. It didn't take long for Drystan to realize this was different from the times he'd spent with women back in Alton. His chest hurt when they were apart, and he would count the minutes until he would be able to see her again.

Vire help him, he loved this girl.

As Genna's sister's wedding drew ever closer, so too did Phillip Kalon's plans to rob Baron Venbarra. Genna also began asking more questions about Drystan's life—something that he dodged when he could or gave half-truths when he couldn't. He couldn't be completely honest with her, no matter how much he wanted to. He couldn't betray his family like that.

But whenever he did tell her something about his life—forging documents, bar brawls, working with his father's crew—Genna never shied away from it. She was curious, always wanting to know more.

"Teach me how to hold a knife," she said one day. "A lady ought to be able to protect herself." She was right, so he taught her, giving her one of his own daggers to keep in her room. "Teach me how to throw a punch," she asked. He worked with her whenever they had time. When she learned he had rudimentary skill in picking pockets, she demanded he teach her the basics. And he was happy to do it, because each thing she wanted to learn meant he got to spend more time with her.

The wedding was two months away, and Drystan's father was becoming increasingly agitated. As Drystan ducked out of the house to go meet with Genna, he was stopped by his father's booming voice.

"Where is the invitation, Drystan? Why haven't you secured one yet?"

Drystan couldn't tell his father that his dating Genna was a secret to her family, that she knew he wasn't a lord, and that there was no way he'd be invited to attend the wedding on her arm. If he did, his father might ship him straight back to Alton. Or worse. Either way, Drystan would never see Genna again if his father knew the truth.

"I'm working on it," he said instead.

Phillip's eyes narrowed on his son. "You had better be. We have come too far for you to fuck this up now. Do you understand me?"

"Yes, sir."

"Good. Your mother's not here to coddle you, so stop behaving like a child and finish the job."

"Yes, sir." He swallowed hard. "I will."

Drystan hurried to the manor. He snuck in as usual and made it to their spot inside the hedge maze as night fell. The midsummer air was much less humid and uncomfortable within the garden walls. Drystan tried not to think about his father's seething words as he waited for Genna. About the threat lying within them.

When Genna arrived, she was wearing a skirt of simple brown cloth and a light pink blouse. She wore no jewelry, and her hair, which had long since returned to her natural pale blond, was pulled back in the most straight-forward braid Drystan had ever seen on her.

"Take me into the city," she said once she reached him.

"What?"

"Take me into the city. Sneak me out of the manor. I want to see the city."

Drystan's mind hurried to catch up. "You've never . . . ?"

Genevieve tossed her hands out to the sides. "My father never lets us off the grounds," she said. "Not until we're married and sent safely off with our husbands. We're prisoners here, Drystan. I'm trapped. But I want to see what I've been missing." She took his hand and squeezed it. "Take me into the city."

She was a prisoner in her own home.

"Alright," he said, gripping her hand tightly. "Follow me."

A gilded cage was still a cage, after all.

Drystan took Genevieve through the kitchens and out the servants' entrance. No one paid any attention to the two of them as they walked with purpose. Sevrun proper was a couple miles away, so it took them the better part of half an hour to reach the edge of the city.

"Keep your head down," Drystan instructed as the walls of Sevrun greeted them.

Music spilled into the street from a nearby tavern, and Genna tugged Drystan toward it. He couldn't help but smile as he let himself be led inside. The place was crowded and lively, with a group of musicians riling up the crowd with a raucous song. Genna stared at it all in wide-eyed wonder.

Even in Sevrun, Phillip Kalon had a reputation, and word had spread over the last few months that he and his sons were in town. A couple seats at the bar opened up as soon as Drystan even glanced in their direction. He guided Genna to one of the stools and took the one beside her.

Genna watched the patrons whose seats they were now in as they hurried to other parts of the tavern. "What was that about?"

"Nothing," Drystan said quickly. He flagged down the bartender and ordered an ale for himself and a glass of wine for Genna.

"No." She set her hand on Drystan's. "I want the same as you."

Drystan nodded at the barkeep. "You heard her." As the barkeep rushed off, Drystan swiveled on the stool to face Genna. "I didn't know you liked ale."

"I don't know if I do," she said with a gentle shrug. "I've never had it."

When their drinks came, Genna sampled the ale with enthusiasm, her nose scrunching up in that adorable way she had—much the same as she'd done the first night they met.

"Oh, that's terrible," she said, her mouth twisting in disgust. "You *like* this?"

Drystan laughed before taking a healthy swallow from his own mug. "It grows on you."

Her nose scrunched up again. "Why would you want it to?" She waved to get the bartender's attention, and Drystan watched with amusement as she pushed both mugs of ale back toward the bewildered man and insisted on two glasses of wine instead.

As the musicians finished their song, everyone cheered and whooped before settling into their various conversations.

Genna watched the bustling tavern, her eyes sharp and cunning. She missed nothing of what was happening. Then she turned those sharp eyes on Drystan. "What were you really doing at the manor that night? At the ball?"

Drystan swallowed the wine in his mouth, nearly choking on it at the drastic shift in her tone. All merriment and wonder had seemingly evaporated, leaving only the cunning behind.

"You're some sort of thief, right?" Genna whispered before he could answer. "You were trying to steal something that night, weren't you?"

He could lie. It was easy for him—he did it all the time. And he'd gotten good at it, too. But he didn't want to lie to Genna. He'd been trying to avoid this very topic so he wouldn't have to make this decision, but it seemed he'd run out of time.

"No," he said. "I wasn't trying to steal anything that night. But I was on a job. I . . ."

He couldn't hide forever. What kind of future could he hope to build with her if he couldn't trust her? He had to take the leap. He had to trust her.

"My father is Phillip Kalon."

He held his breath as Genna stared at him. Finding out he wasn't nobility was one thing, but discovering he was the son of one of the most famous—and vicious—cutthroats in the kingdom? If she slapped him and stormed out, he'd understand, and he'd have no one to blame but himself.

"Phillip Kalon," she repeated. She tossed her head back with an impatient huff. "Is that name supposed to mean something to me?"

Drystan's breath left him in a sharp exhale. She didn't know who his father was. He couldn't remember the last time he'd told someone his father's name and they hadn't either shrunk back in fear or glared at him with open disgust.

Drystan's stomach twisted as he briefly explained who his father was and the kind of business he dealt in. "My father plans to rob your father the night of your sister's wedding," Drystan said at last. "I was at the ball to secure an invitation."

"How would being at the engagement ball provide you with an invitation to the wedding?" Her breath caught as her eyes narrowed on him.

She missed nothing.

"Unless . . ." Genna stiffened, her shoulders pulling back. "Unless you became acquaintances with someone at the party. Someone with whom you could cultivate a relationship to such a degree that you'd be all but guaranteed an invitation." Lifting her chin, she stared down her nose at him. "You said you were there to meet me. Wooing me was your job that night, wasn't it?"

"It was," he admitted. "But when I met you, I didn't realize that you were *you*. I gave up on the job for just the chance to speak with you." He hoped she would understand. Everything had changed the moment he saw her. "I love you, Genna."

The words tumbled out before he could stop them, but why would he? If he wanted her to know the truth, this was part of it. Genevieve was the one bright spot in his life. He wouldn't keep his feelings from her.

Drystan prayed he hadn't just ruined everything. Genna was silent, her jaw tense.

He braced for her to leave.

"I want in."

Drystan stared at her.

She set a delicate finger under Drystan's chin and closed his mouth. "I want in," she repeated. "On the job."

By now the musicians had begun playing again, though the tune was a much calmer one than earlier. Drystan leaned closer to Genna. "You don't know what you're asking."

"I do," she said, a hardness around her usually soft mouth. "I'm not allowed to leave the manor, I'm told where to be and what to wear. Soon enough I'll be told who to marry." She fixed her gaze on Drystan, twining her fingers with his. "I won't have a say in that, either."

"But then what?" This was crazy. And Drystan was crazy for even considering it.

She squeezed his hand. "Then, I leave. With the money my father has, I could go anywhere. I could live my own life. Don't you see? This is my chance to be free."

"You don't understand—"

"Stop telling me what I *understand*," Genna snapped. "Or what I *know*. I know I'll do whatever it takes."

"What about my father?" he asked. They weren't just talking about bringing Genna in on the heist . . . They were talking about betraying his father. No one walked away from that. Not even family.

Especially family.

"You could run too." Her eyes were bright. "We'll get my father's money, and we'll leave."

She would leave. She would leave her life behind and run away.

With him.

Drystan's heart squeezed tight in his chest. "I-I can't do that," he said.

"Why not?"

He opened his mouth to explain the obvious reasons why he couldn't abandon his family. Why he couldn't just *leave*.

But the words didn't come.

She watched him expectantly.

He'd worked hard to get where he was—to finally be a member of his father's crew. And even if he was only being used for his size and strength, he had the opportunity now, with this job, to prove he was more than just a brute. It was what he wanted. It was what he'd *always* wanted.

"Are you happy?" she asked.

"Of course," he replied, squeezing her hand.

"No, I don't mean with me. I mean, with your life."

He stared at her.

"Drystan, are you happy working for your father?"

"I . . ." Drystan looked down at where her hand still held his. He could start over. He could have a life like the ones he used to read about. With Genna.

But was that worth betraying his father? His brothers? Why was this even something he was considering?

Was he happy? "I . . . don't know," he said.

"Oh." Genevieve's face fell and Drystan's heart twisted in his chest. He never wanted to hurt her—never wanted to cause her pain.

He squeezed her hand tightly between both of his. "I want to be with you." Nothing had ever felt more true—more real—in his entire life. "I just . . . It's not a simple thing. I think I need some time . . ."

"I understand." She leaned closer to him, the scent of her rosewater perfume surrounding him. "You need time to decide what's important to you."

"No, that's not—"

"It's alright." Her lips found his in a kiss that was both chaste and yet promised many unchaste things later. She barely pulled away, her lips still brushing his softly as she said, "Take all the time you need."

CHAPTER 7

DRYSTAN AND GENEVIEVE SAT in the tavern for hours. Although they tried to regain the pleasant mood of earlier, a somber cloud hung over the rest of their evening. Genna lamented all the things she wanted to do but hadn't yet had the chance. With each story of how trapped she was in her own life, Drystan's chest tightened further.

While they spoke, she also mentioned a few areas where she'd be able to help Drystan with the heist—should he decide to bring her in—such as providing better inside information about her father's security measures around the vault. Those details would help him stay on his father's good side, Genna explained, giving them time to work out their own plan.

Their own plan. Was she only talking about the heist? Or the future? *Their* future.

The future Drystan would never have with her unless he took this chance.

Once the tavern closed, Drystan was going to walk Genna home, but he had no way of sneaking her back onto the grounds so late. They'd have to wait until closer to dawn, when some of the servants and staff who lived in town would be heading to the manor for their workday. And they'd need to pass the few hours until then.

Neither of them had any trouble thinking of a way to distract themselves.

By the time Drystan got Genna safely back into the manor and made the long walk back to his family's safe house, it was late morning, and his limbs were heavy with exhaustion. But tucked into his back pocket was an invitation to the wedding.

"Where have you been?" his father snapped as soon as Drystan stepped inside.

He saw no reason to lie—at least not yet—so he said, "I was with Genevieve."

"Again?" his father arched a brow. "Be cautious not to wear out your welcome. The gods know how easily it is for a woman to lose interest, especially if she feels she's being pursued too hard."

Drystan nodded, biting his tongue.

"It's a miracle you got her attention in the first place," Phillip continued. "You need to make sure you don't act too much like yourself."

His jaw tightened, but he forced it to relax as he said, "What do you mean, father?"

"I mean you're too eager. Too excitable. Too . . ." He surveyed Drystan, seeming to search for the right word.

"Happy?"

His father stepped closer, peering down at him, and Drystan's blood ran cold as he realized he'd said the thought out loud.

"Soft." Phillip's voice was sharpened steel. "I've tried hard to break you of those traits, and I thought I'd made progress, but it appears you're slipping back into your old ways." His tone dropped to a dangerous pitch as he said, "Do *not* fall for this girl, Drystan."

Oh, it was far, *far* too late for that.

"You must remain calculating," his father went on. "You must keep your wits about you and remember the part you're playing here. Someone like Lady Venbarra would never be interested in someone like you."

Only she *was* interested in him. She wanted to run away with him. Drystan clenched his teeth to keep himself silent, but his father's eyes narrowed as he marked the subtle movement.

"You have nothing to offer her, Drystan. She's a lady, the daughter of a baron. You're a brute whose only usefulness lies in following my orders. You hurt people. Kill people. What use would you be to her?"

It wasn't anything Drystan hadn't heard a hundred times before. He knew it was true. Yet some part of him wanted to believe that he could be more.

"You understand that she would have to give up her entire life for you, don't you? Do you really think you're worth that?"

Drystan's shoulders sagged. "No, sir," he ground out.

"You cannot develop any sort of attachment to her. She is nothing but a means to an end. Do you understand?"

"I understand." As Drystan moved to pass by his father, he reached into his pocket and withdrew the invitation. "I'll just drop this off with Gray then," he said, a little of his anger sliding into his tone.

Phillip grabbed him by the wrist and snatched the invitation from his fingers. Drystan tried to pull away, but his father held him in place, his grip like an iron shackle.

"You may be bigger and stronger than your brothers," Phillip said, his voice lethally calm, "but you would do well to remember that you are *not* bigger or stronger than me. And I won't tolerate you fucking this up or making a mockery of me or this family." His hand on his son's wrist tightened further. "You told me you could handle this. You told me that I could trust you. Can I trust you, Drystan? Can I trust you not to fuck this up?"

Drystan swallowed hard, willing himself to stand tall in the face of his father's piercing glare. He could lie to his father if he needed to, but he was never sure how much his father could read him.

He opted, instead, to stay within the truth. "I know what I'm doing."

"You'd best hope so, Drystan," Phillip said, releasing him. "For your sake."

"Yes, sir."

His heart was racing, but before Drystan could get more than a few steps away, his father said, "Stop pursuing this girl so hard. You're going to spook her. When are you supposed to see her again?"

"A few days," Drystan lied.

His father nodded. "Good. I have need for you to return to Alton to handle a few things. You'll be gone a week."

"What? Why?"

Phillip's glare caused Drystan to shrink back a step. "Watch your tongue. Don't think for a moment that you're not still a part of this family. If I need you to return to Alton, then the only proper response is to pack your bag."

Drystan swallowed. "Yes, sir."

"Good. You leave in an hour."

He hurried up to his room before his mouth could get him into any more trouble. So much for getting any sleep. An hour wasn't nearly enough time to do everything he needed to. Not when he'd be gone a whole week! He'd need to get a message to Genna, to let her know he'd be gone, but how? The manor was in the opposite direction from Alton, so there was no way he'd be able to pass by on the way and drop a note with one of the staff he'd befriended. He couldn't trust any of his brothers to get a message to her, that was certain. He'd have to just pen her a letter, drop it in the town post, and pray it reached her. And he'd need to be discreet.

Drystan wrote as concise a note as he could while still conveying what he needed. He hoped she'd be able to read between the lines.

Drystan had just dropped the letter in the post box on the corner and returned to the house when his father stepped into the kitchen. "Are you ready?"

"Yes, sir," Drystan said, nodding to the small knapsack, packed and ready on the kitchen floor.

"Good." He handed Drystan a folded piece of paper. "This is the list of what I need handled in Alton. See that it's done."

"I will."

Phillip Kalon took the measure of his son before waving a dismissive hand. "Hurry up. Before you lose any more daylight."

Drystan rushed off without another word.

It was at least a day's ride to Alton, but of course his father had made no particular arrangements for Drystan, leaving him to fend for himself. Drystan was on the road for two hours before he happened upon a small caravan of wagons pulled over on the side of the road. It didn't take long for the problem to become apparent.

One of the wagons had thrown a wheel, and three of the travelers were arguing among themselves. Two were demanding they empty the wagon so they could repair the wheel, while the third was arguing that they could just repair it without taking the time to empty it, if the other two would stop whining. They paused in their bickering as Drystan approached.

"Good day," Drystan said, trying to sound cheery despite his fatigue.

"Move along," one of the men said, waving Drystan down the road. "This ain't a sideshow."

The woman in the group swatted the man in the stomach. "Don't be rude," she snapped.

Drystan looked over the scene. If he could prove himself friendly and useful, perhaps they'd let him travel with them. "Can I help?" he offered.

While he sometimes tried to make himself appear smaller and, therefore, nonthreatening, now he made sure to stand at his full height. He hefted his pack onto one shoulder, leaving his thumb looped in the strap so the muscles of his forearm and bicep were more prominent.

The small group eyed him. "You look like a strong fellow," the man who'd been arguing for not unloading the wagon said. He nodded to the wagon with the broken wheel. "You think you could help lift that? I've got two able-bodied folks willing to help, but I reckon we'll need a third to make this go smoothly."

Drystan smiled the friendliest smile he could muster. "That shouldn't be a problem."

As it turned out, Drystan was able to lift the cart's weight on his own, though not for very long. One of the women traveling with the group insisted on helping as well, which was fine by Drystan. She was surprisingly strong, and between the two of them, they had it well in hand, leaving the others to fix the wheel. Drystan and the woman stood on either side of the broken wheel. With her help, Drystan could have held that cart up for hours.

The woman appeared around the same age as Thomas, or maybe Gray, with dark hair braided in tight rows against her head, and deep brown skin. Her clothes were all shades of gray: pants and a fitted top, plus darker calf-high boots.

When they were finished, the woman approached Drystan. "Thanks for your help, friend," she said. "Where are you headed?"

"Alton," Drystan said.

"Us too. Care to travel with us?" She smiled warmly as she added, "Seems like you might be a useful one to have around on the road."

"Thanks." Drystan shouldered his pack. "I'd like that."

Drystan kept to himself throughout the rest of that day's travel, and was grateful that he could grab a seat on the edge of one of the carts for the hottest part of the afternoon, even getting a chance to rest his eyes for a while. The next day was more of the same. The caravan planned to stop for the night when the sun set, which would put them in Alton by noon the following day. That suited him just fine.

They passed another train of wagons heading the opposite direction just before sundown, and the two groups decided to circle up and share a meal and make camp together. Safety in numbers, and all that.

As folks were bedding down, a shout rose from one of the wagons. "Someone stole my necklace!" a woman cried. Everyone gathered as a shorter woman, one of the ones from Drystan's group, hurried toward the campfire. She was a little older than Drystan, with dark brown hair and fair skin. Her clothes were finely tailored and high quality. "My necklace!" she shouted again, approaching a panic. "It's gone!"

The woman in gray who'd helped Drystan lift the wagon the day before stepped forward. "Take a breath," she said as she set a hand on the other woman's arm. "Tell me what's happened."

"I had a pouch," the woman started, forcing words through sniffles and sobs. "It had a necklace in it. Gold, with an emerald and two sapphires. It was my mother's. Please, it's all I have left of her." The woman's hands flew to her face as she fell into sobs.

The woman in gray put an arm around her shoulders while she surveyed the assembled travelers.

"It must be one of them," someone in their group said, pointing to the new arrivals.

Shouts echoed back and forth, but the woman in gray simply focused on each person in turn. Her attention lingered on Drystan no longer than on anyone else.

"Is anything else missing?" she asked the crying woman.

She nodded. "There was some gold in there too," she said. "But I don't care about that. I just want my mother's necklace back!"

The gold that had been in that pouch was easily a week's worth of wages to most folk. The woman was wealthy—there was no denying it with a reaction like that. Drystan had known she was from the start.

It was why he'd stolen from her specifically.

"Listen up!" the woman in gray shouted. Every person there fell silent at the command in her voice. "Here's what we're going to do. I'm going to leave a small sack open near one of the wagons tonight. Inside, I'm going to place twenty gold. Whoever took the necklace can place it in that sack anytime before dawn and take the twenty gold. Plus, you can keep the rest of the stolen gold, no questions asked." She cast a withering look around the group. "If the necklace hasn't been returned by morning, I will search every person here until both the necklace and the gold are recovered, and the thief will arrive in Alton in my custody. Is that clear?"

"Who are you to make such demands?" someone shouted.

The woman in gray pulled down the collar of her shirt, revealing the symbol of two swords crossed over a burning brazier, branded into her dark skin. "I'm a Warden of the Flame."

Murmurs ran through the group as Drystan's pulse quickened. He'd never met a Warden of the Flame before.

"Why offer up more gold to a thief?" someone else asked. "Why not just search everyone now?" A few others chorused their agreement.

The Warden surveyed those standing around her. "Because times are hard. And I don't see any bad people gathered here. I see only hardworking folks trying to do the best they can with the lot they've been given." She regarded the crying woman for a moment before she said, "If anyone here stole that necklace, I believe they did it only because they felt they had no other choice. And I believe everyone deserves a second chance to do the right thing."

CHAPTER 8

Drystan lay awake, the gold necklace held tight in the palm of his hand. He'd thought it would make a nice gift for Genna—something lovely that would look as though it belonged on her. It was a hell of a lot nicer than anything he was able to get her himself. But he hadn't known how much it meant to the woman who owned it.

Why was his stomach so knotted up?

When he was certain everyone was asleep, Drystan crept to the bag the Warden had left open. Inside, the gold coins she'd promised glittered in the moonlight. He could take them—she'd said as much.

With one last glance to ensure no one was watching, Drystan placed the necklace on top of the coins in the bag.

He hadn't made it more than a couple steps toward his own blanket when a whispered voice stopped him. "You didn't take the gold."

Drystan spun on his heels to face the Warden, who was peering into the bag at her feet. "No," he said. His heart skittered as he considered whether he'd be able to outrun the Warden if she tried to arrest him. "You said if I returned it—"

The Warden raised her hands. "I did," she said quickly. "And I won't breathe a word to the others. I swear on my honor." She moved a little closer to him, though she stopped when he took a step back. "I am wondering why, though. Why take the necklace but not the extra gold?"

"You said no questions asked," he pointed out.

"You're right. But I am curious." When he didn't say anything, she sized him up, the corner of her mouth curving as though his silence amused her. "You're an interesting one," she murmured before turning away from him. She rounded the wagon.

Drystan's shoulders sagged as soon as she was out of sight. Aetherann's breath. He'd better be on his best behavior for the rest of the trip. Being scrutinized by a Warden was not something he needed. His place in his father's good graces was tenuous enough; if Drystan ended up with a Warden poking around, he could only imagine the hellfire his father would rain down on him.

Drystan kept his head down the next morning, avoiding the Warden as best he could for the last few hours to Alton. As soon as their little caravan passed through the town gates, Drystan ducked away from the group without so much as a goodbye and hurried home.

His mother answered the front door when he knocked. "Drystan!" she exclaimed, her face alight. "What are you doing back?" She rose onto her toes, throwing her arms around his neck. He dropped his pack and stooped to embrace her.

"Hi, Ma." He took a moment to just breathe in the scent of home. "Dad sent me back to take care of a few things."

Her lips drew tight, but she forced a smile. "Come inside," she said. She pulled him into the house and closed the door. "Why don't you go clean up and I'll make you something to eat."

"I'm alright, Ma," he said, but she was already shoving him toward the stairs. "Go change. Get settled, sweetheart."

After he washed up and changed his clothes, Drystan ate some of the food his mother laid out for him, though he would have thought she was trying to feed him *and* all of his brothers with the amount of food she'd prepared. The spacious, white-painted kitchen looked so empty without half the crew hanging around at any given hour, and seeing the food laid out on the table instead of maps, plans, and coded ledgers was a welcome sight.

For once, it was nice being home. Without his father or his brothers there to take up his time and space and energy, he could relax and spend time with his mother, just the two of them. They so rarely got to spend more than a few minutes together.

Sitting at the table and picking at the remnants of his lunch, Drystan reviewed the list of tasks his father needed him to do. Apparently, the lieutenant left in charge wasn't handling everything to Phillip's satisfaction—and a *meeting* with him was on the list. There were a handful of payments to be collected, of course, and a few other visits to some of the local business owners to ensure his father's hold over them was enforced. But then Drystan's eyes snagged on the last item on the list. There, in his father's code, was an address and three words.

Burn it down.

Drystan tucked the note into his pocket. He would worry about the list later, he decided. Although he was anxious to get back to Sevrun so he could see Genna again—he missed her so much already—there wasn't anything so urgent that it couldn't wait until tomorrow. For now, he would enjoy a rare, quiet night where he could relax.

That evening, after they'd had a pleasant dinner together, Drystan followed his mother into the sitting room. She sat in her favorite chair, and Drystan lit a few of the candles and oil lamps around the room, giving the space a warm glow. He hesitated for only a moment before he sat at his mother's feet, ignoring the scolding tone of his father's voice in his head.

He watched the flames dance on one of the nearby lanterns while his mother read silently. Her hand rested on Drystan's head, her fingers idly combing through his hair as her nails scratched gently at his scalp. She used to do that all the time when he was little. If he was sick or scared, he would curl up on her lap and she would gently scratch his head with her long, manicured fingernails until he was soothed and fell asleep. Even now, the motion settled something in his chest, and he closed his eyes and leaned against her leg a little more.

"What tasks does your father have for you?" she asked, just before he'd dozed off completely.

"The usual," he said through a yawn. He didn't want to worry her, so he left it at that.

His mother's hand stilled. "I think I'm going to get some sleep," she said. She leaned forward and placed a kiss in his hair. "It's nice having you home. I'll see you in the morning, sweetheart."

Drystan stayed on the floor in front of his mother's chair for a while longer, thoughts of his family and of Genna swirling through his mind.

Chapter 9

Drystan's time in Alton seemed to drag on, yet it also went by far too quickly. He spent the mornings with his mother before heading into the city proper to tend to his father's business. After a few collections and a few beatings for those unwilling or unable to pay what they owed, Drystan would make his way to his favorite tavern. As long as he didn't spend what was owed to his father, he could blow as much of his own money on ale and whatever else caught his fancy as he wanted. Then he'd stumble home in the early hours of the morning, collapse into bed, and do it all again the next day.

Halfway through the week, Drystan was at the tavern as usual, though that night he was drinking to dull the throbbing pain of a split lip and a bruised rib from one of his father's debtors who'd opted to fight back. Most of the regulars at Simon's knew who he was and gave him a wide berth. And yet a voice rose up from the stool beside him.

"If you won," a woman said, startlingly close, "I'd hate to see the other guy."

Drystan paused in mid-drink. Then he turned to regard the person beside him. He blinked, needing a moment for the reality of what he was seeing to snap into place in his brain.

"Evening, Warden," he said.

The Warden from the caravan smiled. "Ah, you do remember me."

"Hard to forget," Drystan mumbled into his ale as he took another long swallow.

"So, did you?" the Warden asked.

"Did I what?"

"Win." She gave him an upward nod. "The fight."

"Yeah," he said. "I won." He took his drink and moved to an empty table in the far corner of the room. The last thing he felt like doing was talking. Hopefully the Warden would take the hint and—

"Mind if I join you?" The Warden pulled out the chair beside Drystan and sat down before he could answer.

"Yes."

She didn't move to stand, though she nodded toward his drink. "You've been at that for a while."

Drystan set his mug down hard. "What do you care?"

"I suppose I shouldn't. I have no reason to. I don't know you after all." She leaned back in her chair. "But back on the road, you were ready to return that lady's necklace even before my offer, weren't you? Before the reward—that's why you didn't take it. As soon as you realized you'd hurt her, you were ready to give it back. Am I right?"

"Look, it doesn't matter," Drystan said, his stomach twisting at the memory of the woman's pain-stricken face. He dropped a coin on the table and moved to leave, his beer unfinished. "I gave it back, didn't I?"

"Who are you, kid?" the Warden called after him. "What's your story?"

His story? His story, he was coming to realize, was a dark mess, punctuated with only the single bright spot of a girl he'd met at a masked ball.

Drystan didn't answer the Warden as he left Simon's and wandered into Alton.

There was one job left on Drystan's list, and he'd been putting it off for most of the week. Research into the situation and the target was needed, he'd told himself, but he'd been stalling. He was supposed to head back to Sevrun the day after tomorrow, and this was the last thing left to do. Factoring in time to allow for adjusting his plan if something went wrong, he couldn't delay it any longer.

His mother pulled a light shawl around her shoulders as she watched him leave the house with his bow slung over one shoulder and a quiver on his hip with a single arrow. She'd grown quieter over the week he'd been home. Perhaps his father had been right—perhaps he did have a tendency to wear out his welcome.

Drystan shook the thought from his mind as he crossed the city. It was midafternoon, and the streets were crowded. He needed to focus.

A new crew had moved into Alton a couple months ago and had been slowly encroaching on Phillip Kalon's territory, Drystan's digging had uncovered. Drystan's father had given the man a warning, but apparently the man had decided to double down on his stake in the city. Now that Drystan's father was beyond negotiating, Drystan's orders were clear.

Burn his house down.

It had been no trouble to find where the man lived with his wife and two small children. Nor had it been difficult to find a nearby building that was tall enough to provide the correct vantage point.

Drystan climbed onto the roof of the storefront he'd selected. It was a few buildings away, and he approached from the alley to avoid being spotted. While doing something like this in the daylight meant more potential witnesses, it also meant that the flame on his arrow would be less noticeable from the street.

Drystan waited as long as he could, but if the sun started to set, it was more likely he'd be spotted. He couldn't delay anymore. He used a small piece of flint to light the oil-soaked arrow he'd brought with him. His target was the second-floor window on the right side. It was open about two inches, and from Drystan's reconnaissance, he knew it was the man's office—lots of papers and documents ready to be set alight.

Drystan took aim at the narrow opening and held his breath. The arrow loosed and flew high, shattering the window. Shards of glass fell to the ground, and shouts rose up from the streets, even before smoke began to billow from the broken window.

Drystan sprinted across the roof and scaled down the side of the building, back into the alley the way he'd come. When his feet hit the ground, a voice that was becoming frustratingly familiar greeted him.

"Nice shot."

Drystan stared, dumbfounded, at the Warden in gray. "Have you been following me?"

"Yeah," she said flatly. "Pretty much."

More cries rolled through the surrounding streets, along with alarm bells and shouts of fire.

Drystan turned to run, but the Warden blocked his path.

Yet, she didn't move to apprehend him.

His heart raced. "Are you going to arrest me?"

The Warden angled her head. "Walk with me. And ditch the bow. You can come back for it tonight, but if anyone spots you with it, you'll be sunk."

He didn't trust her, but he had little choice. Drystan dropped the bow behind a stack of crates and followed her. The Warden led him out of the alley, keeping to the smaller side streets as they moved away from the fire.

"In here," she said, holding open a door. When Drystan hesitated, she added, "If I were going to arrest you, I'd have done it at the crime scene."

Drystan ducked inside. It was a shop of some kind, with trinkets and odds and ends lining the rows of dusty shelves. The old man behind the counter simply nodded to the Warden, who led Drystan through a curtain into a back room and down a narrow flight of stairs.

"What is this place?" Drystan wondered aloud.

"A safe house, of sorts," the Warden said. She lit a few candles, illuminating the sparse stone room. Before Drystan could ask any other questions, the Warden faced him, crossing her arms. "I know who you are, Drystan Kalon."

Drystan's stomach clenched. *Shit, shit, shit.* He took an instinctive step toward the stairs.

"I already told you," the Warden continued, raising her hand as though to steady his rising anxiety. "I'm not going to arrest you."

"Then what do you want?"

"I just want to talk." She studied him a moment more before she said, "You're one hell of an enigma, you know that?"

Drystan bristled. "I'm really not."

The Warden counted off on her fingers. "You steal a necklace from the wealthiest woman in the caravan, only to return it the moment you find out it means something to her. You run enforcement for your father, but drink yourself into a stupor after every job. And you saved the lives of a whole family today."

"What are you talking about?" Drystan's face heated. "I-I didn't—"

"You could have set fire to that house at night, when that entire family would have been tucked in their beds, sound asleep."

"The flame from the arrow would have given away my position," he said weakly.

The Warden shrugged. "Sure. Maybe that's true. But the children were at school, and the wife was at the market, wasn't she? Only the husband was home. Working in his office. Where your arrow landed."

"It's where his records were . . ."

"Of course it was. But it also means the fire wouldn't go unnoticed for very long, would it? And just in case you had poor timing and he was out of the room, you made sure to call attention to it by shattering that window on purpose." Her lips curved into a small smile. "Didn't you?"

Drystan swallowed hard. How could she possibly know any of that? She couldn't know that Drystan was skilled enough with a bow that he could've hit that opening from twice the distance. "I don't know what you're talking about," he said, though his voice was scarcely more than a whisper.

"I'm sure you don't. All I know is that when I see someone trying so hard to do the right thing, it usually means they want to do the right thing. You're not suited for your father's life, Drystan."

"Now *you* don't know what you're talking about," he muttered. She was wrong. But even if she wasn't . . . "What does it matter anyway?"

"It matters because you have a choice. You can choose to stay or choose to leave your father's world in the dust." The Warden watched him, her mouth twisting in consideration. "Have you ever given any thought to joining the Wardens?"

Drystan laughed, low and hollow. "You've got to be kidding. You're trying to *recruit* me?"

"I'm serious," she said. "You've got skills, but you're obviously being wasted doing your father's dirty work. With the Wardens, you could help people. You could do some good in the world."

"You just saw me try to burn someone's house down, and you think I could help people?" Drystan scoffed. "Are you mad?"

"You *tried*," she admitted, "and purposefully failed. And because of that, you did help people. Whether you realized what you were doing or not."

Drystan shook his head, taking another step away from her. "If you know who I am, then you know who my father is. He'd never—"

"He doesn't get a say," the Warden interrupted. "You're probably not familiar with the Warden's oath, but when you join, you swear to forsake all ties to inheritances, lands, titles . . ." She paused for dramatic effect. "Family connections."

He rolled his eyes. She couldn't be serious.

"The other day in the tavern, I asked about your story. Look, I know you couldn't choose how it started, and you can't choose how it ends, but what you can choose are all the parts that happen in the middle."

Drystan crossed his arms over his broad chest. "Are we done?"

"Think about it. That's all I'm asking. If you decide you're interested, come back to this shop and tell Myron at the front that you need to speak with me. He'll know how to reach me."

Drystan turned toward the stairs. This was ridiculous. Wardens were noble. Honorable. Vire's hells, they were heroes, for fuck's sake. That wasn't him.

You're a brute, his father always told him. *You hurt people. Kill people.*

And he was right. Drystan wasn't Warden material, not by a long shot.

"Remember, Drystan," she said, halting his steps. "No one's born a Warden. We've all come from another life. You wouldn't be the only one with a dark story who used the Wardens as a chance to start over."

Drystan took the stairs two at a time, leaving the Warden with only the flames casting shadows on the wall. He hurried back to the alley to retrieve his bow. Stories of Wardens, heroes, and villains wove through his mind as he rushed home.

Chapter 10

Drystan couldn't risk going back into town that night, in case he'd been spotted during the attempted arson, so he stayed at home. And since the Warden seemed to enjoy tailing him, at least he'd avoid running into her again too. He stayed in his room, thoughts turning themselves over and over in his mind. There was no way he could ever be a Warden, but . . . But *could* he leave? With Genna?

Could he betray his family?

When he didn't go downstairs for dinner, his mother brought him a plate of food. He took it and thanked her quietly, though he barely touched it.

In the morning, Drystan skipped breakfast. He thought about packing for the trip back to Sevrun, but he wasn't leaving until the next day and he'd only brought his small knapsack. It wouldn't take him long to get his belongings in order.

"I never wanted this for you, you know."

Drystan spun to find his mother standing in the open doorway to his room. "What?"

"When I married your father, I was so young. I knew a bit about who he was, but I didn't know everything." She stepped into the room, and sat on the end of Drystan's bed. She smiled up at him, her green eyes shimmering. "By the time I realized the extent of it, I already had you. I wanted to shelter you from the life he led, but he wouldn't entertain it for a moment." She blew out a quiet sigh as he sat beside her. "Not to mention that you looked at your older brothers with such admiration when you were little—I knew there'd be no keeping you from it."

It was true. Drystan had wanted nothing more than to be just like Elias. Like Thomas. Like Gray.

Her voice cracked. "I'm sorry I didn't try harder."

"Ma, it wasn't—"

"I'm sorry I couldn't protect you from it. I never wanted this for you," she said again, and there were tears in her eyes. "If you ever get the chance to leave, I want you to take it, Drystan. Understand? If you're able to run away, then you *run*. Don't look back. Don't even tell me where you're going."

Drystan had never seen so much emotion from her—had never seen her cry—and it pulled at his heart. His throat tightened. "Wh-why are you saying this?"

"Because I want you to be happy, and I don't think you can be here." Her voice trembled as she took her son's face in her hands. "If one day you disappear, I'll know you made it out. And I'll be so proud of you."

Drystan swallowed hard, his thoughts darting back to Genna and the job in Sevrun. Was his mother right? Could he be happy somewhere else—with Genna?

Did he owe it to himself to try?

"Alright, Ma." The words nearly caught in his throat. "I will."

"That's a good lad." Her hand caressed his cheek as she blinked rapidly, ushering the tears away. A tight smile pulled across her lips until she looked calm and even, just as she always did, though for the first time, Drystan recognized her placid demeanor for what it truly was.

A mask. A shield that she used to protect herself.

And him.

The realization tore through him, and he wordlessly stared at his mother as she rose, smoothing the fabric of her dress. She wasn't happy. But she'd done everything she could so Drystan would have a chance to be.

She smiled down at him. "Let's head downstairs, sweetheart. Let's not waste any more of this beautiful day."

On the morning he was due to leave Alton, a knot of uncertainty had settled in Drystan's stomach. He wasn't sure how he would do it, or what the future would hold, but he was certain of one thing—he would leave with Genna.

Drystan hugged his mother goodbye, holding on to her for a long time. "Thank you," he said over the top of her head. "For . . . everything."

Her arms tightened around him. "Take care of yourself, sweetheart," she said. The same words she'd said to him when he'd left for Sevrun a few months ago, but he could now hear the meaning behind them.

"I'll try," he said. He turned and walked away from his mother, and from the home he grew up in.

Despite the tension wound through him, Drystan was eager to return to Sevrun and to Genna. His father wasn't expecting him until the third morning at the earliest, so Drystan rushed the last leg of the journey, making it back to the city at dusk on the second day. But instead of heading to his family's safe house, he kept walking straight to Baron Venbarra's estate.

He managed to make it onto the grounds without raising any suspicions, but he doubted he'd even get through the kitchens in his current state, covered in road dust and a thin layer of grime. He headed toward the gardens, where he might pass as a gardener cleaning up after a long day's work. He hid in the hedge maze until the sky reached full dark before he made his way toward the manor.

Trellises of ivy lined the inner walls of the gardens, and he'd learned by now which of the many balconies above was Genna's. Drystan hid his pack in one of the bushes and climbed the trellis, his arms burning as he navigated the overhang of Genna's balcony.

The gossamer curtains to her room were drawn all but a sliver. Through the narrow gap between the flowing fabric, Genna stood by her door, talking to someone in the hallway, out of view. As Drystan watched, she closed the door and crossed toward her washroom, pulling her thin dressing gown more tightly closed and readjusting the tie around her waist.

Drystan set his hand against the window and tapped a light rhythm. Genna's head snapped up. The curtains pulled back sharply and there she was—blond hair loose, her dressing gown barely clinging to her shoulders, hardly hiding the curves of her body. Her sharp eyes were wide.

She unlocked the glass door and pushed it open. "What the hells, Drystan?" Her words were a harsh whisper. "Get in here." She stepped to the side to allow him entrance into her room. She closed the door and drew the curtains again. "How long have you been standing there?"

"I just got back," he said, moving toward her.

Genna took a step back, halting him in his tracks. "Where have you been?" she demanded.

"I-I had to go back to Alton," he stammered. "I wrote you a—"

"Yes, I got your note," she said flatly.

He blinked. If she got his note then . . . "Then why are you upset?"

Her brows rose, her face red with anger. "Why am I upset? Drystan, I asked you to bring me in on your job, and you told me you needed time to think. Then the next day you disappear with only a chicken-scratch note saying that you were called away on *family business*. I thought you ran away."

He was such a fool. He should have considered how it would look from her perspective. The timing, the cryptic message—all of it. Of course she'd thought he'd left.

"I'm sorry," he said, helpless. "I was foolish."

She lifted her chin, defiant, bold. Gods, he loved that about her.

He took another hesitant step closer, his lips curling as his eyes landed on the V of her robe where it started to fall open again, dipping low between her breasts. "Can I make it up to you?"

Genna tugged her robe closed again, crossing her arms to hold it in place. "Don't play coy with me. You should have come to tell me in person instead of sending a stupid note."

"I know. But I didn't have time."

"You should have made the time for me."

"You're right. I'm sorry." He inched closer. Lanara's tears, he wanted nothing more than to wrap his arms around her and never let her go. "I'm sorry, Genna."

Her gaze slid over him, much as it had the first night they'd met. "Did you even think about me while you were gone?"

"Every day," he said immediately. "I thought about you every second of every day. And . . . And I decided that I want to run away with you."

Genna's arms fell to her sides. "You do?"

He inhaled deeply, steeling his nerves. "I do. I love you." He took another step closer. She didn't move away, but she didn't close the distance either. "Can you forgive me?"

"I forgive you," she said at last. "But gods above, you are absolutely filthy!" She scrunched her nose up in the delightful way she often did. "Go get cleaned up. Meet me in the maze tomorrow night, ninth chime. We lost a week of planning. We need to get started, and you've got a lot of work to do to make it up to me."

"Of course," he said. She was right again—he should have gone home to clean up first, rather than tracking road dust into her room, but he'd been so excited to see her.

Too eager, his father had said.

Drystan turned, opening the door to the balcony. "I'll see you tomorrow. Goodnight, Genna."

But she was already heading to her washroom. As Drystan scaled down the wall of the gardens and made the walk back to Sevrun proper, he began to formulate a plan for how the two of them would betray Phillip Kalon, the most notorious criminal in Weryn.

CHAPTER 11

DRYSTAN SPENT NEARLY EVERY moment he could with Genna, as often as her own schedule would allow. He'd memorized the maps and plans his father had for the heist, so he redrew them for her, and she pointed out where the maps were outdated, and where the guard schedules had changed. In turn, Drystan brought that information back to his father, earning himself an appreciative nod.

In addition to reviewing his father's plans, Drystan and Genevieve developed some of their own. They needed to reach the money first, after all, and they needed to get well beyond the manor grounds before anyone noticed they were gone. It would require strategically feeding Drystan's father a few false details buried amid the truth.

"We have to be careful," Genna said one night while they reviewed the plans again. The wedding—the job—was only a week away. "If my father catches us—"

"He won't." Drystan took her hands in his and brought them to his lips.

"But *if* he does . . . Drystan, I don't think you understand what he could do. What he's capable of. And the manor guards . . . He hires cruel, ruthless men to work for him."

Drystan had spent all his life around cruel, ruthless men. He wasn't afraid of them. "We'll be fine, Genna." He leaned in close, nuzzling a kiss into the curve of her neck. "We have a good plan. It'll work."

"Let's go over it again," she said, though her body leaned into his.

He kissed her again, sliding his hand through her hair. "We've been over it five times tonight already."

"And we're going to make it six." She set her hand on his chest, pushing space between them. "Or seven, or eight, until I'm satisfied. I'll do whatever it takes to ensure nothing can go wrong."

"Alright, alright." He straightened up from where he'd been reclined with her on her bed among the scattered maps, notes, and schedules. "The wedding will be taking place in the main ballroom," he recited. "You'll be there, along with the rest of your family. My father, brothers, and I will be there as wedding guests."

"How are the invitations coming?" Genna interrupted.

"Almost done," he said. "Gray's finishing them up in the next couple of days."

"I want to see one when it's finished."

"If I can sneak one out, I will."

Genna's gaze sharpened. "This isn't a game, Drystan. I helped design the invitations for my sister's wedding myself. I need to know that these forgeries are perfect."

"I know it's not a game, Genna. I have just as much at stake here as you do."

She rose from the bed. "Don't snap at me."

"I'm not—"

"You *are*," she continued. "This is very stressful and I don't appreciate the tone you're taking with me."

Drystan breathed deeply. He didn't think he'd been taking any kind of tone with her.

"I'm sorry," he said, running a hand along the back of his neck. "You're right—this is stressful." Drystan hadn't realized how much it must be affecting him.

Her face softened. She moved closer and set a gentle kiss on his cheek, though she stayed standing. "Thank you." She paused before waving her hand, gesturing for him to continue. "You were saying. About the plan."

He blew out a sigh, trying to focus. "While we're at the party, I'm supposed to step away and distract the guards at the tenth chime, but I'm actually going to go distract them at five minutes before the *ninth* chime. While I'm distracting them, you'll go to the vault and empty out as many of the most valuable things as you can. You'll leave the vault key in the second-floor hall credenza on your way back to your room. I'll pick up the key there and bring it to my father."

"How are you getting the key in the first place?" she asked as she paced the room.

Drystan bit back another sigh. "Part of my father's plans are for me to lift the key off the seneshal at quarter to the tenth chime. I'm going to lift it early and hand it off to you before I go distract the guards." Drystan had been practicing his sleight-of-hand for months to pull this off. It was a critical piece of both plans.

Originally, his father had wanted Elias to swipe the key, as he was the best pickpocket on the crew, but he was also the best shot next to Drystan, so his father had elected to put him on sniper duty, where Drystan would've otherwise been. Gray wasn't nearly subtle enough to pick anyone's pockets, and Thomas was needed to work the room with Phillip and ensure no one suspected anything. So that left Drystan.

"Good," Genna said. "Continue."

"You'll change out of your gown and into the traveling clothes I brought for you. Then I'll meet you at the servants' entrance off the kitchen. Together, we'll go to the stables, where we'll take two of the horses intended for my father and brothers, and we'll run."

"How will you distract the guards?"

Drystan walked her through every trick he knew that would serve as a long enough distraction for Genna to empty what gems and coin she could from the vault.

"And you know the best things to take from the vault?" Drystan asked. They'd need to make sure everything Genna put in the knapsacks he provided would be light enough for her to carry alone.

"Of course," she said, rolling her eyes.

"It's just that gold is very heavy, but gems are—"

"I know what's valuable in my own father's vault, Drystan. Don't you trust me?"

"I do." He rose from the bed and crossed to her, reaching for her hand. "I just thought—"

"It's fine." Genna twined their fingers. "We're both on edge. I . . . I can't let this fail." After a moment, she set her other hand against his chest. His skin warmed beneath his shirt. "I know I'm not as experienced with this sort of thing as you are." She leaned against him. "But it hurts a little that you don't trust me."

Drystan encircled her with his arms. "I *do* trust you." He stared into her eyes, losing himself there. They were so sharp, so stunning. "I love you," he said.

Genna rose on her toes and kissed him, long and sweet and far from chaste.

When he caught his breath, Drystan smirked. "So . . . Was six times enough, or do you need me to go for seven?"

She kissed him again, drawing his lip between her teeth before she said, "I'd like to see if there's anything else you think you can do six times tonight."

Gods be damned to Vire's hells, this girl was going to be the death of him.

Chapter 12

Drystan moved through the crowded ballroom. The air was stifling, with hundreds of guests filling the manor and spilling into the gardens. Although there was music and dancing, it was all slow and stilted and terribly proper. Even the gowns worn by most of the women were in dull, muted colors. Drystan couldn't imagine Genna staying somewhere like this for the rest of her life. That bright spark of her soul would be smothered into darkness.

He pushed the thought from his mind. The baron's vault key sat heavy in his pocket; it was nearly time to meet Genna at the servants' entrance. The last thing he needed to do was hand off the key to his father.

Drystan spotted him in the manor foyer, as they'd planned. A blond wig and some facial hair served as a sufficient enough disguise that no one would recognize the notorious Phillip Kalon. Not in a place like this. He was laughing among a group of wedding guests, and they were laughing with him as though he'd just said something funny. It never ceased to amaze Drystan how many different roles his father could play, switching between them as effortlessly as if he was donning a hat.

"Excuse me a moment, sirs," Phillip said as he spotted Drystan. His tone was pleasant and cheerful.

Once his father had separated himself from the group, Drystan approached, sliding his hand into his pocket. "Have a fine evening, sir." He extended his hand to his father as he said the scripted line, the key tucked tight against his palm.

Phillip clasped his son's hand, still smiling, and turned them both. As soon as Phillip's back was to the group of wedding guests, his face hardened, losing that joyful warmth from only a moment before. The swiftness with which his expression could change was always startling, and Drystan had to force himself not to step back.

"I'll admit," his father said, not yet releasing Drystan's hand. "I didn't think you had it in you before tonight."

"And now?" Drystan asked. He didn't know why he needed to know, but had he finally proven himself a capable member of the crew in his father's eyes?

Phillip Kalon regarded his youngest son, giving the question due consideration. "I suppose even a broken clock is right twice a day."

Drystan's mind snagged on his father's words. "Sir?"

"I only allowed this dalliance as a favor to your mother," Phillip continued. "We're not going to make a habit of this little role reversal. An attack dog doesn't stop being an attack dog just because you dress it up. Understand?"

It didn't matter. Drystan would be gone in only a few more minutes, leaving this part of his life behind forever. It didn't matter what the fuck his father thought of him. And yet knowing it hadn't been enough . . . Even after everything Drystan had accomplished for this heist—everything he'd done to prove himself worthy—it hadn't been enough . . .

He would never be enough.

Something inside him cracked, but he didn't let it show. He shook his father's hand, pressing the key into his palm. "I understand," he answered dutifully.

"Good." Phillip pocketed the key. "Now, see to your girl until it's time to distract the guards. *Don't* be late."

Drystan spun and headed toward his meeting place with Genna without another word to his father.

Genna was late. They needed to be on the road by the time his father discovered that Drystan wasn't distracting the guards like he was supposed to be. They were rapidly running out of time, and Genna was nowhere to be seen.

Something was wrong.

Drystan moved as quickly as he dared through the shadows of the gardens. Maybe she'd been delayed somehow and was still in her room. Their escape plan could still work, so long as they stuck together. Drystan climbed up the ivy trellis beneath her window and levered himself onto her balcony. Candles flickered behind the drawn curtains. He pulled open the glass doors and stepped inside.

"Genna?" Even the whisper was sharp in the silent room. His stomach twisted into a knot. He knew this kind of stillness. It wasn't the stillness of an empty room, or even the stillness of sleep. The strange stillness of death hung in the air. "Genna?" he tried again, urgency seeping into his voice. *Lanara's tears, please don't let her be—*

"Dead." Genevieve appeared in the doorway to her sitting room. Her dressing gown was pulled tight around her, and her silver-blond hair was unbound and wild about her shoulders. Her eyes were equally wild as she looked at Drystan. "He's dead."

"It's alright," he said, even though that seemed to him to be the farthest thing from the truth. "Show me."

Unblinking, Genevieve retreated into the sitting room, disappearing into the shadows. Drystan swallowed down his trepidation, as well as the voice in his head telling him to run, and followed her.

Several candles lit the sitting room, illuminating the body of a servant that lay in the middle of the floor. A pool of crimson surrounded him, soaking into the carpet. A bloody dagger lay nearby.

"Gods, Genna, what happened?"

"It's not my fault," Genevieve pleaded. "Please, you have to believe me."

"What *happened*?"

She stomped her foot. "Don't shout at me!"

"I'm not—" Drystan took a deep breath. It would be alright. He could fix this. He closed the distance to Genevieve and set his hands gently on her arms. "I'm sorry, but this is important. Are you hurt?"

She shook her head.

"Good." He rubbed her arms. "Now, please tell me what happened."

Genevieve inhaled sharply. "It was awful. He came into my room to tend to the fire, and then he started asking me all these questions about why I wasn't downstairs at the party." Her voice was steady. "As though he had a right to know any of it. And . . . And it all just happened so fast." She was remarkably calm, not panicked as he would have expected, despite her wide eyes. But shock could do strange things to a person.

He pulled her into his arms, though she remained stiff against his chest. "It'll be alright. But, Genna . . ." There was one question he still needed to ask. "You weren't at the meeting spot. Why weren't you where we said?"

Genevieve shoved Drystan back. "I was attacked! I could have been killed, and you're blaming me?"

"I'm not blaming you," he said, trying to keep his tone even, "But—"

"But what?" she demanded.

What did it matter? What did any of it matter? At least she was safe. "You're right. But we need to take care of this. Quickly." Gods above, they were running out of time. "We need to hide the body—somewhere he won't be found until we're long gone." The thought churned his stomach. He hated that he couldn't give the man's body the respect owed the dead . . . but he'd attacked Genna, and they needed to buy themselves some time. He swallowed, bile burning his throat. "Then we can get out of here. Like we planned."

Genevieve smiled, sliding her hands into his. "Together?" she asked.

"Together."

She stood on her toes and kissed Drystan. "You're perfect."

"I love you." He squeezed her hands before sliding off his suit coat and draping it over the couch. "Can you find something we can clean the floor with?" he asked as he rolled his sleeves up to his elbows.

"Of course. I'll be right back." Genevieve darted into the bathing room, leaving Drystan to deal with the body.

A body, Drystan had learned when he was younger, weighed the exact same amount as a living person, and yet, somehow, carrying one always seemed so much harder. Perhaps, he wondered in the vain hope of distracting himself from his gruesome task, it was because a living person could offer at least some small amount of assistance—they could hold on or lean one way or the other. But a dead body, well . . .

Drystan dragged the servant into the bedroom. Unfortunately, under Genna's bed would be the best hiding spot he could manage under the circumstances. After all, he wanted the man to be found eventually. He set the man down on the floor, laying him on his stomach so the wound on his back wouldn't leave a streak of blood on the carpet as he shoved him under the bed.

Wait—

Drystan returned to the sitting room. The blade was where he'd last seen it, discarded on the floor. He crouched beside it to take a closer look. It wasn't a standard household knife. It was the dagger he'd given Genevieve.

"Genna," he called. Her soft footsteps sounded on the tiled floor of the bathing room, though he kept his eyes on the dagger. "Why does he have a wound in his back?"

"What?"

"You said he attacked you. Why did you stab him in the back?"

When there was no answer, Drystan peeled his attention away from the blade. Genna stared at him from the doorway of the washroom.

"Why did you stab him in the back?" he asked again.

"It doesn't matter."

Drystan stood, crossing the distance to the woman he loved. "It does," he said. "It matters to me. Did he attack you or not?"

Genna smoothed the fabric of her dressing gown, leaving faint trails of blood. "He did not."

Drystan blinked, floundering for words, for thoughts. "Then . . . then you thought he was going to?" He took her hands in his. He needed something to steady himself. "You were afraid for your life?"

She shook her head.

"Vire's hells, Genna. Then why? Why'd you kill him?"

Genevieve's gaze went cold and distant. "I needed to know what I was capable of."

Thoughts flooded Drystan's mind faster than he could keep up. "You . . ." She'd killed a man just to know whether or not she *could*? "You . . . what?"

"If I was really going to leave—to be free—I needed to know that I could survive on my own."

No, no, not Genna. She couldn't—

"The world is a dangerous place, Drystan." Her voice was deadly calm as she squeezed his hands so tightly her knuckles turned white. "I needed to know that I could do what had to be done."

"So you stabbed an innocent man in the back?"

"I needed to know that I could protect myself."

"But *I* can protect you!" Drystan cried. "You didn't need to— You don't—"

Another thought struck him, and it pulled the breath from his lungs. He met Genevieve's eyes, which were still so calm and cold. Calculating.

He'd always been awed by the sharpness in her eyes.

"You were going to leave," he murmured. "Alone. That's why you weren't at the meeting spot." His vision swam as the pieces clicked into place. "You were going to take the coin and run."

Genna's lips—the lips he'd kissed a hundred times—curved into a sad smile. She cupped his face in her hands. "You taught me what I needed to know," she said softly. "And for that I will forever be grateful. But I can't be free if I'm just trading one master for another."

"But I'm not . . . I never wanted to . . ."

Genna's words from that night in Sevrun echoed through his mind. *I could go anywhere . . . I could live my own life . . . I'll do whatever it takes.*

"This was always your plan." Drystan's chest tightened painfully. He couldn't breathe. "This was your plan from the start, wasn't it?"

"I never meant for you to be here," she said, and it sounded more sincere than anything she'd ever said to him. "Please believe this was never part of the plan."

"Wait, Gen—"

Genevieve screamed.

CHAPTER 13

SHOUTS ROSE FROM THE hallway as the echoes of Genevieve's scream faded.

"What are you doing?" Drystan yelled. This couldn't be happening. No, not Genna. They were going to run away together. He had risked everything for her. He'd betrayed his father, his brothers, for her.

Everything had been for her.

Genevieve shook her head. "I'm sorry, Drystan. Please understand. You've given me so much. But I'm afraid there's one last thing I need from you." She gave him the pitying smile she might give a lost puppy. "A distraction."

He tried to process what she was saying, but her face shifted from pity to terror as he watched. She screamed again, and several guards burst into the room.

Genevieve pointed at Drystan. "Help! Help me please, he— He killed him! He—" Her words devolved into hysterical sobs as the guards advanced on Drystan.

"No, wait!" He held up his hands . . . which were covered in the servant's blood. And that was Drystan's dagger on the bloody carpet.

Genevieve had set him up.

She was still sobbing as Drystan bolted for the balcony. He threw the door open with such force that it shattered against the outer wall as he jumped onto the railing and leapt over. Pain shot through his ankle when he hit the grass, but he rolled with the landing. He scrambled to his feet. Nothing was broken. He could still run.

And Drystan ran. He sprinted across the gardens and through the main gates, shouts and cries and alarms roaring behind him. He didn't look back.

The estate was surrounded by rolling hills, with Sevrun to the south and the forests and river to the north. His family's safe house was in town. If he was followed, he could lead the guards straight there. And if the guards didn't murder him, his family certainly would.

Drystan hooked north. It was at least two miles to the forest, only a bit farther than town, but maybe if he made it to the tree line, he could lose his pursuers in the darkness.

He ran. He ran until his legs ached and his lungs burned. Horses' hooves pounded behind him with the baying of hounds.

Shit.

The river. His only chance was the river.

The thundering of the horses grew louder until Drystan was certain he'd be trampled at any moment. He didn't dare look back.

Something solid struck him hard between the shoulder blades. Drystan stumbled and fell, tumbling. A hand grabbed the front of his shirt and hauled him to his feet. Drystan stood into the pull, sending the guard off balance, and followed through with an upper cut to the man's jaw. Something cracked as the guard's head snapped back.

Another guard reached for him. Drystan ducked the grab and ran. He couldn't let them catch him. If they caught him, they'd throw him in jail. Or worse, depending on what Genevieve told them.

The trees were just ahead. Drystan pushed forward, digging down for a burst of speed he wasn't sure he had left. He was nearly there.

As he ran, Drystan's foot snagged on a tree root, sending him sprawling. His chest struck the ground hard, and he gasped for the air that was knocked from his lungs.

"You're fast, kid," a deep voice said as Drystan struggled to regain his breath. A guard gripped him by the shoulder and rolled him onto his back. "You like running, eh?"

The guard drove his boot down on Drystan's knee. There was an explosion of pain as a sickening *crack* reverberated through his whole body.

"Can't have you trying that again," the guard said, raising his leg for another stomp.

Another sharp snap of bone tore a scream from Drystan. His vision darkened except for a narrow pinprick of light as nausea rolled through him.

"What're you doing?" another voice called from nearby. "Get him up. Venbarra's going to want to deal with him."

"Just giving the bastard what he deserves," the first man said. Drystan was lifted off the ground by his shirt before something solid struck his face, knocking him back into the ground. Then a third *crack* sounded as the man sent a kick into Drystan's side.

Drystan gasped and wheezed. He curled up on himself as best he could, tucking his arms into his sides and covering his face with his hands.

"Quit playing around," the second guard shouted. "Get him up, dammit."

"Alright, alright," the first grumbled. He grabbed Drystan's shirt again. "On your feet, you piece of shit."

Drystan tried to pull away as the man hauled him up.

"Fine," the guard said, laughing. "You wanna run? Go ahead. Run." He released Drystan. Searing pain lanced through his ruined knee as he collapsed with another anguished cry. Drystan's vision flashed white and then black as the world faded away amid the sounds of barking dogs and laughter.

Drystan opened his eyes. The world spun and his stomach roiled. Each movement was agony, and nausea crashed into him as he lifted his head. Where was he?

He was surrounded by dirt, blood, and filth where he lay on cold, gray stone. Hazy light filtered in through a small window somewhere above him, and metal chains scraped against the stone when he shifted. He touched his face, swollen and bruised, and a sharp pain lanced through his side with every breath.

He couldn't bring himself to look down at his knee.

Gods, this was it. He was never getting out of this cell. He was going to die here, and it was all because he had trusted Genevieve. He had trusted her—he had loved her—and she had used him to get what she wanted. His father had asked Drystan what use he could be to her.

It seemed he now had his answer.

Tears welled in his eyes, the salt stinging the cuts on his face.

He was going to die here.

Fear settled in his chest. His jagged, fragmented thoughts drifted to an old prayer his mother had taught him when he was a child.

Taerna of the earth on which I walk, deliver me. Aetherann of the air that fills my lungs, deliver me. Lanara of the water that gives me life, deliver me. Pyrannis of the fire that fuels my heart, deliver me.

He prayed and prayed and prayed, until boots thudded against the stones nearby. Drystan couldn't tell how many.

"Grab him," a voice ordered. There was a clang of metal and then hands were on him as two guards hauled him to his knees. Drystan couldn't stop the yell that tore from his throat at the violent movement. Someone fisted his hair and yanked his head up. A few feet away stood Baron Miles Venbarra. A scowl darkened his noble features, and he was still wearing his formal attire from the wedding.

"Where is my money?" he demanded. "Where is my daughter?"

So, Genevieve had escaped during the distraction of Drystan's capture. Just as she'd planned. She'd told him exactly what she was going to do. A dozen times, she'd told him. He never listened.

"Your money and your daughter?" Drystan rasped. "In that order?"

Venbarra turned his attention to one of the men holding Drystan's head up and gave a nod. A fist crashed into Drystan's jaw, snapping his head to the side. His vision darkened, but the hands holding him jerked him upright again as the room resolved into blurry view again.

"I know who you are," Baron Venbarra sneered. "You're one of Phillip Kalon's sons. Which means he's here somewhere. I don't suppose you have enough sense of self-preservation to tell me where he is."

There was no chance his father and brothers were still at the safe house. Not after the chaos that had no doubt erupted at the manor after Drystan's attempt to flee. But even if Drystan knew where they'd gone, would he have had it in him to betray his family a second time in as many days?

Drystan spit a wad of blood and phlegm on the ground.

Venbarra's lips twisted in disgust. "I figured as much. This is your last chance, boy. Tell me where to find my gold and my daughter, and I'll grant you the mercy of a swift death."

Drystan looked up at the baron, silent. Even if he knew where Genevieve had gone, Baron Venbarra would never believe him.

Venbarra looked over his shoulder. "Prepare the gallows," he said to someone out of sight. "Tomorrow we'll make an example out of him."

CHAPTER 14

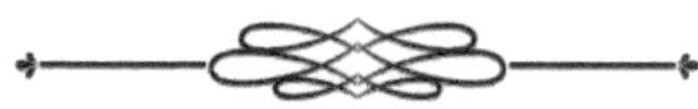

D RYSTAN'S WORLD WAS NOTHING but shifting, rolling shades of gray that faded in and out with his consciousness. At some point he was vaguely aware of his hands being bound behind his back before he was hauled across the stones and up some stairs.

The daylight singed his eyes as the murmur of a gathered crowd reached him. *We'll make an example out of him*, Baron Venbarra had said.

Someone was speaking as Drystan was dragged up the gallows' steps. A list of charges. He only caught every other word, but most sounded fabricated. Not that it mattered.

They stood him up, and he was forced to use his right foot for balance despite his broken knee. Just touching his foot to the wooden platform was agony. Drystan gritted his teeth to keep from crying out. He wouldn't scream. Not here. If this was to be his fate, he would meet it head on.

The Warden from Alton had told him that he couldn't choose how his story would end. That was true, but Drystan had always known it would come publicly at the end of a rope. If he were lucky, it might come at the end of a sword with fewer witnesses. But he was never destined for the luxury of dying an old man alone in bed or surrounded by a family who loved him.

His vision resolved as the voice continued. Sevrun's magistrate addressed the crowd, which pressed in against the base of the gallows. It seemed everyone wanted a good view of the show.

As his gaze wandered across the crowd, Drystan's eyes locked onto a familiar figure.

Gray.

Drystan's oldest brother stood closest to the stairs, his dark hair pulled back, something like sadness creasing his face.

"Drystan Kalon," the magistrate said. "Son of Phillip Kalon."

Whispers of awe ran through the crowd. Drystan kept his focus on Gray.

"You are hereby sentenced to hang from the neck until dead. Do you have any last words?"

Not for any mortal ears, he didn't.

Taerna of the earth on which I walk, deliver me.

"Very well," the magistrate declared. The noose was placed around Drystan's neck and pulled snug. The rough fibers scratched his throat.

Aetherann of the air that fills my lungs, deliver me.

Gray's mouth moved, his lips forming silent words. *"I'm sorry, brother."*

Lanara of the water that gives me life, deliver me.

The crowd fell eerily silent. The executioner grabbed the wooden lever that would drop the floor from beneath Drystan's feet.

Pyrannis of the fire that fuels my heart, deliver—

"Stop!" The booming voice cut through the silence of the square. A woman in a hooded cloak stepped through the crowd, which parted for her like a stream around a boulder. She bounded up the steps of the gallows, her hood falling to reveal deep brown skin and dark hair pulled back in many small braids.

Drystan blinked, trying to clear his vision. It couldn't be possible, could it?

"I'm Warden Cora Sylus." The woman tugged aside the collar of her shirt to reveal the symbol of the Wardens of the Flame branded on her chest. "This man is with me."

The Warden from Alton.

"W-Warden Sylus," the magistrate stammered. "But you—"

"You will release him into my custody," she commanded, "where he will serve the Wardens until justice has been done."

Drystan's mind raced to catch up, even as the rope around his neck loosened and lifted over his head. The iron shackles fell from his wrists.

As he struggled to comprehend what was happening, the Warden moved to his side. "Lean on me," she said quietly, ducking under his arm. She was at least a head shorter than him, but she was sturdy. The Warden wrapped her arm around his waist and muttered something under her breath. As she did, a pressure encircled his leg as though it were wrapped in a thick blanket. His knee still hurt like hell, but whatever the Warden had done, he found he could lean on her and hobble without feeling like he was about to pass out from the pain.

"What'd you do?" Drystan whispered as she helped him down from the gallows.

"Not here. Keep moving."

At the bottom step, Drystan stumbled. The Warden's arm tightened around him to hold him up, but another set of hands caught him by the shoulder, balancing him.

Drystan met Gray's eyes.

Would his brother try to stop him? Would he kill Drystan for betraying them?

But Gray only helped Drystan straighten. His hand lingered on Drystan's shoulder, though he stepped back as the Warden pulled Drystan into the crowd, which parted for her again.

Though now that he was in the middle of it, he could hear their murmured frustration, the tension rippling through them. They'd been denied their morning's entertainment.

How long before they reached the conclusion that a hundred townsfolk could take down a single Warden of the Flame?

Around the corner, the Warden steered him toward a horse that was tied to a post. "You're going to need to ride," she said. Her tone did not give the impression there was room for him to argue, so he nodded.

Getting onto the horse was easier than he expected, though the Warden had muttered a few words again as she helped him get seated behind the saddle. Then she untied the reins and swung up in front of him.

"Hold on to me," she instructed. "We need to move fast."

Before he could respond, she spurred the horse into a canter, and they were off through the narrow streets of Sevrun. Drystan held on to the Warden, wrapping his arms around her waist as they left the city at a gallop. The adrenaline was wearing off, the pain and dizziness returning as the horse's gait jostled his bruised and broken body.

"Drystan!" the Warden snapped. "Don't let go!"

Drystan tightened his grip, which he hadn't realized had begun to loosen. His vision was darkening at the edges. "I don't think I can do this," he shouted over the thundering hooves.

"You have to," she said. "A little longer."

Drystan tucked his head against the Warden's back. *A little longer*, he repeated to himself. *Hold on just a little longer.* "Hey," he called. He needed something to distract himself so he didn't black out. "What did you do back there?"

"I used magic to stabilize your leg," the Warden said into the wind.

"Magic? You're a mage?"

"Not formally trained or anything, but I know a few tricks." She glanced over her shoulder. "Have you seen much magic before?"

Drystan shook his head. "Not really," he admitted. "Not up close."

"What'd you think of it?"

"It was incredible." The horse leapt over some small obstacle and the landing jostled Drystan's broken bones. "I just wish it lasted longer," he said through clenched teeth.

"Sorry 'bout that," the Warden said. "We're almost to the camp."

Drystan swallowed down a wave of nausea. "Camp?"

"The Wardens set up a camp just on the southern side of the Mistvale Mountains," she said, nodding toward the rising mountains to the north. "Westhold declared war on Aethir about a week ago. They attacked the College of Magi. Burned it to the ground, along with a few of the smaller mountain towns. We're helping the survivors as best we can."

He swayed and tightened his grip around the Warden's waist again.

"We're here," she said quickly. The horse slowed, though it didn't stop. She tapped Drystan's arm. She must have felt him starting to slip. "Hang on just a moment more, alright?"

He nodded, trying to get his vision to focus. Shouts rose up, first from the Warden and then from others nearby. It all sounded terribly muffled and distant.

"Need some help over here! Where's Theo?"

"Gods above, he looks terrible."

"Someone get him down."

Drystan's vision darkened further, and he gripped at the Warden to keep himself upright.

"It's alright," the Warden said. She sounded impossibly far away, but hadn't she been right in front of him just now? "It's alright. You're safe now, Drystan. You can let go."

And Drystan let go.

❋

When next he opened his eyes, Drystan was lying on a cot surrounded by the canvas walls of a tent. His head and face ached horribly, and he couldn't move, though with the stabbing pain in his knee and his side, he hardly wanted to. He tried to look to see if he'd been bound again, but nothing would respond. He couldn't even wiggle his fingers. His pulse quickened.

"Hey." The Warden appeared by his head. "Try to relax, Drystan. You're safe. The medics gave you something to paralyze your muscles so they could patch you up. It'll start to wear off soon."

"Wh-where am I?" he asked, testing his voice. His throat was raw.

"You're in the Wardens' camp," she said. "On the border of Weryn and Aethir. But, Drystan . . ." She paused as though searching for the right words. "I need to talk to you about your injuries." The Warden slid a stool over to the side of the cot and sat. "You have a concussion, two broken ribs, and . . . your knee was shattered. It's beyond what our medics could heal on their own. However, we have a devout of Ainam who has, on more than one occasion, been able to work healing magic. He's scheduled to arrive in camp tomorrow. I think he might be able to help repair some of the damage that was done."

She swallowed, and her voice was gentle when she continued. "I'm going to be honest with you. I think you're likely to have a lot of pain for the rest of your life without his help. And possibly a good deal even with it, too. I'd like to ask him to come by and see you. Would that be alright?"

Did he deserve help from the Wardens? Did he deserve to be prayed over by a devout of Ainam—to be granted the miracle of healing magic? Did he deserve any of this? His choices had led him to the end of a rope in Sevrun. That was what he deserved.

But his knee felt as though a knife were jammed into it. The idea of living with that kind of pain forever was terrifying. And so he looked up at the Warden and said, "Yes."

Even though that made him a coward.

The Warden nodded, satisfied. "I'll arrange everything."

"Warden?" he asked, catching her before she could stand to leave.

"Cora," she said. "Call me Cora."

Drystan licked his lips. His mouth was so dry. "Am I . . . a prisoner?"

Cora chuckled. "No, not at all."

"But you . . . said . . ."

"I said you would serve the Wardens until justice has been done." She crossed her arms over her chest. "What'd you do? I mean, I heard what they were accusing you of, but what'd you *actually* do?"

He saw no reason to lie. "I tried to rob Baron Venbarra's vault."

Her brows rose slightly. "That's it?"

"Y-yeah."

"Then as far as I'm concerned, you've paid for your mistakes. I don't feel the need to make you pay any more than you already have."

Drystan stared at her, not fully comprehending her words.

The confusion must have been evident on his face, because Cora set a hand on his shoulder. The weight of her hand was strangely comforting. "You'll stay here at the camp until you're healed. And then, you'll be free to go where you wish." Her mouth quirked into a small grin. "Though I'd recommend against Sevrun. Or Alton." She gave his shoulder a reassuring squeeze. "Your recovery won't be an easy road, but I'll be here to help you along in any way I can."

"Why?" Drystan asked. He couldn't make sense of any of it. "Why did you help me?"

"Because you're more than just your father's son." Cora's face relaxed into a soft smile. "And because I believe everyone deserves a second chance."

CHAPTER 15

DESPITE HIS EXHAUSTION, DRYSTAN got very little sleep that night. The effects of whatever they'd given him to lock down his muscles finally abated, and every time he drifted off, some spasm or muscle cramp jolted him awake. Then he would lie there in the dark for an hour or more, listening to the sounds of the camp. It was mostly quiet, but there were occasional moans and sobs—the sounds of the injured and the dying. Victims of the war Westhold had just declared on Aethir, Cora had told him.

Drystan bit his lip to keep from making any noise, even when he twisted in his sleep and the pain hit him, swift and sudden. The others in the camp were survivors—innocents. He had no right to be there among them, taking up space and resources and the healers' time. So when the pain rolled through his body, Drystan gritted his teeth and gripped the edges of the cot until his knuckles ached.

As the sky lightened outside, the tent flap opened. Cora ducked through carrying a tray and a bundle of blankets tucked under one arm. "Good morning," she said softly. "Were you able to get any sleep?"

"A bit," Drystan said. He didn't sound very convincing.

She set the tray on the small side table near the bed. "I brought you a little breakfast if you're hungry. And I didn't know how you take your coffee, but there's no cream in the camp anyway, so I just brought a little sugar in case you want it."

Drystan eyed the tray. "I don't know," he said. "I've never had coffee."

Cora's brows climbed. "Really? Well, damn. In that case, I wish I had better to offer you. The stuff we've got here is pretty terrible, to be honest with you."

He couldn't help but smile.

"But here," she continued, spooning some of the sugar crystals into the cup. "I'll make it the way I would take it—without the cream, sadly—and you can let me know what you think."

She laid the meager breakfast out on the table, then moved to Drystan's side and helped him sit up. He squeezed his eyes tight, though she was far gentler with him than he'd expected. Even still, he was breathing hard by the time they were done.

"How are you feeling?" she asked as she propped the blankets she'd brought and a couple pillows behind him to keep him upright.

"Like I was run over by a carriage," he said, though it was weak of him to admit it.

"Only a carriage? I'd have figured several carriages, at least. Possibly before falling off a cliff."

He was so caught off guard by her words that he laughed, which he immediately regretted. His hand flew to his side, and he lowered his head, gritting his teeth.

"Lanara's tears, I'm sorry," Cora said. "My instinct when people get hurt is always to make them laugh. I usually stay away from the ones with broken ribs for just that reason."

"It's fine," Drystan ground out. He nodded toward the tray. "Pass me that bread and we'll call it even."

Cora chuckled and handed him the bread. "That seems fair."

The bread was hard and a bit stale, but it was food, and Drystan ate it without complaint. Then he tried the coffee.

"This is really good," he said. He took another sip.

"It's better with cream." Cora pulled up the stool. "If I can get my hands on any, I'll let you know."

She sat with him while he finished his breakfast, and she filled the silence with random bits of conversation and stories.

But it wasn't right. She shouldn't be wasting her time here with him. She was a Warden of the Flame. She was important. She should be off helping someone who actually deserved it.

"You . . . don't have to stay," Drystan said after a while. "I mean, thank you for the food, but I'm sure you must have better things to do with your time."

A crease appeared in the middle of Cora's forehead. "I'm not here because I have to be, Drystan. I'm here because I want to be. I want to help you. I may not be a healer, but I can talk, and I can listen." She leaned forward, her elbows coming to rest on her knees. "Look, I know. I know from when I spoke to you in Alton that you don't think you're worth the time or the trouble. But you are. And I don't have anywhere else I need to be right now, so I'm choosing to be here."

Drystan swallowed back everything else he'd considered saying. This Warden, this stranger, had thought he was worth something back in Alton. She'd tried to recruit him, for Vire's sake. Somehow, she still thought he was worth helping now, and for the life of him, he couldn't figure out why.

"I don't know what to say," he said quietly.

"You don't have to say anything," Cora said. "Sometimes having someone nearby is all you need. But if you want to be alone, just say the word and I'll go. Alright?"

Drystan nodded.

Cora told a few more stories of her time in the Wardens, but then she let the silence stretch on for a while as she cleaned up the remnants of breakfast. "I'll be right back," she said, ducking out of the tent with the tray.

She returned a few moments later holding a wooden crutch. "This is for you," she said. "I had to guess at the height, but I think it should work, at least for now." Cora gestured for Drystan to sit forward more. "Give it a try."

He winced at the thought of moving. "I don't think I can."

She held out her hand. "Just try, alright? You need to be able to move around."

Drystan clasped her hand, using it for balance and to take the pressure off his broken ribs as he moved the blanket away and carefully swung his legs over the edge of the bed. He didn't know where the clothes had come from, but he was wearing a loose gray shirt and lightweight linen pants with the right leg rolled up.

He inhaled deeply and finally looked at his knee. It was splinted on either side, held fast with bandages that made it impossible to bend. In the gaps between the cloth and wood, the skin was purple and misshapen. His heart pounded in his chest. What if it never healed? What if it always felt the way it did now?

"I can't."

"Here," Cora said, pulling his attention. She held the crutch upright. "Pull yourself up."

"I can't," he said again. No, it was too soon. Far too soon. What if he twisted wrong and fell? What if he only made it worse?

Cora put one hand up in concession before leaning the crutch against the tent wall. "Alright, alright. I won't push you."

Gods, he was such a coward. As Cora helped him bring his legs back onto the cot, he mumbled, "I . . . think I'd like to be alone now."

The Warden watched him for only a couple seconds before she nodded and turned to leave. "Theo, the healer and devout of Ainam I told you about, arrived this morning. He's settling back in, but I'll send him over this afternoon." She pushed the tent flap open but lingered there for a moment. "Get some rest, Drystan. I'll come by again soon." Then she left, leaving him alone with his thoughts.

Drystan leaned against the blankets and pillows Cora had tucked behind him and tried not to think about the last few days. There was an ache in his chest that he couldn't name, but it hurt the more he focused on it. He wanted to ignore it, but it was hard not to replay every moment he'd spent with Genna, searching for all the signs he'd missed. Eventually he tried to sleep, but everything hurt, and he didn't dare move enough to lie down again.

He'd finally managed to nod off, still sitting propped against the pillows, when a voice roused him. "Are you Drystan?"

He startled, lightning shooting through his side and his leg as he jerked awake.

"Oh, Ainam's glory, I'm so sorry," the man said, rushing to his bedside. "I didn't realize you were asleep."

"It's alright," he groaned. Drystan cracked his eyes open and peered up at the man now fussing over him.

He appeared around the same age as Cora, maybe a little older, with fair skin and dark hair that was pulled back and twisted into a bun. His kind eyes surveyed Drystan.

"I'm Theo North." The man adjusted one of Drystan's pillows before rummaging through a satchel he'd dropped on the ground. "Not the best first impression for a healer, I'm afraid. Here." He offered Drystan some sort of root from his bag. "Chew on this. It'll help."

Drystan did as he said, the bitter sap of the root coating his tongue and throat.

"May I examine you?" Theo asked.

Drystan nodded, and Theo helped him to lie back on the small cot. Theo checked him over, holding up fingers for him to count, asking him questions, and searching what felt like every inch of his skin for cuts and bruises. He spent the longest time hovering over Drystan's knee.

After ages, Theo returned his focus to Drystan's face. "I'll pray to Ainam to heal you. But before I do, I must tell you two very important truths. The first is that just because I pray for Ainam's grace, there are no guarantees Ainam will grant my request. The second is that Ainam's healing, while powerful, doesn't come without cost."

Drystan's pain had eased slightly, thanks to the root Theo had given him, and for that relief alone he wanted to grovel at the man's feet. But if Theo could take the pain away completely? Or, at least, mostly? He would do anything.

"Ainam's healing is *imprecise*," Theo continued. "We've come to understand that Ainam's power makes little distinction between things that move but shouldn't—broken bones, for example—and things that move but *should*, like joints. The result for a situation like yours where the joint is affected can sometimes mean that the bones might fuse too far, in which case we'll need to correct it before the true healing can begin. It will be painful until it heals, but I believe you could eventually fully recover." He set his hand on Drystan's. "I know this is a lot of information, so if you want to take some time to think about it, I can come back."

But what was there to think about? His choices were either pain for the rest of his life, or only a chance of pain for the rest of his life.

"No," Drystan said, his voice cracking. "Do it. Please."

And so, Theo began to pray.

Chapter 16

The next time Drystan woke, Cora's dark eyes stared down at him. "Pyrannis's flames," she cursed. "You scared me, kid."

Drystan blinked slowly. It was dark save for a glass-hooded lantern on the table beside the cot. His mind was a haze of gray. "Did I?" His voice was hoarse, his throat raw.

"You don't remember?"

Well, he hadn't until she asked. Then the memories flooded back. Pain like he'd never felt, popping bones and snapping tendons. Somewhere amid the agony, he'd passed out.

He risked a look down. His knee was wrapped in white linen, though it was bent slightly with pillows tucked beneath it.

"Theo said you might be out of it for a little while, but it's been a touch longer than *a little while.*"

"How long was I out?"

"About thirty-six hours." She lifted a clay cup from beside the lantern and held it out to him. She smiled. "Glad to see you're still with us."

Cora *cared* about him. For some inexplicable reason, she cared about what happened to him. Drystan's heart squeezed in his chest. "Thanks," he murmured.

He took the cup, and Cora helped to angle him up slightly so he could drink. The pain in his side was still there when he moved, so he took his time. The water soothed his parched throat.

"Theo's been checking on you pretty regularly," Cora said. "He wanted to stay, but we have many others in the camp that need his care, unfortunately, and he needs to sleep when he can. But he asked me to tell you that you're going to have to work with him every day to rehabilitate. He said you'll have to move it as much as possible to stop it from locking up." Cora took a breath, her eyes darting to the tent wall behind Drystan as she took the cup from him.

He angled his head and spotted the object that had her attention. The crutch she'd brought him that first morning in the camp. Its shadow danced mockingly in the lantern light. He swallowed hard. "Cora, I—"

"I swear to Pyrannis, Drystan, if you say you *can't*, I'm going to . . . I was going to say *hit you*, but that seems a bit rude, considering."

Drystan's face heated, and he snapped his mouth shut.

"Just try. I'm here with you, alright? You're not alone." She offered him her hand.

"Now?" Drystan's eyes darted to the sliver of space between the tent flaps. "It's the middle of the night."

"And?" Cora's hand still extended toward him. "You have something else to do?"

Lacking any reason not to besides cowardice, Drystan took her hand, and Cora carefully helped leverage him up. She reached past him and grabbed the crutch.

Drystan swallowed down the fear until it sat like a lump in his gut. His side twinged as he pulled himself up to stand, but that was the worst of it.

"Good," Cora said. "Keep your weight off that leg for now. We'll let Theo manage that part. Just try taking a few steps with the crutch. Put it on your left so you can counterbalance."

He did as she said, and his shoulders hunched a little as he moved the crutch a few inches forward and hopped first one step, then another. It was uncomfortable and incredibly slow, but it worked. He could get himself from one side of the tent to the other.

Turning, on the other hand, was a different matter entirely. When he tried to turn around to head back to the cot, the crutch got crossed with his leg, tripping him up. Stabbing pain shot through him as his right leg brushed the ground, and he twisted to try to keep from falling on it completely. He braced to hit the dirt, but strong arms caught him.

"You're alright," Cora said, practically in his ear as she held him up, keeping his weight off his wounded leg. "You're alright. Just breathe. Breathe, Drystan."

Was he not? Drystan forced himself to suck in a breath.

Somehow Cora got him back to the cot, though he wasn't sure how. He was too focused on trying not to vomit. Mostly because vomiting with broken ribs was high on the list of things he never wanted to experience.

"That was good," Cora said once Drystan's breathing had steadied. "You did well."

Drystan cracked one eye open. "I nearly fell flat on my face," he groaned.

"True." A twist of a smile curled Cora's lips. "But you did much better than I did my first time."

The week tumbled on. The first few days of meeting with Theo were agonizing, so he gave Drystan a day off to rest, but that only made his return to Theo's exercises even worse. The healing magic was still working, Theo explained, and would continue trying to solidify the moving bits of Drystan's knee for a while, until things settled down. Every time the joint froze, they had to force it to move, which just felt like breaking it all over again. Theo assured him he was doing well, but Drystan couldn't see how.

Cora visited him frequently and kept him company when she could. He appreciated having her around to distract him. Whenever he was alone, his thoughts pulled toward Genna, spiraling inward, down and down, until he landed on a single irrefutable truth—he'd loved her, and he'd been too much of a fool to realize she'd never loved him back.

And if Genna wasn't the one plaguing his thoughts, it was his family. Had Gray told them about his rescue from the gallows? Would his father come looking for him? What would his mother think about what he'd done?

Before long, Cora needed to travel for a couple weeks to pick up supplies from one of the Warden outposts in Southreach, and Drystan wasn't sure what to do with himself. His sessions with Theo had moved to the healing tent, but beyond the slow walk it took him to get there, Drystan had nothing to occupy his time.

"Have you made any friends around camp?" Theo asked during one of their early afternoon sessions. Drystan lay on his back, staring up at the beige ceiling of the large healers' tent. His right leg was extended while Theo pressed Drystan's foot to slowly bend his knee.

Drystan breathed through the pain as Theo had taught him. "Friends?"

Theo let out a soft snort. "Yes, *friends*. You know, people you talk to besides me and Cora." He stepped into a different position, bracing the side of Drystan's knee with one hand. "I mean, I know you can't get enough of me right now." His smile turned serious as he focused on what he was doing. "Alright, now straighten your leg."

Cora had only been gone a few days and Drystan had already felt his mood souring. He had too much time alone, too much time to think, and that was the last thing he wanted.

Drystan tried to straighten his leg, but Theo was holding it steady. "I can't," he ground out between clenched teeth. "You're pushing on it."

"I'm giving you a bit of resistance," Theo said, though the pressure lessened. "Try it now."

Drystan did as Theo instructed. "No," he managed once his leg was mostly straight again. "I haven't met anyone else yet."

"There are dozens of people in the camp," Theo said, helping Drystan repeat the exercise. "Maybe meeting a few others who are staying here would do you some good."

"Maybe," Drystan conceded.

"I know you've only been with us for a couple weeks, and I don't know much about what you must've gone through, but I've seen enough hurt to know that not all of it's physical. Maybe meeting some new people might help you a bit with the other kind."

Theo finished the session soon after and wrapped Drystan's knee in fresh linen before sending him on his way with a reminder not to neglect his morning exercises. "Same time tomorrow," he said, as he always did. Though he hesitated a moment before he added, "But let me know if you need anything before then. I'll be around."

Drystan bid him a silent farewell and began his hobbling trek back to his own tent. He took his time, concentrating on where he was putting the crutch so he didn't fall. The camp was arranged in neat, orderly rows of tents in white, beige, and shades of green. Many of them were the same size and style as Drystan's, while others were larger to house supplies or provide communal spaces, like the healers' tent, the mess hall, and a makeshift temple. There were also a few canvas awnings and pavilions set up to provide additional shelter from the weather.

Up ahead of Drystan, a few people were heading his way. All three had visible bandages, and one had her arm in a sling, but they were walking unaided, and there was no Warden accompanying them. They were likely some of the refugees from Aethir or the mountain border towns in Weryn.

Drystan paused in his hobbling and straightened as they approached. *Everyone deserves a second chance*, Cora had told him. Maybe he really could start over. Maybe he just needed to take the first step and talk to people, as Theo had suggested.

He gave the group a warm smile. "Hi there," he said. "Beautiful day, isn't it?"

The man and one of the women exchanged a confused, wary look, while the other woman glanced at the sky before giving Drystan an appraising once-over. Judging by the unpleasant curl to her lip, she must have found him wanting.

"It's cold and cloudy," she said, clearly finding that anything but beautiful.

Drystan shrugged one shoulder. "I've always liked the dreary days myself." He held his smile. "I'm Drystan, by the way."

"Oh, we've heard of you," the man said, taking a step back.

A muscle ticked in Drystan's jaw. "I'm sorry?" Maybe he hadn't heard them right? Or maybe—

"We heard about you," he repeated. "You're Phillip Kalon's kid."

One of the women tugged on the man's arm, pulling him back. With one more judgmental backward glance, the three of them retraced their steps to avoid him.

Something like guilt or shame tugged at his heart as Drystan watched them walk away.

Everyone deserves a second chance. Cora had helped him—had saved him from the gallows—because that was what she believed. She'd offered him a second chance, but Drystan had been naive to think he could leave his old life behind just like that. His father's deeds, *his* deeds, would always follow him.

Would he ever be able to run far enough to escape them?

The next week held more of the same. Every time Drystan left his tent, furtive, suspicious gazes followed him from the refugees and even from some of the Wardens. He missed Cora. Theo was pleasant enough to talk to, but he was often too busy for more than a quick chat.

Drystan sat alone in the mess hall where the least injured refugees ate together. He'd taken to listening in on the nearby conversations to stave off boredom, and today's meal was no different. Though the words that made their way to him this time piqued his interest more than usual.

"Honestly," one of the refugees was saying, "I don't know why the Wardens are even bothering. The girl's a lost cause. It's disturbing."

"What do you mean?" another asked.

"Have you *seen* her? I poked my head in her tent once. Gods above and below!" Laughter rolled across the table.

"And she won't talk to anyone," the refugee continued. "She won't even look at anyone. I overheard one of the Wardens saying she hasn't said a single word since they brought her here. I think it's been at least a month."

"Tell them about the screaming," someone else said.

"Oh, yeah," the first said. "I've heard that there's some trash in her tent from when she was brought here, and if anyone tries to take it away, she screams like she's being murdered."

Quiet mumbles filled the space. "That's insane," someone said.

"It is!" the first agreed. "I'm telling you, that girl's brains are scrambled. She's just taking up the Wardens' time and resources. They could be helping others instead of wasting their time on her. Just be sure to steer clear of that green tent on the edge of camp, alright? She's beyond help."

Drystan ate his food in silence, turning their words over in his mind. He knew the tent they were talking about. He passed by it on his daily loop around the camp, though he hadn't known who it belonged to or what it was used for. He'd only ever seen healers going in and out; no other Wardens or anyone else visiting.

A plan began to take shape while he finished his meal and crutched his way to the healing tent for his afternoon session with Theo. That should be just enough time, Drystan reasoned, for him to talk himself out of it.

CHAPTER 17

HIS CRUTCHING WAS EVEN slower that afternoon as he crossed the Wardens' camp. His knee was throbbing. He was making progress, Theo said, but he had a long way yet to go if he hoped to walk on his own again. He detoured from Theo's tent to the makeshift temple—the priest there had a small collection of books for the Wardens or others in the camp to borrow. Drystan had considered stopping by before but had kept finding excuses not to. He hadn't read anything in years, though this seemed as good a reason to start up again as any.

With a small book tucked under his arm, Drystan slowly hobbled toward the one green tent on the outer edge of camp. The one only the healers ever seemed to enter. The tent was sparsely furnished, much like his own, with a cot, a small side table, and a stool. Drystan lingered in the entranceway, building up the courage to step inside.

A girl lay on the cot. She was young and thin and frail, with alabaster skin and reddish-brown hair that lay untamed around her head. He couldn't guess her exact age, but she looked young—maybe a few years younger than he was himself. Her face and neck showed the remnants of healing cuts and bruises, but her arms were completely bandaged.

Drystan inhaled deeply and approached, blinking as his eyes adjusted to the dim light within the tent. No, her arms weren't bandaged. They were *gone.* White linen wrapped her chest and around her left shoulder, which was unnaturally even with her narrow torso. On her other side, her arm was missing below the elbow, the stump wrapped just as neatly.

Drystan hesitated. The girl hadn't turned to look at him, hadn't acknowledged him in any way, just as the other refugees had indicated. Was she even aware of his presence?

"Hi," he tried. His voice cut through the silence of the tent, almost startlingly loud in the small space. "I'm Drystan."

The girl didn't react at all. Her dull eyes stared blankly up at nothing. Drystan made his way over to the small stool and pulled it closer to her bedside.

"I hope you don't mind if I join you for a little," he said as he lowered himself onto the stool with a quiet groan. It felt good to take the weight off his leg. He leaned his crutch against the small table. "I brought a book. I thought I could read it aloud, if that sounds alright. I'll admit, I have no idea if it's any good. Honestly, I . . . sort of just picked one at random, so I'm not even sure what it's about." Drystan forced a smile, but there was still no response from the girl, no reaction at all.

What was he doing? He felt foolish, like he was talking to himself instead of another person, but at the moment, it wasn't enough to deter him. Theo was right: he needed someone to talk to. Even if that someone could never answer him back.

It was selfish of him, but . . . This girl seemed to be alone. Maybe she needed someone too.

Drystan opened the book, turning to the first page. "*The Midnight Lark*," he began. "Chapter one."

The book, it turned out, was about a folk hero who called herself the Midnight Lark. She wandered from place to place, helping the small villages she came across with whatever trouble they were having, whether it was an overbearing town constable, or a band of roaming undead causing a disturbance. Drystan read aloud to the girl for an hour before he closed the book and grabbed his crutch again, promising to return the next day to read more. And he did.

He visited her tent every day. He would read for a while, then talk a bit longer before heading out again. She never reacted or gave any indication that she heard him, but he didn't mind too much. It still helped distract him from his loneliness, and it kept him from dwelling too long on his failings. And besides, when he asked Theo about the girl, the healer said that even when people couldn't respond, sometimes they still heard what was happening around them. Drystan liked to think that was true for the girl.

Late one night, Drystan awoke from a dream about Genevieve and the heist—about when she betrayed him. In the dream, his brothers were the ones who caught him and beat him after he'd tried to run, with his father delivering the blow that shattered his knee, all while Genevieve looked on and laughed. Drystan couldn't get back to sleep after that, and his session with Theo later that day only served to reinforce his already foul mood.

He decided to skip his visit with the girl that afternoon—he'd seen her every day for almost two weeks—and was about to pass her tent when a medic exited hurriedly, muttering something under her breath.

Something tugged at Drystan's soul, spurring him into the tent instead of past it.

The girl was in the same place she always was, lying on the cot, her hair splayed messily about her pillow. The bandages on her shoulder and her arm looked fresh, but other than that, it didn't look like much had changed.

Drystan hobbled to the stool and took a seat. He hadn't even brought *The Midnight Lark* with him, so he sat in silence for a long time. "I wasn't going to come by today," he admitted at last. "I had a dream last night about . . . about what happened before. The reason I'm here, at this camp, I mean." He rubbed a hand along the back of his neck. "And I guess it's kind of been bothering me all day."

Drystan told her the story of what happened to him that night, of Genevieve and how he'd been so drawn to her that he hadn't even noticed all the signs. She'd told him exactly who she was. She had from the very beginning. He'd just been too blind to see it. And in the end, he had no one to blame but himself.

When he reached the end of his story, Drystan inhaled deeply. He felt lighter for having talked about it, like some small weight had been lifted from his shoulders. Other than the brief parts he'd shared with Cora and Theo, he hadn't told anyone the whole tale of what had happened that night. It felt good to talk about it, even if it was only to a girl who couldn't even acknowledge that he was there.

The girl continued staring straight ahead, her occasional blinks and the slow rise and fall of her chest the only signs she was alive.

"Thanks for listening," Drystan said quietly, shifting his gaze toward the open air outside. He took up his crutch and rose from the stool. "I promise I'll bring the book again tomorrow."

Drystan finished reading the book to the girl before long and turned to telling her stories of home. Some were funny tales that had happened to him or one of his brothers somewhere along the way, while others were about more heartfelt subjects, like his mother, or his difficult relationship with his father. On the day he shared a story about his father, Drystan was feeling dejected and melancholy. He still couldn't walk without a crutch, despite it having been more than a month since he first began working with Theo, and his session that afternoon had felt more like five steps back rather than making any progress at all.

"I've heard it said," Drystan mused, mostly to himself, "that the Lord Ainam bestows trials on the children he favors." He chewed on his bottom lip for a moment before adding, "It would be nice if he favored the two of us a bit less, wouldn't you say?"

Shame quickly warmed his face as he realized he'd just compared his self-inflicted plight to whatever horrors this girl had endured. Had he truly just spoken those words aloud? Was he really such a fool?

"I'm sorry, that was—" His sentence cut off as he saw the girl's face.

There was a little curl at the corner of her mouth. It faded again as he watched. She'd smiled.

It wasn't a large smile by any stretch, but it was there.

Drystan stared at her a moment longer. Theo was right. "Y-you can hear me," he murmured.

The next day, he hobbled into her tent, a fresh book tucked under his arm. "You won't believe this," he started by way of greeting. But the rest of whatever he was about to say never made it past his lips.

The girl was looking at him. Her eyes, brighter now than they'd been, tracked his movement as he stepped into her tent.

"Hi," he said, the word coming out much higher than usual.

Again, the slightest curve of her mouth. Half a smile.

Drystan cleared his throat, returning his voice to his normal register. "I wasn't expecting . . ." His eyes darted to the floor. "I'm sorry," he said, flustered. "This is a pleasant surprise."

Suddenly much more self-conscious of his movements, Drystan limped to the small stool and pulled it closer to the cot. He leaned the crutch against the little table, as he always did.

Drystan held the book's cover toward her. "I found these old fairy tales. I thought they might be fun."

He stayed longer that day, reading from the book of fairy tales until the girl's eyelids began to droop, and Drystan's legs and back were aching from sitting too long. "I'll let you get some rest," he said at last.

She was asleep before he'd left the tent.

Drystan decided to see the girl early the following morning instead of after his session with Theo in the afternoon as he usually did. He was approaching her tent when agonized shrieks cut through the camp. Drystan wasn't sure what made him worry about the girl, but he picked up his pace as he headed toward her tent.

One of the medics he didn't know stood outside as the screams from within ebbed.

"Is she alright?" Drystan asked, breathing hard.

The medic eyed him sidelong but nodded. "I don't know what set her off this time," he said, running a hand over his tired face. "But I just gave her something to calm her. She should settle down soon."

Settle down? Like she was an animal in need of taming, or a small child running wild. "Did you ask her what was wrong?" Drystan demanded. A muscle ticked in his jaw as the medic raised an eyebrow.

"What?"

"Did you try to talk to her before you drugged her? Did you even tell her what you were giving her?"

"She's not at home," he said, tapping his own forehead. "Why do you care anyway?"

Drystan's fingers tensed around his crutch. "I care because she's scared and alone. Why don't you?" Of course, Drystan himself was also both of those things, but that was hardly the point. He brushed past the healer before the man could think of something else to say, just as the girl's cries softened into anguished sobs.

"Hey," he said, grabbing the stool and pulling it to her side. "Hey, it's alright."

Her sobs caught in her throat as she heard his voice, and she struggled to focus on his face through the haze of whatever the medic had given her.

Drystan leaned forward and brushed away a tangle of hair that had stuck to her forehead. "I'm here," he said, his throat tightening. "I'm here, alright?"

A frustrated cry tore from her as she tried to fight off the sedation.

"Just relax. I'll be here when you wake up. I promise."

Her clouded eyes found his before her head sagged and she stopped struggling, drifting off to what Drystan fervently hoped would be a restful and dreamless sleep.

It was a few hours before the girl stirred, blinking slowly as consciousness returned. Drystan's shoulders finally relaxed when she opened her eyes fully.

"See?" He gave her as reassuring a smile as he could muster under the circumstances. "I told you I'd be here."

That small smile returned to her face as she let her head settle back onto the pillow.

"Are you alright?" Even though he knew he wouldn't get a response, he had to ask.

The girl shut her eyes tight but gave a tiny nod.

Drystan's own breath caught. That wasn't her little smile of recognition or tracking his movement with her eyes. That was an *answer*. He'd asked her a question, and she'd answered him.

He tried again. "Do you want me to stay?"

And again, she nodded.

So Drystan stayed. He told her stories of home—funny pranks his brothers had played on him growing up—and jokes he'd heard in the taverns back in Alton.

Anything to make her smile.

Chapter 18

"I was asleep when it started."

Drystan had just positioned the stool in its usual spot when the girl spoke. It was only the day after her run-in with the healer. And her voice was shaky but strong.

Drystan held his breath.

"One of the knights woke me up. He tried to get me out. We ran. But the soldiers found us. They . . ." The girl closed her eyes, a tear slipping from beneath her lashes as she swallowed hard. "He's dead, because of me." Her voice cracked. "He was protecting me. And all I did was get him killed." When she opened her eyes again, another tear chased the first. "I don't even know his name. I don't know his name. And . . . And the soldiers were everywhere." She looked at Drystan, and her eyes were wide with the horror of her memory. "I burned them. I burned all of them." Her breathing and her tears were coming faster now. "I burned it all."

Drystan leaned in and brushed his thumb across her cheek, wiping away her tears.

She waved her right arm toward something behind Drystan. "That's the only thing I have left," she said.

Drystan turned and spotted something metallic on the far side of the tent. A broken sword.

"They laughed when I picked it up," she continued. "They laughed. But I burned them all, and they stopped laughing."

Drystan's mind reeled, shaken by her words. Soldiers and fire . . .

On the ride to the Warden's camp all those weeks ago, Cora had said Westhold declared war on Aethir by attacking the College of Magi. It was why the Wardens were in this part of Weryn in the first place. Had this girl been there? It didn't seem much of a stretch.

This girl had had to kill soldiers to survive. It wasn't fair. It wasn't right.

"I'm sorry that happened to you," Drystan said. It felt worthless, considering everything she'd been through, but it was the only comfort he could offer.

"Verity." Another tear slipped down her cheek. "My name's Verity."

"Verity," he repeated. "My name's—"

"Drystan," she said. "You told me."

So she really had heard everything from the very beginning.

"I'm sorry for what happened, Verity," Drystan said again. Searching for something else to say, he opted for what was in his heart. "You must be very strong to have made it through that."

"I'm not," she said quietly. "I could barely even lift a broken sword."

"That's not the kind of strength I'm talking about."

A tortured, bitter laugh escaped her, like she didn't believe him. But she'd survived! A teenage girl against trained Westholden soldiers, and she'd killed them, and she'd *survived*. That took more strength than he could imagine.

"You are strong, Verity," Drystan said. "I'd wager you're a hell of a lot stronger than you think you are." He fell silent, wanting to give her time to cry and grieve for what had happened to her. Though perhaps she would rather be alone with her grief. "Do you want me to leave?" he asked.

"No," she said quickly. "Please stay, Drystan."

Please stay, Drystan. Gods above, hearing her speak—hearing her say his name—how could he do anything but exactly what she asked?

Verity sniffed back another sob. "Did you bring the book?"

"I did." He stooped to pick up the book where it had been momentarily forgotten.

"Would you read to me?"

Drystan's chest tightened. "Of course."

A few months passed in the Wardens' camp, and the cool autumn weather soon gave way to cold winter mornings. Drystan was walking on his own again, albeit still with some pain and a noticeable limp. He'd taken to helping out around the camp when he could, delivering fresh linens to Theo, or helping serve meals in the mess tent. He still got the occasional odd look, but many of the refugees who'd always given him dirty looks had moved on, leaving him mostly in peace.

Verity's own recovery had come a long way, though she still rarely spoke to anyone beyond Drystan. He was bringing her a meal one evening when he found her sitting up in bed.

"Are you alright?" he asked, rushing as quickly as he could to her bedside. "What's wrong?"

"Nothing," she said quickly. "Nothing's wrong. I just . . . I couldn't sit still."

Drystan set the tray of food down on the small side table beside her cot. "I can certainly understand that. Do you want to go for a walk?"

Verity's head jerked up at the question, and her deep brown eyes met his, her brows furrowing. "Out there?"

"Well . . . yeah." Drystan couldn't help a grin from appearing. "I mean, I guess we could do laps around the cot, but we might get bored *real* quick."

Verity rolled her eyes, though the amusement flickered out as she seemed to catch a glimpse of the sky through the tent flaps behind him. "I-I don't know," she stammered. She looked down at the bandages tight around her left shoulder.

Drystan sat beside her, taking the opportunity to stretch out his knee. "What are you worried about? They're not going to hurt you, Verity."

"I know," she said, her voice almost a whisper. "But what if . . . they . . ."

"Are you worried they're going to stare at you?" he asked gently.

Verity nodded.

"I can't promise they won't. But I can promise I'll be right there with you. Every step of the way." Drystan nodded toward the outside. "There's still a bit of daylight left. Let's work up an appetite before dinner, yeah?"

Verity took a deep breath. "Alright."

"Do you want me to help you stand?"

She swallowed hard before answering. "Y-yes . . . Please."

Drystan stood and set one hand on Verity's elbow, just above the bandaged end of her arm, and the other on her back. "Is this alright?" he asked.

She nodded and, pushing her arm into Drystan's hand for leverage, stood slowly. Verity wobbled as soon as he let her go, so he grabbed onto her again to steady her.

"It's hard to balance," she murmured, almost to herself. She focused on her feet. "It feels odd."

"I'll help you," he said. He repositioned his hands as he draped a blanket around her. Verity's breath shuddered on her inhale, and Drystan offered her a smile. "I won't let you fall."

As they stepped outside the tent, Verity squinted against the setting sun. She was unsteady on her feet, and Drystan took his time, careful of his knee. If he went down, he'd take Verity down with him, and that was something he couldn't ever let happen.

Thankfully, most of the people they passed on their slow walk were Wardens, but even so, a few of them stopped to stare, and still others whispered to one another as they passed. There was more than one pitying look as well, and Verity tensed with each person who walked by.

They cleared one row of tents, and as Drystan prepared to turn them around the corner to the next row, Verity stopped. "Take me back," she demanded.

Drystan looked up, following her line of sight. In a clearing at the edge of the camp, a bonfire had been set up, surrounded by several benches and cots populated by a host of newcomers. They were soldiers, by the matching crimson and gold colored tunics. There were about ten of them, all varying degrees of wounded. A few Wardens were assisting them, and some of the less hurt soldiers were helping to tend to their more injured friends.

Verity's face was white. "Take me back," she said again, her voice breaking. "Take me back."

Drystan didn't ask questions. His knee twinged as he rushed to spin them around, but he gritted his teeth and led Verity back the way they'd come. She was shaking by the time they made it back to her tent. Drystan let go of her with one hand so he could push the tent flap open, and when he did, Verity turned and vomited into the grass.

She fell to her knees, sobbing, and Drystan lowered himself to one knee as quickly as he could. He helped her balance as she was sick again, but he wasn't sure what else he could do, so he set his hand on her shoulder. He squeezed gently, just enough to let her know that he was there—that she wasn't alone.

"Take me inside," she said, her voice small and trembling.

Drystan stood, biting back a groan of pain, and lifted Verity with him. He wrapped his arm around her and brought her into the tent. She sank down onto her cot, curling her knees up to her chest, crying into her small pillow.

What could he say to her? What could he *do*? He was helpless. "Verity, I—"

"Please, just go," she sobbed. "Leave me alone."

Drystan didn't move. When had Westholden soldiers arrived at the camp? He never would've suggested she go outside if he'd known they were there. He never would've walked her straight into them!

"I'm sorry, I didn't—"

"Go!" she screamed.

His heart hurt as he turned and left. He wanted to confront those soldiers, but part of him knew it wasn't their fault the Wardens had brought them here.

After the horrors Westhold had committed, why *had* the Wardens brought soldiers into the camp?

Drystan's hands clenched into fists as his anger found a new target.

CHAPTER 19

Drystan found Cora Sylus as she was heading out of the mess tent. "What the hells, Cora?"

A few other Wardens paused and looked over. Cora waved them off as she took Drystan by the elbow and led him a short distance away. "Nice to see you too, Drystan," she said, lowering her voice. "What seems to be the problem?"

"There's a dozen Westholden soldiers in the godsdamned camp!"

"Yes. There are."

"What the fuck are they doing here?"

Cora's tone was even as she said, "They were injured in a battle across the border. When the Westholden forces were forced to retreat, a handful of their wounded were left behind."

"But *why*?" He stared at her, his jaw set. "They attacked innocent people. Why help them? Why do they deserve it after what they did?"

Cora nodded solemnly, taking in his question and seeming to give it due consideration. "We help them," she said gently, "because we're Wardens. Wardens of the Flame are neutral. We don't take sides in war. We help those who need it. And as for your question about why they deserve our help . . ." She set her hand on Drystan's shoulder, meeting his hardened gaze. "There were some who asked me that question about you."

Drystan stepped back as Cora's words hit him.

"Is this about that girl you befriended?" she asked. "The one we brought back from the College?"

"Her name is Verity."

Cora nodded. "I'm sure finding out there were men here from the army who attacked her home and nearly killed her was very difficult for her. I'll talk to her, Drystan. I'll tell her the same thing that I'm telling you: these soldiers are not the same ones who hurt her, and they are not the ones pulling the strings, giving the orders. They have families, they have hopes and dreams, just like you. Just like Verity. As Wardens, our role is to help them, as we helped the both of you." Cora cast a glance in the rough direction of the soldiers, though they were well out of sight from here. "If they step out of line, we will deal with it, but for now they need help. And unless they give us a reason to mistrust them, they're guests here. The same as you."

Drystan tried to swallow down his rage, though it didn't fade entirely. "So, what? They get a pass because they were following orders?"

"No," Cora said quickly. "No, part of taking orders is knowing who to take orders from. Orders or not, they've done horrible things, and they'll need to atone for those deeds someday, to whichever god they favor. But that's not my job. My job is to help heal their wounds and get them back on their feet. And maybe—just maybe—if they see the compassion shown to them by a group of strangers, perhaps they'll find a measure of that compassion within themselves."

"And what if they don't?" Drystan asked. "What if you give them this second chance and they run straight back to Westhold and go back to the war? What if they hurt more people?"

"I can't know what they're going to do when they leave here," Cora said. "But I won't judge someone for something they haven't done yet. If they throw away the second chance they've been given, that says more about them than it does about me. And when the day comes when they have to stand before Death's Gates, that'll be something they'll have to face."

She squeezed Drystan's shoulder as she stepped past him. "I'll go talk to the girl. Verity. I'll make sure she's alright, I promise."

Cora's words settled in Drystan's chest. He didn't know what else to say, so he let himself sink into the silence as Cora left. Even if Verity wouldn't speak with her, Drystan hoped that Cora's presence might give her some small measure of comfort. Yet he worried about it on the walk back to his own tent and all through the rest of that night.

Drystan rushed through his morning chores around the camp. He wanted to finish everything as early as possible so he could check on Verity. He hoped she was alright. He hadn't heard anything after he'd spoken with Cora the day before.

Ignoring the ache in the side of his knee, he hurried to her tent. He didn't even stop to grab the book he'd been reading to her. Verity was lying on her cot when he arrived, staring up at the ceiling. She looked so much like she had when he'd first come to see her that his chest tightened.

"Verity?" His voice barely came out as a whisper. "Can I come in?"

Relief flooded through him as she nodded.

"Are you alright?"

She inhaled deeply but only nodded again.

Drystan pulled up the stool. He sat in silence, his jaw tight as he held back the string of rambling thoughts that threatened to emerge. He wouldn't push her to talk if she didn't want to—no matter how much he might need it. He would just be here if she wanted his company, and he would leave when it was no longer wanted.

"You told Warden Sylus about what happened?" Verity asked after a few minutes. She still stared straight up, not bothering to look at Drystan.

"No," he said. "I asked her about the soldiers. She guessed why I was asking and said she would come check on you."

Silence filled the space between them again, and Drystan let it.

"I'm going to go home," Verity said at last.

Drystan practically fell off the stool. "What?"

"I asked Warden Sylus to send a message to my parents, and they wrote back almost immediately." She angled herself onto her side and levered herself up until she was sitting cross-legged on the bed, though she stared at the ground at Drystan's feet. "They want me to continue my recovery at home. And I want to go."

Drystan's heart nearly dropped out of his chest. It had only been a few short months, but next to Cora and Theo, who were often busy with their Warden duties, Verity was his only friend at the camp.

She was his only friend anywhere, if he was being honest.

He didn't want to lose her—the companionship and trust they'd built. But he wouldn't try to keep her from doing something she needed to do. He would be happy for her, even if it broke his heart to see her go.

"That's wonderful," he managed. He hoped it sounded genuine. "When do you leave?"

"Soon," she said. "Warden Sylus is making all the arrangements. I'll need someone to escort me, of course." Her gaze darted to her bandaged arm and then back to the floor, still avoiding looking his way. "But . . . I need to ask you for a favor."

Drystan slid the stool closer. "Anything."

She finally looked up at him for the first time since he'd walked into her tent. "I want it to be you."

"You want me to—"

"I want you to take me back to Aethir," Verity said, inhaling sharply as though steeling herself. "I want you to help me get back home. My parents said they'd send someone for me, but I . . . I'm not sure that I'd trust anyone else."

Drystan blinked. "You trust *me*? To get you all the way to Aethir?"

"I do."

Gods above, she knew about the things he'd done. "Why?" he asked. Why in Vire's hells would she ever trust someone like *him*?

Verity's brow furrowed, like she was deep in thought. She was silent for so long, Drystan thought maybe she was going to change her mind. Finally, she said, "Because you've looked out for me. And because when you look at me, you see *me*. Not what happened to me. Not . . . what I'm missing. But *me*. I don't know another person who's looked at me like that since I've been here."

Just like how Cora had been the first person to see *him* as more than just his father's son.

Drystan swallowed hard as he rubbed his knee, which ached from all of his frantic hurrying about that morning and the twisting from the day before. "I don't know how useful I'd be," he admitted. "And I don't think I can travel very fast—"

"I'm not looking for the fastest trip," she said. "Or even the safest. I need . . . I need to get out of this godsdamned camp." Her voice cracked and she swallowed, taking a deep breath. "I need to get home, and I need someone I can trust to help me get there." She watched him carefully for a moment, her eyes searching his. "I need your help, Drystan. Please."

Drystan sat up a little straighter on the stool. She needed his help. And what's more, this could be his chance. It was an opportunity to get away from his past and to move forward somewhere new. He could bring Verity home and then stay in Aethir himself. It was unlikely anyone there would recognize the son of Phillip Kalon. He could start a new life.

"I'll do it," he said, his resolve set. "I promise I'll get you home."

CHAPTER 20

THE NEXT DAY, DRYSTAN headed toward Theo's tent, the dull ache in his knee growing sharper with every step. He'd overdone it the last couple of days and was paying for it now. As he passed the mess hall, Cora jogged over, tossing up her hand in greeting.

"Morning, Drystan. Do you have a moment?" Her tone and face were both unreadable.

"I've got a session with Theo," he said cautiously.

"That's fine. I'll walk with you." She fell into step beside him. "You've really come a long way."

"Thank you. Though I can't imagine that's what you wanted to talk about."

"It sort of is." Cora looked out across the camp as they walked. "I'm sure you've heard that the girl, Verity, is leaving us to return to her home in Aethir."

Drystan's jaw tensed. "Yeah, she told me."

"I understand she was planning to ask you to escort her." Drystan kept silent as Cora eyed him. "She did, didn't she?"

There was no point in denying it. It would be clear soon enough. And besides, he trusted Cora. She wouldn't do anything to hurt him. "She did," he said. "And I agreed."

"Drystan, you have to know that's a bad idea." She set her hand on his arm, stopping him. "I meant it when I said you've come a long way. But you still have a long way to go." She gestured to his leg as he shifted his weight with a wince. "You can't even walk to the healer's tent without pain."

"I overdid it yesterday," he said quickly. "That's all."

"If you overdid it around the camp, how do you think you'll fare on the trek to Aethir?"

Drystan crossed his arms over his chest, closing himself off.

"Look, I know you've gotten close to this girl, and I know you want to help her. But I don't think you realize how hard it'll be on you to travel with her. There's very little she's capable of doing on her own. I know you spend time with her here, and you do a lot to help her, but there are many more things Theo and the other healers do for her. If you're traveling together, you will have to be her *everything*. Is that something you're prepared for?"

Drystan bit the inside of his cheek but didn't answer. He knew it would be a hard journey, but he hadn't considered all of what she would need.

"Her family offered to send people to get her," Cora went on. "My advice to you, for the sake of your own recovery, is to let them handle it."

"She doesn't trust anyone else to do this." His voice was sharper than he intended. "She trusts me. She asked me and I'm going to help her."

Cora studied him, staring deep into his eyes until he had the urge to look away. But he held her gaze. He wouldn't back down from this.

After a long moment, the Warden sighed, scratching between the braided rows of her hair. "I can see you've made up your mind. I'll do what I can to arrange for the safest, easiest journey for the two of you. But Drystan . . . May I offer you another piece of unsolicited advice?"

Drystan let his arms fall to his sides, his shoulders moving away from his ears. She wasn't going to try to stop him. She wanted to help, just as she always had. He nodded, but he wasn't prepared for the words Cora spoke next.

"You have *got* to stop falling in love with every girl who shows you kindness."

His face heated. "I . . . I don't—"

"It's alright," Cora said, lifting her hands to ward off his rising defensiveness. "It isn't fair, the lot you were given. You deserve so much more—so much *better*. You have a huge heart, Drystan, and I mean that in the best way. But if you keep giving it to people who haven't earned it yet, it's going to keep getting broken."

Drystan stood there, floundering, unsure what to say—what to think.

"Just be careful," she said, clapping him on the arm. "That's all I'm saying. Be careful. Guard your heart. Protect it."

With a kind smile, she turned and left him standing alone in the middle of the camp.

Drystan rubbed the back of his neck. Cora wasn't wrong that the trip would be difficult, but he could talk to Theo and figure out what he'd need to know to help Verity along the way. He could do it.

She trusted him with this. Just because he didn't want to let her down, that didn't mean he was in love with her. He didn't fall in love with every girl who was kind to him.

That was ridiculous.

Cora was true to her word: she chartered Drystan and Verity passage on a ship out of Fordryn, Weryn's capital city and port. Although the Wardens' camp was near the border of Aethir, neither Verity nor Drystan would be capable of making the journey through the treacherous mountains unassisted, and the Wardens couldn't spare anyone to send with them. Verity's parents were less than thrilled that their daughter refused to wait at the camp but agreed to meet the ship when it arrived in Whitehollow.

Cora also provided horses to get them to Fordryn, and a buckled strap of leather for Verity that would attach to her saddle's pommel and help her to keep her balance while riding.

When the day came for them to leave, a few Wardens came to see them off that morning, including Theo and Cora. Theo had a satchel slung over one shoulder, which he held out for Drystan as he approached.

"What's this?" Drystan asked as he took the bag.

"Medical supplies. Such as we can spare. Linen for Verity's bandages, and for your knee in case you need the extra support. You remember everything I taught you?"

Drystan couldn't help but smile at Theo fussing over him like a mother hen. "I remember."

"And be sure to take care of yourself too. Don't push yourself too hard." Theo extended his hand to Drystan, who clasped it firmly.

"I won't," he said. "Thank you for everything, Theo."

"Move over," Cora said, using her elbow to give Theo a playful shove out of the way. "My turn." She held a small pouch that jingled pleasantly. "Here. I want you to have this."

Drystan hesitated a moment before he reached for the pouch. It was heavier than he expected. He didn't own anything anymore and certainly didn't have any of his own money. If he was going to get Verity safely to Aethir and then start over somewhere new himself, having some coin to his name would go a long way to making that happen.

"You don't have to do that, Cora."

"I know. But I want to. Oh, and there's one more thing." Cora stepped around the side of the closest tent and returned a moment later holding a bow and a quiver of arrows. "I want you to take this too."

Drystan's fingers twitched, his muscles remembering the motion of drawing back the string. He hadn't shot a bow since before the disastrous job with Genevieve. It was part of his old life. It had once been something that brought him peace, sure, but his father had stripped that away.

He stared at the bow but made no move to take it.

"Look," Cora said. "You can waste your skill to spite your father, or you can use it despite him. You can use it to do something good."

"I don't want it," he said quietly.

"Do you know how to wield a sword?"

". . . Not really."

"Then take the damn bow, Drystan." She grinned despite her sharp words. "I want to make sure you're safe out there, and the way I know how to do that is by giving you money and something to defend yourself with."

As Drystan's fingers touched the bow, memories rushed into him. Every shot he'd ever taken at his father's orders—every shot that had ended someone's life—flashed through his mind. His hand flinched back.

But Cora was right. He needed to be able to keep Verity safe on the road. He swallowed down the nausea climbing from his stomach and took the bow and quiver in a firm grip. "It'll be useful if we need to hunt for food," he said, more to himself than to Cora, though she nodded.

"There you go," she said. She sobered quickly, her lips forming a thin line. "Drystan . . . Be safe out there, please. I know you're focused on taking care of the girl but listen to Theo and take care of yourself too. And I meant what I said to you back in Alton. I still think you'd make a hell of a Warden. If you ever decide you want to take the oath, come find me. I'd support your pledge in a heartbeat."

Drystan wished he knew what she saw in him. There was no way he could ever cut it as a Warden of the Flame. And there was no way they'd let someone like him in, even with Cora vouching for him.

An attack dog doesn't stop being an attack dog just because you dress it up. "Thank you," he said around the tightness in his throat.

"Wait!" Verity cried. Her eyes were frantic. "The sword. Where's the sword?"

A few of the Wardens nearby exchanged looks; they'd likely never heard her speak before.

"Don't worry," Drystan said, keeping his voice calm and even. "Wait with Cora. I'll be right back."

Drystan headed toward Verity's tent, moving as quickly as his knee would allow. He tried a slow jog and was pleased to find that he could manage it for a few dozen yards. The broken sword lay in Verity's tent, just where it had been every time Drystan had visited. He grabbed it and hurried to where Verity was waiting.

"Got it," he called as he came around the last tent.

Verity blew out a long breath. She looked like she'd been approaching a panic. Theo stood beside her, his hand on her back.

"What do you want to take that rusty thing with you for?" one of the other Wardens asked. The question earned him a sharp look from Cora.

"It's not *rusty*," Drystan snapped, carefully tucking the sword in with the rest of their gear. "And what does it matter to you if she takes it or not?"

Between Drystan's comments and Cora's glare, the Warden mumbled something and skulked off.

"Don't pay him any mind, dear," Theo said to Verity. "Best of luck back home. I'm proud of how far you've come."

Verity remained silent as she moved to Drystan, and he helped her mount the gentle horse Cora had picked out for her. Cora offered to lend a hand, but Drystan needed to be certain he could do it himself while they were on the road. It took him a couple tries to find the best method, but he managed. He then tethered the horses together so he could direct them both.

"Take care of yourself," Cora said again as she wiped quickly at her eyes. Theo put his arm around her shoulder and, pulling her into his side, set a gentle kiss on her cheek.

Drystan angled his head, looking between the two of them. "Wait, are you two—?"

Cora chuckled as she leaned into Theo. "We don't make a show of it. He usually hates any sort of public displays."

"I do," he said softly. "But I thought you could use it today."

Cora's smile was genuine as she stepped toward Drystan. "I truly hope I have the good fortune to see you again someday."

"Thank you," Drystan said, his eyes stinging at the corners. He held his hand out to her. "For everything. Y-you saved—"

Cora pulled him into a hug instead. "Alright, now get out of here before you make me cry," she said. When she stepped back, her eyes shimmered, but she blinked rapidly as she turned to Verity. "I'm sorry I didn't get to know you better while you were here, but I wish you the best in your life back home."

"Thank you," Verity said quietly.

Drystan mounted the other horse and spurred them both forward, leaving the camp and the Wardens behind.

CHAPTER 21

THEIR FIRST NIGHT ON the road, Drystan set up a campfire, then helped Verity with her food before eating his own meager dinner. Verity was quiet, as she'd been through most of the day's journey. Drystan had been focused on the path ahead of them, so he hadn't pushed her to talk, though now he worried something was bothering her.

As they sat in the glow of the fire, Drystan was about to ask her if she was alright when Verity cleared her throat. "Could you help me with something?"

"Of course." His mind started running through every task Theo had told him about that hadn't yet come up, from basic to more specialized.

"Would you mind . . . brushing my hair?"

"Oh." Drystan hadn't even considered something as simple as that. "Sure."

Verity gave an upward nod toward their things. "There's a comb in my bag, toward the front."

Drystan found the comb without any trouble and set to brushing Verity's hair, which was thick and knotted from the day on the road, despite having been tied back. "Sorry," he muttered every time the comb snagged on a tangle.

"It's alright," she mumbled quietly.

The silence was maddening, so he told Verity a story of home, of when he used to sit by his mother's knee while she combed her hair before bed. He was only half paying attention to what he was saying; the rest of his focus was on his task.

He fell silent again after reaching the end of his story, or at least what he hoped was a reasonable end to his rambling tale.

"I don't suppose," Verity said after several long minutes, "that you know how to braid?"

Drystan huffed a laugh. "I have three brothers."

"So that would be a *no*, then?" There was a note of amusement in her voice that made him smile.

"That would be a no." Then after a moment he added, "Sorry."

"It's alright," she said. "I was just thinking it would help keep it manageable while we're traveling."

"I'd be willing to learn, if you could teach me."

Verity turned to look at him over her shoulder. "Really?"

"Really," he said, tugging the comb through the last of the tangles. "You're right—it would make this much easier on both of us."

She seemed to consider it for a moment, but then her face fell, her shoulders hunching. "Except that I can't show you how to do it," she said, her voice small again. "I could try to explain it, but I won't be able to see what you're doing, so I won't know if it's right."

"What about this?" Drystan moved to kneel in front of her. "May I try something?"

Verity nodded, and Drystan reached behind her and gathered her hair, gently pulling it to cascade over her shoulder.

"You tell me what to do," he said. "And this way, you'll be able to see if I'm doing it right. What do you think?"

A small smile graced Verity's lips, like the ones she used to give him when he was first visiting her. "Alright."

Verity's instructions were quite clear, and it wasn't long before Drystan had successfully completed a braid that certainly wouldn't win any competitions for looks, but would hold and keep her hair tamed and under control.

"Thank you," Verity said. "Really. This means a lot. The healers at the camp . . . they'd sometimes comb my hair, but I never dared ask anyone to do anything with it. This . . ." She inhaled deeply, her eyes shimmering with tears. "Vire's demons, it's such a stupid thing to be emotional about."

"I get it." Drystan leaned in and brushed a tear from her cheek with his thumb. "Did you used to wear it like this before?"

"Well, not exactly like *this*"—she nodded toward how the braid hung over her shoulder—"but yes, I wore it braided a lot."

"It's something normal," he said. "And there's very little that has been for . . . well, for a long time."

She sniffled softly and nodded. "Thank you."

It felt nice to be able to do this for her. He was already doing a lot, he knew, but this was something small that made a difference in how she felt in her own skin—how she felt moving through the world. Seeing how much it meant to her warmed something deep in his chest. "You're welcome, Verity."

Drystan jolted awake as a scream tore through the still night air. He scrambled to his feet, his mind racing with the rush of adrenaline.

He instinctively found Verity in the flickering firelight. She was thrashing in her blankets, screaming like she was being attacked. Drystan dropped to his knees beside her. Pain shot through his leg as he hit the ground, but he didn't care.

"Verity!"

She didn't respond. Her arm smacked into him as he leaned over her.

Drystan didn't want her to hurt herself, so he gripped her elbow with one hand, his other hand pressing against the left side of her chest to hold her down. "*Verity!*"

Her eyes snapped open, and she flinched away from him with another cry.

He let her go, holding his hands open. "You're alright," he said quickly.

Verity's face shifted from terror to anguish. "Gods, I'm sorry," she sobbed.

Drystan pulled her up so she was sitting, keeping his hands on her shoulders to balance her. He wanted her to know she was safe. He wanted her to know he would protect her. But he didn't know how to say it, so Drystan wrapped his arms around her. Maybe he didn't need words. Maybe his presence could be its own kind of comfort.

"I-I should have warned you," she mumbled between sobs. "I'm s-sorry."

"It's alright," he said. When she lifted her head to look at him, he asked, "Do you want to talk about it?"

She shook her head, tears still falling.

"Then I'll just be here." He shifted to sit beside her. "For as long as you need."

The rest of the journey to Fordryn was quiet, save for the nightmares that plagued Verity. As with everything else on their trip, Drystan fell into a routine with these too, waking with her when they struck and sitting with her until she fell back asleep.

The two of them boarded their chartered ship in Fordryn as planned, and their time at sea was a welcome reprieve, though it was short-lived. In less than two weeks, they docked in Whitehollow.

Whitehollow's port was full of ships, beyond which were white stone buildings that rose up and stretched into the distance. The air was colder here than in Weryn, but the sun shone overhead, glittering off the bay. It was stunningly beautiful, and Drystan couldn't help but admire it as he leaned against the railing and breathed in the scent of the sea.

Once they docked, an entourage of a dozen liveried soldiers and half a dozen young ladies gathered around the ship expectantly.

"Ainam's glory," Verity muttered, though it sounded more like a curse of annoyance than relief.

"Friends of yours?"

He'd meant it in jest, so he was shocked when she said, "Kind of . . ."

Drystan's mind reeled. Who were Verity's parents that they could pay to send eighteen guards and staff from the middle of Aethir to Whitehollow and back? He'd never asked her about her family, and she'd never said, though he'd talked about his own plenty. Like a damned fool.

Too eager, his father had said. *Too excitable.*

As soon as Drystan helped Verity down the steep ramp leading from the ship, one of the soldiers strode up to her, followed closely by the eldest of the women.

"Miss Corallan," he said with a bow. "Your parents have sent us to escort you home." The man didn't acknowledge Drystan's presence at all, so he stepped out of the way, hefting his and Verity's meager belongings over his shoulder.

Verity didn't look back. Her already quiet demeanor intensified as she seemed to withdraw into herself. "I thought my parents were coming themselves," she said, barely audible over the bustle of the port.

"They had urgent issues to attend to," the woman said, stepping closer to Verity. "They've missed you and they're very eager to see you once we arrive back home." The woman held her arm out for Verity to walk with her.

Verity paused, watching the rest of the gathered group. "Why are there so many?"

"Your father wasn't sure what kind of care you were going to need," the woman said. "He wanted to make sure you were well-attended on our journey home. But you seem quite well, Miss. The letters from the Wardens had made it sound like you were . . ." She trailed off, her face reddening as she no doubt sensed she was treading into unwelcome territory.

Verity moved to follow the woman.

"Do you have any bags, Miss?" the woman asked.

Verity turned and found Drystan where he'd been keeping back. The woman and the soldier both followed her gaze, their attention landing on him with such suddenness that he took another step back.

"Thank you, lad," the soldier said, reaching for the bags. "That'll be all."

"He's not a porter, Justice," Verity said, her tone sharpening. "He traveled with me from the Wardens' camp."

Verity had hardly acknowledged him since they docked. Was she ashamed of him? Knowing who he was—who his father was . . .

Back at the camp, she'd said she trusted him, but had she only said what he wanted to hear so he'd help her? So she could get what she needed out of him?

Like Genevieve . . . ?

The soldier eyed him suspiciously, his nose wrinkling like he smelled something foul.

Drystan's face heated. What had he thought would happen when they arrived?

"I suppose you'll be wanting some sort of payment then?" the man, Justice, asked as he began checking his pockets.

"I didn't do it for money," Drystan said, his voice small. He'd been too trusting again, hadn't he? Too eager.

"He's coming with us," Verity said. There was a command in her words that Drystan had never heard from her before, and it pulled him out of his spiraling thoughts. "He's my friend."

Drystan's heart warmed, even as shame made his ears burn. He knew Verity. She wasn't like Genevieve. She *wasn't.* She wouldn't use him like Genevieve had.

Verity's attendants gave each other a pointed look, but neither argued. The woman gestured for Verity to walk with her. "Alright then, let's be on our way." She moved to set her hand against Verity's arm as though to guide her.

But she was on Verity's left side. With her traveling cloak draped over her shoulders and pinned tight, Verity's injuries were invisible. The woman's hand brushed the cloak and the notable absence of an arm beneath. Her hand twitched back, and Verity flinched. It was only a little bit, but Drystan had to stop himself from rushing to her side.

"What's your name, lad?" the soldier asked, pulling Drystan's attention.

Shit. This far north, would people here have heard of Phillip Kalon? Would a soldier, whose job was protecting people?

Was that a risk he could take?

"Drystan," he said, hoping the man wouldn't ask for his surname.

Justice gave Drystan an appraising look before waving him toward the rest of the soldiers. "We'd best be off."

Several of the women swooped in around Verity, ushering her away from the docks and toward a carriage that waited nearby. Together they climbed in, leaving a few of the younger women and the soldiers—as well as Drystan—outside.

He fell in line with the others around the carriage. A pair of young women were just ahead of him, their long skirts sweeping the ground.

One leaned in close to the other. "I'm surprised she hasn't yelled at us yet," she said, her voice hushed.

The other snorted a quiet laugh. "True. Maybe she finally got taken down a peg."

Adjusting their bags over his shoulder, Drystan kept his mouth shut. He followed in silence, his thoughts drifting. It was the first time, he marveled as the realization struck him, that he'd even set foot outside his home kingdom of Weryn. He'd done it.

He'd made it out.

He hoped his mother would be proud of him.

Chapter 22

Getting into Aethir from Whitehollow was slow going. The carriage, pulled by only two horses, took its time along the roads. The pace served Drystan just fine, who had to walk the whole way alongside the soldiers. He barely saw Verity while they were on the road. If they were moving, she was cloistered up in the carriage, and if they were stopped or camped, she was practically swarmed with her attendants. Drystan overheard a few more comments when Verity wasn't around, and he bit his tongue so as not to cause any trouble, but otherwise the trip was uneventful enough.

By the time the soldiers announced that they were entering the Corallans's lands, Drystan's knee was aching with every step, and his limp, which was more pronounced now than usual, had him lagging toward the back of the group.

The estate finally loomed ahead—a sprawling manor with gardens and stables and so many other buildings, Drystan had no idea what they could all be used for. It rivaled Baron Venbarra's estate for size and sent a sinking feeling deep into the pit of Drystan's stomach. Was Verity the daughter of some sort of duke or baron? Did they have those in Aethir?

The carriage stopped, and Drystan only caught a glimpse of Verity's hair as she was whisked inside. Drystan was ignored as everyone spread out to handle their individual duties. It would be dark soon, and he wasn't sure where he should go or even where the nearest town was. Besides, Verity had wanted him to come with her here. He didn't want to leave without at least saying goodbye.

Before he could worry too long over what to do, Justice, the last to depart, cast a glance at Drystan over his shoulder. "Come on," he called. "Temperance will find a room for you, I'm sure."

"Thank you, sir." Drystan limped after the guard and followed him inside.

They'd barely entered the massive foyer, all dark wood and bright marble floors, when a woman hurried in from an adjoining hallway. Justice waved a hand toward Drystan as though to tell the woman *he's your problem now.*

The woman smiled pleasantly. Her hair was dark with several small streaks of gray, and her olive skin had only a few soft lines around her eyes and mouth. "Welcome," she said, sounding a touch out of breath. "I'm Temperance, lady's maid to Miss Verity. It's a pleasure to meet you, sir."

"Call me Drystan," he said.

Temperance showed him to a modest room on the lower level of the manor, down one of the service corridors. "I'm sorry I can't provide you with anything finer."

Even this room was larger than his room had been back home, though the furnishings were simpler in design. It was nothing fancy, but it certainly beat his tent at the Wardens' camp, so he said, "This is perfect. Thank you."

"We should be the ones thanking you, sir. Thank you for bringing Miss Verity back to us."

Drystan smiled tightly. The lady's maid was the only person he'd seen who genuinely seemed to care about Verity.

"Unfortunately, we're past the dinner hour," Temperance continued. "But you're welcome to help yourself to whatever you can find in the kitchens just down the hall. In the morning, I'll speak with Magistrate Corallan and we'll go from there."

Verity's father was a magistrate? The memory of a noose around his neck made Drystan's throat tighten. He swallowed hard. "Thank you," he managed. He dropped his bag near the door, though he held the other out toward her. Back in Fordryn, Drystan had bought some thick canvas to wrap around the broken sword, and had attached it to the side of Verity's pack with makeshift fastenings. Only the very end of the hilt stuck out from the canvas. "This belongs to Verity. Can you see that she gets it?"

Temperance eyed the sword as she took the bag. "Alright."

"It's very important to her," Drystan said. "Please see that she gets *everything*."

The woman nodded gravely. "I understand. I'll bring it straight to her now."

Once Temperance left, Drystan made his way to the kitchens, which were still warm from the smoldering embers in the massive hearth. A few staff were cleaning up from the day, but no one seemed bothered by his presence. He scrounged up some bread, an apple, and what looked like a slice of leftover meat pie, and by the time he'd eaten and returned to his room, he could barely keep his eyes open.

Despite his exhaustion, sleep eluded him for most of the night. The pain in his knee was a constant distraction, as were the worries about what would happen to him now that he was on his own in Aethir. Maybe he could talk to Verity about it in the morning. She might have some suggestions for him.

Shortly after dawn, Temperance returned, a frown creasing her face. "Magistrate Corallan and his wife thank you for bringing their daughter back," she said solemnly. She held out a coin purse to him. "Please accept this as a token of their thanks. They've also paid for accommodations for you in town. I'll provide you with all the information before you go."

"Oh, that's very kind, thank you," Drystan said, hiding his disappointment. He didn't move to take the purse. "But I didn't do it for any money."

"I know, dear," Temperance said. "But it's the least we can do. Please, take it."

Drystan hesitated before finally taking the pouch. "Can I—That is, would it be alright if I said goodbye to Verity?" She'd wanted him here. He needed to at least make sure she was settled in before he left.

The woman's frown deepened, her lips thinning. "I don't think that would be a wise idea," she said. He wanted to ask why, but Temperance ushered him toward his bag. "It'll be for the best, dear. You'll see. You've done her a great service, but she's home now, with the people who care about her. She'll be fine."

I care about her too. But Drystan stopped the words from forming. Maybe Temperance was right. This was Verity's home. She'd be well taken care of in a manor like this, with servants to attend upon her every need, parents to care for her, and healers should she need help.

What use would he be to her? What could he offer her that she didn't already have here? Verity didn't need him for anything anymore.

"I understand," he said, his voice quiet. "Would you mind telling her goodbye for me? And, um . . . That it was really nice getting to know her?"

"Of course." Temperance led him down the hall and to a small door at the back of the manor. "Town is two miles that way," she said, gesturing east. "Follow the road. When you get there, head to the inn. There's only one. Give the owner this." She handed him a sealed note. "It'll give you two-week's lodging. That should be enough to get yourself on your feet. Halcyn may not be a huge city, but there's work enough for those who look for it."

Drystan took the envelope and placed it carefully in his pocket. "Thank you," he said. Then he turned and headed east.

The town of Halcyn was larger than Drystan had been expecting, with buildings that stretched three, four, or even five stories into the sky. Temperance had mentioned that there was only one inn, but she hadn't mentioned that it was massive and sprawling—certainly different from the grimy establishments Drystan had stayed in before. As he stepped inside, his stomach rumbled as the smells of smoked bacon, coffee, and fresh bread surrounded him.

He found the owner easily—a portly man with thinning hair and a pleasant smile—and handed him the note from the Corallans. Before long, Drystan was settled into one of the nicer rooms he'd ever stayed in. How much must something like this cost? He had better make good use of his two weeks here, he decided. There was no way he'd be able to afford to stay here on his own.

But that would be a problem for another day. Today, Drystan would eat and rest his leg and lie on the soft, plush bed in his room, daydreaming about what the future might hold. What could he do, now that he was free? Free of his father and free of his former life. He didn't know the answer, but he was excited to find out.

He wished he could talk to Verity about it.

CHAPTER 23

HALCYN WAS VERY DIFFERENT from Alton. Drystan had heard stories of Aethirian cities, where the streetlamps came on by themselves and carts drove themselves along the roads. He saw no phantom-driven carts, but the lanterns certainly lit themselves at dusk and extinguished themselves at dawn. There was also a massive building at the center of town, which Drystan soon learned housed thousands of books that could be borrowed by anyone in town, so long as they gave a name and an address where they could be found.

Drystan spent the first few days combing the stacks of books and finding a dozen or so to read. They were mostly adventure stories, which had always been his favorite, though one of them had the heroine falling in love with a farmhand and taking him with her on her adventures. It was as much about their love as it was about their heroics, and Drystan found it captivating.

He also inquired around town for work, but it seemed the citizens of Halcyn were leery of anyone from beyond Aethir's borders—apparently they didn't get too many travelers from neighboring kingdoms. Drystan made the mistake of telling one or two business owners that he was from Weryn, and it wasn't long before word spread of the tall, broad-shouldered boy from away.

Two weeks came and went, and he was forced to vacate the room Verity's parents had paid for. Luckily, the inn had rooms at several price points, and he was able to secure another that he'd be able to afford a while longer on his own, thanks to the money they'd given him, as well as what he had left from Cora. His new room was much smaller, and much closer to what he was used to back in Alton, but it had a bed, a blanket, and a small trunk where he could store his meager belongings. That was enough for now.

The following week, Drystan finally found a job at one of the farms on the outskirts of town. It was hard work, and by the end of the first day, Drystan's entire leg ached, and he could barely walk. A few shots of whiskey helped dull the pain though, as it did the next day, and the next. But without enough time to rest, Drystan had trouble keeping up with what needed to be done.

They let him go after a week, and he was back where he started.

After another week, his money had nearly run dry. He had no prospects and nowhere else to go—he could leave Halcyn, he supposed, but the coin he had left wouldn't get him very far. And besides, would any other city in Aethir be much different from this one? So Drystan turned to the taverns scattered throughout the town. A number of them had games one could bet money on, like dice or cards, and Drystan's father had taught him how to count cards when he was seven.

His *luck* at cards bought him another week's stay and enough whiskey to keep himself comfortable, but he needed to be careful. If he were caught, they'd run him out of town so fast it would make his head spin. Unfortunately—or fortunately—Drystan's talents caught the attention of one of the local businessmen.

"Tell me, do you do any mercenary work?" the man asked. The gold rings on his thick fingers glittered as he slid a whiskey over to Drystan. "I've got an establishment that's in need of some security. Keeping out the riffraff and ensuring the clientele behave themselves. I may also have a few odd jobs that would suit someone of your stature. What do you say?"

Cora had told Drystan that he couldn't choose how his story started, and he couldn't choose how it would end, but he could choose the parts that happened in the middle. Well, it seemed he couldn't even do that right, because that was how, after a month of freedom, Drystan found himself exactly where he'd been before—hurting people for money.

Another month went by. Drystan had earned a reputation in town by then. You didn't want to be on the wrong side of his fists, people said. The work was less physically demanding than the farm work had been, and so Drystan's knee finally started to feel better, and he didn't need the whiskey to keep it at its usual ache. He did, however, need the whiskey to help him ignore the sinking feeling in his gut that nothing had changed in the slightest. He was still just a brute, stuck in the same rut as before.

And now he was wasting his second chance.

That feeling—that he was squandering the gift Cora had given him by saving his life—hurt more with each passing day. The whiskey helped, but not enough. Women helped a little too. A stranger sharing his bed—or him sharing theirs—gave him something else to focus on for a time. And if they were gone when the dawn came, then all the better.

A sharp knock on Drystan's door woke him. His head spun and his stomach churned with the alcohol he'd drunk the night before. He rolled onto his side, curling in on himself. How much had he—?

The *clunk* of an empty bottle falling from the bed answered his question.

Another knock.

Drystan could ignore it. There was no one who needed him at this time of the morning—or any time during daylight hours, really. And considering he'd only got to sleep a couple of hours earlier, ignoring the problem until it went away seemed the best course of action.

The knock sounded again, more insistent this time. Drystan wasn't sure he could stand even if he wanted to, but if whoever was on the other side of his door was in such a hurry to talk to him, fine.

"It's open," he groaned, half into the pillow.

The door latch clicked, and two sets of footfalls entered the room. There was another sound of a glass bottle rolling across the floor. The footsteps hesitated by the door.

"Drystan?" Verity's voice was quiet.

Drystan jerked his head up, causing his vision to swim. But that was definitely Verity standing just inside his room, a traveling cloak pulled tight around her, as always, and her reddish hair braided over her shoulder the way he'd done it for her on the road. Beside her was Temperance, her dark hair pulled back in a bun. Both women appeared horrified.

"Verity." He swallowed the bile that climbed his throat as he sat up and swung his legs over the side of the bed. "What are you doing here?"

"Looking for you." She eyed the mess of his room, her gaze lingering on discarded bottles, mugs, plates, and half-finished meals. "Are you alright?"

Verity was asking if *he* was alright? He should have asked her the moment she walked in. But she looked good. *Well*, even. Drystan rubbed his face, trying to sober himself a little.

"Yeah," he murmured as he dropped his hands. "I'm fine." He hoped it sounded believable. Nothing about the last few months had gone how he'd hoped. And now Verity was here, staring at him like he was a street dog in some back alley. His stomach turned again and this time it wasn't only from the liquor. He didn't want her to see him like this, but it was the pity in her eyes that hit Drystan the hardest. Genevieve's face flashed in his mind, along with the pitying look she'd given him right before she'd screamed. Drystan's knee twinged. He shook his head to clear the memory but only succeeded in kicking off a headache.

"Get cleaned up," Verity said, turning toward the door. Temperance was close behind her, as though she couldn't leave fast enough. "Meet me downstairs."

The door closed as both women hurried from the room. Drystan flopped back down onto the bed. He hadn't seen Verity in months—not since she'd been home. What could she possibly need him for? Had she been thinking about him the way he sometimes thought about her? Had she missed him?

Drystan dragged himself to his feet. She came here looking for him—he'd better not keep her waiting.

Downstairs, Drystan found Verity and Temperance sitting at a table off to one side of the common area. Verity's traveling cloak was unpinned, and some sort of prosthetic arms were visible now. They were very pale, even paler than her own skin, and the hands rested in her lap, almost fading into the soft pink of her dress.

The noise of the common room was deafening, sending spikes through Drystan's head as he approached their table. Once he was seated, Temperance pushed a mug of water toward him. He downed it in several quick gulps while Verity stared at him.

He wiped his mouth with the back of his hand. "You look great," he said.

"And you look terrible. What happened to you?"

"Nothing." He dragged his fingers through his hair, pushing it out of his eyes as his face heated with shame. He could only imagine the image he presented, even with having taken a few moments to change his shirt and wash his face before leaving his room.

Verity watched him for another moment. But then she raised her chin as though she'd come to a decision. "Drystan, I need your help."

Temperance cleared her throat. "Miss Verity, might it be better if we—"

"Would you excuse us for a few minutes, Tempie?" Verity asked, though her tone made it clear that it wasn't a request.

Temperance looked between the two of them once before she stood and moved to the other side of the room.

Verity leaned toward Drystan. "I can't stay here."

Drystan tried to process her words through his rapidly rising hangover. He couldn't have heard her right, could he?

"They're smothering me here. I can hardly get a moment to myself to think—they won't let me study." She held up her right arm, where the pale material attached to a cloth sleeve that was pulled over her elbow. "My parents had these made for me," she said. "They're porcelain. *Porcelain.*" When he didn't say anything, her face hardened, anger flashing in her eyes. "Drystan!" she snapped. "Are you listening? They're dressing me up like a doll, keeping me locked away like I'm going to break. And these"—she indicated her arms with a derisive jerk of her head—"are useless. I need something else. Something better." She took a breath, shaking a wisp of hair out of her face, though it fell back immediately. "And I need your help to make it happen."

Drystan was doing his best to follow her hurried speech. "Something better?" he asked. "Like what?"

She shook the hair out of her face again. "In there." She nodded toward a bag resting beside the chair Temperance had vacated, and the stubborn locks fell into her eyes again.

Drystan slid into the empty chair, putting himself beside Verity, and tucked the rogue strand of hair behind her ear before he thought about what he was doing. As his fingers brushed her fair skin, he jerked his hand away.

"I'm sorry," he muttered. "I shouldn't have—"

"No," Verity said quickly. "I appreciate it. Thank you."

He couldn't help but smile as he reached into the bag at his feet and withdrew a red fabric-bound book. A ribbon marked a place about a third of the way through, and he flipped it open to that page.

Rough sketches of hands filled the page, diagrams showing details of joints and fingers with gears and cylindrical parts connected together.

Drystan looked over the pages. There were notes in the margins as well, but it looked like some kind of shorthand. He couldn't make it out. "What's all this?"

"Temperance has been helping me with the sketches and notations," Verity said. "But these are some ideas I have for functioning arms."

"*Functioning*?" Drystan tried to blink away some of his hangover. He failed. "As in, they would move?"

"Yes. But it's all just theoretical until I can find someone who can build them."

Drystan flipped the page to find more sketches, more notes. "You did all this in the last two months?" It was an incredible amount of work.

"No, no, definitely not," Verity said. She leaned a little closer, as though checking to see what page he was on. "It took a while for me to even think of the idea, and then I had to get Tempie to write it down for me. I started working on it in earnest a couple weeks ago."

Drystan's mind reeled. *Weeks?* "That's incredible, Verity. But . . . What do you need me for?"

She gave an upward nod at the book. "Next page."

Flipping the page as instructed, Drystan read the information listed there. "Noel Torin, Snowfeld. What's that?"

"Not *what*," Verity said, her eyes lighting up. "*Who*. And also, *where*. Noel Torin is a famous mechanist. He was the first to combine clockwork with forged metals to create some of the most complex engineering designs on the continent. He built the lifts at Embercliff. We studied him back at the . . ." Her gaze went distant for a moment before she cleared her throat. When she continued, her voice was shaky. "He was exiled from Pyrrah and lives up in Snowfeld, at least as far as anyone knows. He's apparently a bit of a recluse." Verity sat up straighter, her back going rigid as she held her head high. "I need you to take me to him."

Drystan's brows shot up. "You want me to take you to Snowfeld to find a reclusive engineer?"

"Yes."

"I don't even know where Snowfeld *is*."

"It's northwest from here." She paused. "*Very* northwest. I have maps."

"I don't have any money."

"I can fund the whole thing."

Drystan wanted to help. Really, he did. Seeing her again brought the other parts of his life into sharp focus. He hadn't quite realized what he'd been missing when he couldn't talk to her. But he cared about her too much to jump blindly at this opportunity to see her again. He needed to be certain that she knew what she was getting into. That she was sure about leaving.

"But you only just got home," he said as he closed the book. "Would your parents be willing to reach out? Maybe contract with him to build these according to your designs? Or, at least, could they take you there if you need to go in person?"

Verity's chin dipped. "My parents don't see the point. They say they'll take care of me—of everything I need. That I won't need to worry about anything. It sounds good on paper, but . . . I don't want to have everything done for me. I don't want to waste away in a room with pretty flowers on the nightstand and no way to do anything on my own. I don't know *what* I want to do, but I know it's not that."

"You want to live," Drystan said softly. "You don't want to just *survive*. Or *exist*. You want to *live*."

She looked at him, and there was a shimmer of silver in her honey brown eyes. "Yes," she whispered. "There's no one else I trust to take me. Will you help me, Drystan?"

He swallowed around the lump in his throat. "Of course I will."

CHAPTER 24

Drystan agreed to use Verity's money to secure horses, food, and gear for their journey to Snowfeld. They'd resupply in Whitehollow and Valda along the way, Verity explained, though the last stretch of the trip would be the most difficult. There was very little besides open wilderness for the miles between Valda and Snowfeld.

It only took a few days for Drystan to get everything in order, including telling his employer he was leaving town. Thankfully, a well-timed crack of Drystan's knuckles ensured that he was paid everything he was owed that same day.

As he packed his belongings, Drystan thought about leaving the bow from Cora—he hadn't used it on the trek from the camp and hadn't even touched it since arriving in Halcyn—but in the end, logic won out over his discomfort. It could still prove useful, especially once they left civilization behind.

On the day he and Verity had set to leave, Drystan took one of the horses the two miles to Magistrate Corallan's estate. He'd barely made it up the walkway to the stables when the manor door opened and Verity stepped into the sunlight. Temperance followed her, along with a short young man who held a couple of bags and something long wrapped in black cloth.

Drystan dismounted and walked the horse closer. He hadn't expected her to be ready to go immediately upon his arrival. But as he approached, the redness around her eyes was clear.

"Verity, are you—"

"Only one horse?" she demanded, stopping short. "Where's mine?"

Her voice was so sharp, Drystan's steps faltered. "This one's yours," he said. "I didn't want to bring everything here in case we weren't ready to—"

"I said we'd leave today, didn't I?"

"Well, yeah, but—"

"Then where's the issue?"

Drystan swallowed hard, but before he could muster an answer, Verity turned to the man carrying the bags.

"That'll be all," she snapped. The young man set the bags down and dashed away as though his ass was on fire.

Temperance frowned, though it shifted to a hard neutral as Verity's gaze turned her way. "Stay safe, my dear," Temperance said. She took a hesitant step toward Verity but stopped when Verity didn't move to close the distance. Temperance glanced at Drystan. "Thank you," she said softly. Then she followed the young man toward the manor.

Verity's jaw was set as she moved toward the horse. Drystan helped her into the saddle before hefting the bags onto his shoulders. He gathered up the cloth-wrapped parcel, which had to be the broken sword that Verity refused to let out of her sight, and tugged gently on the lead rope to spur the horse into motion.

They walked in silence for a while, and Drystan let his thoughts wander, though they circled around Verity. Judging by how fast the young man carrying the bags had run away, and how the women had first spoken of Verity when they'd traveled from Whitehollow, Drystan was beginning to get a picture of how she treated people in her service. But that couldn't be all there was to her. The Verity he'd met in Weryn was quiet and reserved, but also brave, fearless, and kind. Being here, it was like seeing a whole different side of her. It wasn't a side that sat well with him.

"Would you tell me a story?" Verity asked.

"That depends," Drystan said, not looking back. "Are we friends?"

"What do you mean?"

"Are we friends?" he asked again. "Either I'm your hired help for this journey, or I'm your friend, helping you out because I want to." He stopped, stroking the horse's mane as he looked up at Verity. "If we're friends, then sure. Though I'd appreciate you not talking down to me like you did back there. And if you hired me to be a servant then, well, honestly, I'd still appreciate it if you didn't talk down to me like that."

Verity stared at him. "I'm . . . sorry." Her gaze drifted down to her porcelain hands.

"What did your parents say about you leaving for Snowfeld?" he asked. Maybe something had happened before they left that had set her on edge. "Were they angry?"

"Worse," she said quietly. "They were disappointed."

He waited for her to continue, but when she didn't, he cleared his throat. "And?"

"*And* what?"

Drystan rubbed the back of his neck. "You're going to have to explain a bit more, I think," he said with a soft chuckle. "I'm pretty sure I've disappointed my father every day since the moment I was born."

He hadn't meant for it to sound like some horrible thing, but Verity's face fell in sorrow. "That's awful." Before Drystan found any words for a reply, Verity continued, "They think I'm being foolish. They can't understand why I don't want to just stay at home and let everyone do everything for me. I'm trying to be strong, but everyone at home—they just kept treating me like some kind of broken thing."

Drystan smiled up at her, touching her arm where the prosthetic met her elbow. "You're not broken, Verity. You're a survivor. A fighter. And that makes you stronger than any of them." A tear slid down her cheek, and he reached up, rising onto his toes, and wiped it away with his thumb. "Hey, did I ever tell you about the time my brothers dared me to run through the temple of Ainam naked?"

A laugh bubbled out of Verity. "You definitely did *not* tell me about that."

Drystan led the horse along the road as he told his story, enjoying the sound of Verity's laughter behind him.

They gathered the rest of their gear and their second horse in Halcyn as Drystan had planned, then made their way slowly across the northern expanse of Aethir and into Armathain. It didn't take long for the two of them to adjust to being on the road again, even though it had been months since their last journey together.

Drystan was grateful it was spring—he didn't want to think about what the northern reaches of Armathain might be like in the dead of winter. Even still, the storms that sometimes rolled through the plains proved difficult to manage. Drystan wasn't a woodsman or a tracker—he'd been raised in and around cities—so dealing with raging thunderstorms while keeping their gear dry and himself and Verity safe was a challenge he hadn't been wholly prepared for, but he did his best.

Verity still had nightmares most nights, though they seemed somewhat less frequent. His own dreams were a mix of darkened prison cells and gallows ropes around his neck while his father or brothers—and sometimes Genevieve—looked on. Some nights, however, his dreams were more pleasant. Occasionally, he even dreamt of Cora, and of going on adventures with her as a Warden of the Flame.

Those dreams were his favorites by far, fantastical though they were.

When Snowfeld came into view at last, Drystan couldn't wait to be off horseback and to spend time in an actual town—maybe even in a bed. His knee was stiff from so many days of traveling, and an unrelenting ache had set in a few days before. The town walls were visible first, with wooden watch towers rising high, manned with archers. It was midday and, thankfully, the gates were open.

"Let's get settled," Drystan said, turning in his saddle to look at Verity. "We'll find an inn. Then tomorrow we can start asking about Torin."

Verity breathed deep, her eyes wide as she took in the town. It was definitely rustic; probably much more so than anywhere Verity had been before, the Wardens' camp notwithstanding. Most of the buildings were one-story, made of wood and some kind of dried mud or clay. Only a few of the larger buildings were made of stone.

Drystan asked one of the men at the gate about a place to sleep, and he was directed toward a small, two-story building on the eastern edge of town. They passed a few shops and a couple other buildings on the way, including what appeared to be a tiny library. Drystan would have to stop in once they got settled and could relax for a while.

The woman tending the front desk of the inn smiled warmly as they entered. "Welcome to the Frost Field Inn," she said. Her fair skin was covered in freckles, splattered across her nose and cheeks like paint. Her hair was as black as ravens' feathers, and her eyes, with soft lines at the corners, were such a startling crystalline gray that Drystan caught himself staring.

"Two rooms, please," he mumbled.

Verity cleared her throat and nudged him in the side gently with her elbow. "I . . ." She leaned a little closer to him, lowering her voice. "I don't think I could . . ."

"Right." Drystan shook his head, his face heating. "Sorry, one room. Uh, with two beds. Please."

The woman glanced between the two of them, her attention lingering on Verity for a moment before she smiled and moved to retrieve a key from a pegboard on the wall behind her. Her deep rose dress hugged her curvy frame as she stretched for the key.

"Number three, up the stairs," she said as she handed the key to Drystan. "How long will the two of you be staying with us?"

"Likely quite some time," Drystan said. His fingers brushed hers as he took the key.

"And we'll need our horses stabled," Verity cut in. "Do you happen to know of a man named Noel Torin?"

"Ol' Noel?" the woman asked, the rhyme of the man's name rolling off her tongue. "Yeah, I know him. Keeps to himself mostly. Has a cabin about a mile outside the walls, but he frequents the Trapper's Tavern on the other side of town."

Verity nodded, nudging Drystan again before heading to the stairs. "Come on."

Drystan's cheeks burned hot. "Thank you, Miss," he said to the woman. He hefted the bags onto his shoulders again.

She laughed, the sound sending little jolts through his chest. "I haven't been called that in a while. Please, though, call me Addie."

With a soft smile and a dip of his head, Drystan turned and limped after Verity.

He'd barely unlocked their door and dropped their bags by each of their beds when Verity faced him. "Grab the book," she said. "Let's go."

"We just got here. Let's take a little time to—"

"We need to find Torin. Now."

Drystan bristled. His knee was killing him, and he wanted nothing more than to lie down for a few hours. But he couldn't ignore the urgency in Verity's eyes, the nervous energy wound through her whole body. They'd traveled so far, and they were so close to her goal. Could he really ask her to stop now?

"Fine," he said. "Let's clean up, though. We're not going to make a good first impression smelling like horse and road grime."

She groaned but agreed, logic winning out. Drystan helped her wash up and change, then did the same for himself. Verity was waiting by the door when he emerged from the small bathing room, water still dripping from his hair.

"Ready?" she asked. She bounced a little as she inched toward the door to the hall.

Drystan couldn't help but give her a wry smile. "Thank you for your patience," he said as he tied his hair at the nape of his neck.

"Yes, yes!" Verity tossed her head back. "Come on, let's go!"

He ignored the sharp twinge in the side of his knee as he crouched to pull her book out of one of the bags. "Alright. Let's go find your engineer."

Drystan managed to convince Verity that searching the Trapper's Tavern first would be a better option than heading directly for the man's home. If he frequented the place but wasn't there now, someone might know when he would be likely to show up next.

It was a small town, so it didn't take them long to find the place. Only a few people were inside enjoying either a meal or a midafternoon drink. They asked at the bar and were pointed toward an older man with tan, leathery skin sitting by himself at a table toward the center of the room. Verity and Drystan crossed to him.

"Noel Torin?" Verity asked.

The older man glanced up from his meal. He had long, dark hair that was almost as gray as it was black. His clothes were modest and functional, like a woodsman or a trapper. "That depends," he said gruffly.

"My name is Verity. I'm looking to hire a skilled mechanist to make something for me. From my research, Noel Torin is the only one capable enough. Are you him or not?"

Drystan hid his grimace as he slipped into the chair across from the man. He pushed the other chair out for Verity. "Sorry to interrupt your lunch," he said.

They needed this man to like them so he would agree to help, and jumping down his throat at the first opportunity was not the way to go about it. So, despite his exhaustion, Drystan plastered a disarming smile on his face and explained why they were there.

When he was finished, the old man looked Verity over, eyes lingering on the porcelain hands that lay lifeless in her lap. "I'm not a mechanist anymore," he said flatly. "And something like what you're describing would take years. We'd need designs, measurements, and more calculations than I can even think of right now just to get the damn things to bend properly. And that doesn't even begin to take into account how you plan to make them function."

"Let me worry about that part," Verity said, no less prickly than before. "And I've already done the calculations. I just need someone to confirm the viability of my design and to help me build it."

Torin gave Verity another appraising look. "*You?*"

"Please," Drystan said, holding up one hand to delay the rejection he knew was coming, as well as the sharp response that was no doubt about to come from Verity. He set the book on the table. "Just look at her designs. See what you think." If they could let Verity's work speak for itself, that might be their best shot.

Drystan opened the book to the pages with her designs and pushed it across the table. Torin's quick glance at the open pages turned into a deeper study of the diagrams and notes almost immediately. He read through the notes, seemingly understanding the shorthand far better than Drystan had been able to. His brows rose and stayed there.

"How old are you, girl?"

"Verity," she corrected, sitting up a little straighter. "And I'm seventeen."

"You did all this?" he asked.

"Yes."

Torin didn't lift his eyes from the page. "Where did you learn this?"

"I studied at the College of Magi," she said. There was the slightest tremble in her voice as she spoke.

"A first-year did all this?" Torin asked.

"Actually, I was about to graduate before—" Her voice caught, and she blinked rapidly, lifting her chin almost defiantly.

Had news of the attack on the College reached this far north?

Drystan wanted to set his hand on her shoulder—to give her some small measure of support and to let her know that he saw how difficult this was for her and was proud of her for doing it—but he didn't want to undermine what she was doing. He sat back and let her handle it, but pride swelled in his chest as she held her head high.

After a few moments, Torin gave a quiet grunt. Was that approval? He looked at Verity, really focusing on her for the first time. "And how did you find out about me?" he asked.

"We studied you in my class on mechanics and clockwork."

"Hmm . . ." His finger tapped rhythmically against the book as he flipped between the pages a few more times.

"Drystan," Verity said, turning to him. "Would you mind waiting by the bar?"

He'd hoped to stay close so he could help if needed, or offer support, but maybe she needed to know she could do this on her own. One small step along a much longer road. "Sure," he said. He swallowed a groan as he stood, his leg protesting having to move again, and made his way to the bar.

He ordered a drink and tried to give Verity the privacy she'd requested, though he stole occasional glances over his shoulder to make sure she was doing alright. Soon Torin had scooted his chair closer to her and was pointing at different parts of the notes. Verity was answering his questions, the tightness around her lips loosening into a soft smile.

You've got this, Drystan thought. If she needed him, he'd be right here.

Chapter 25

While Verity and Torin's review of the notes and sketches turned into an animated discussion, with Torin even jotting down more notes on a separate page of Verity's book, Drystan enjoyed some quiet time at the bar, as well as a few drinks. Several hours passed before Verity joined him, her face bright with a wide smile. Drystan wasn't sure he'd ever seen her so happy.

"I take it that went well?" he asked. He downed what was left in his glass. After two ales he'd switched to whiskey, and it burned quite pleasantly on the way down. Not to mention it had finally dulled the throbbing in his knee.

"He's agreed to work with me," she said. She kept her voice low, but she was practically vibrating with excitement. "He has some ideas for control as well. We'll start tomorrow."

"That's great, Verity," he said. "I'm happy for you." Drystan paid his tab at the bar, and they headed back to the inn.

"Thank you," Verity said as they walked. "I couldn't have done any of this without you."

"You're very welcome." As they crossed town, Drystan's head was heavy, and even with the alcohol he'd drunk at the tavern, the pain in his knee returned full force. He didn't try to hide his limp, letting himself compensate with his other side. It hadn't hurt this bad in months. Had he pushed himself too hard with the journey to Snowfeld?

"Drystan?" Verity's voice was thick with concern. "Are you good?"

"I'll be fine," he said. "I think I just need to give it a break."

At their inn, Drystan ordered a meal for him and Verity. When he carried the small tray with their dinner to the stairs, the single flight up to their room seemed a daunting task. He paused at the bottom landing and took a steadying breath as he prepared for the climb.

"Do you want to lean on me?"

Drystan looked down at Verity, forcing a smile. She was a full head shorter than him and probably half his weight. There was no way she'd be able to support him. "No, that's alright." He braced his elbow against the wall instead. "I'll take it slow."

And he did. It felt like it took him a quarter of an hour to climb the stairs, though in truth it likely wasn't more than a minute or two. After helping Verity with her food, Drystan inhaled his own. He wanted nothing more than to collapse into bed, but there was still more he needed to do. It wasn't late, but with all the travel, as well as the time at the tavern, he wasn't sure he'd be awake much longer.

"Do you mind if we get ready to turn in now?" Drystan asked. "I'm beat."

"Of course," she said. "No problem."

Drystan helped Verity change into her night clothes, then brushed her hair and braided it over her shoulder.

"You've really gotten good at that," she said as she watched his hands work. "Have you been practicing?"

"Yeah," he remarked cooly. "I posted fliers around Halcyn and had women lining up around the block for me to braid their hair."

Verity laughed. "And here I thought I was special."

She had no idea.

"Drystan?" Verity's voice cut through the darkness of his dreams. "Are you awake?"

He meant to say *yeah*, but it came out as more of a grunt into his pillow.

"It's getting late," she said. "I'm supposed to meet Torin at the ninth chime."

Right. Drystan forced his eyes open, blinking away the sleep. He pushed himself up, but when he rose and took a step, pain like a dagger through his knee dropped him to the floor. It knocked the breath from him, and all he could do was lie there, curling around his leg like he had the night it had been shattered.

"Drystan! Gods, what's wrong?"

He barely heard her. He wanted to answer, but his mind couldn't form words, or even coherent thoughts. He could scarcely breathe.

"Drystan!"

Hardly anything else seemed to exist beyond the pain. There were noises around him, shuffling feet, muttered cursing. Bile rose in his throat, but he swallowed it back, gritting his teeth.

He had no sense of how long he'd been lying there in agony, but at some point a hand gripped his shoulder.

"Breathe," someone said. It was a woman's voice, though not Verity's. "Breathe through the pain."

He drew a gasping breath, forcing it in and out.

"Good," the woman said. "I'm going to help you sit up, alright?"

Drystan opened his eyes. The innkeeper, Addie, crouched beside him. He still wasn't sure he could talk, so he just nodded. Addie's hands slid under his arm and levered him up. Drystan bit back a cry as his leg straightened a little.

"We have a medic in town, though he services all the camps and homes on the outskirts, so I'm not sure if he'll be around today. I'll send for him though, so he can take a look at you."

Drystan nodded again, jaw still clenched tight.

"I'm no medic myself," Addie continued, "but I think you should stay off your leg until he can see you."

Drystan darted a look at Verity. She sat on the edge of her bed, eyes wide. Her face was stricken, and worry creased her brow. Verity was supposed to meet with Torin this morning. He couldn't be the reason she missed it. He wasn't worth her missing this opportunity for, and she needed his help to—

But Verity was already shaking her head. "It can wait," she said. Before Drystan could argue, she turned toward Addie. "Could you help me draft and send a letter?"

"Sure. I've got everything downstairs." Addie set her hand on Drystan's arm. "Do you think you could get into bed with some help?"

He swallowed hard but nodded. He could do this. He couldn't spend all day on the floor.

Addie clasped his hand and stood, bracing herself to pull him up. "Ready?"

"Are you sure?" Drystan croaked.

Still holding his hand, Addie set the other on the wide curve of her hip. "I'm far from a delicate flower," she said, a smirk on her lips. "I've been dragging barrels around this place since I was sixteen." The smile lines around her eyes deepened as she added, "And let's just say I'm pretty sure that was before you were born."

Drystan used Addie and the bed to push himself up, carefully avoiding putting any weight on his leg. Addie eased him back onto the bed, and he couldn't stop the groan of pain as she lifted his leg and propped his knee up on a pillow.

"Thank you," Drystan managed. "And just so you know, I'm almost twenty."

Addie chuckled as she stepped back. "Fine then, I've been dragging barrels around this place since you were *almost* two." She turned to Verity. "Come on, dear, I'll help you with that letter."

Verity stood then, following Addie to the door. "Rest," she said, looking back at Drystan. "I'll be back soon."

As the door closed, Drystan focused on his breathing. Vire's hells, it felt as though his knee had rolled sideways. Had he really pushed himself so hard that this was the result? Had he been that foolish?

He leaned his head against the wall and squeezed his eyes shut.

Yes, he supposed he had.

Verity spent the rest of the day fussing over Drystan—no matter how many times he told her not to worry about him—and Addie sent food up for both of them. Drystan was able to sit up with only a few grunts and one sharp gasp, and Verity used her elbow to push the pillow that had been under his knee to reposition it. From there, he was able to help her with most of the things he usually did, and Addie was kind enough to help with anything else. The door to their room had a latch rather than a knob, so Verity was able to open it with her arm, allowing her to come and go as she needed to, so long as they kept the door unlocked.

The medic Addie had mentioned, Kellan, came to see Drystan early the next day. Thankfully, he said it seemed only to be Drystan's previous injury acting up, but that Drystan needed to take better care of himself, especially on—and immediately after—long journeys. Kellan had added that last part with a pointed look that Drystan took to heart.

Verity was there, having been unwilling to leave to finally meet with Torin until she was sure he was alright, and something on her face was different. She watched him carefully, her brow furrowed, as though working through some difficult problem in her head.

Kellan wrapped Drystan's knee tightly with linen to keep it from twisting when he walked. On his way out, he said he'd have something else sent along shortly to help. Once they were alone, Verity hooked her knapsack in the crook of her elbow, having foregone her porcelain arms since the day before.

"I'm going to head over to Torin's now," she said, though there was a hesitation in her tone. She was looking at Drystan, and yet not. Almost like she was looking at his shoulder rather than his face.

"Alone?" he asked. He didn't want to keep her from doing this—it was the reason they were here after all. But the thought of her going alone—

"Addie has a friend who works downstairs—Isaiah. He's going to walk me over there."

"Alright. Are you sure?"

She nodded, still not quite looking at him. "I'm sure. I'll be back later." She paused at the door for only a moment before she left.

About an hour later, Addie came upstairs. "Verity made it safely to Noel's," she said, leaning in the doorway. "Isaiah let me know. He'll head back over there this afternoon to walk her back."

Drystan blew out a breath, releasing the tension he hadn't realized had been knotting his shoulders since she left. "Thank you."

"Is she your sister?" Addie asked.

Sister? Drystan shook his head. "No, we're not related."

Addie's brows rose slightly. "Oh." At what was no doubt a confused look on Drystan's face, she added, "You worry over her like an older brother." Without waiting for a response, Addie reached back into the hallway before stepping fully into the room. "Kellan sent this over," she said as she held out a crutch in one hand.

Drystan's stomach knotted and turned over itself as his heartbeat quickened. *No . . . No, not this again.*

"What's wrong?" Addie asked. She leaned the crutch against the wall near his bed, within arm's reach. "Have you never used one before?"

Drystan couldn't take his eyes from it. At the camp, his recovery had always felt like two steps forward and three steps back, but this—it was like a thousand steps back. A hundred thousand. It was like he was right back where he'd started, like he hadn't made any progress at all. He'd had to use a crutch for months at the camp. How long would it be this time? Weeks? Months? Or had he managed to undo everything Theo had done, and now it would be this way forever?

Drystan found his voice again, but it sounded hollow to his own ears as he said, "I've used one before."

"Oh." Addie fell silent, her kind face scrunching up. "Can I sit?"

He nodded, and she took one of the narrow wooden chairs and brought it beside the bed. Another pang ran through his stomach. It was so much like what Cora used to do with him. Or what he used to do with Verity.

"I know we only just met," she said, "so you just let me know if you want me to get the hell out of your room and leave you in peace, alright?"

Drystan couldn't help the quirk of his lips.

"I don't know all of what you're feeling, and whatever history you've got is between you and whichever gods you fancy. But I will say this. There's no shame in needing a little help. Or a lot of help, for that matter." Addie gathered up the flowing locks of her dark hair and smoothed them over her shoulder. "There's strength in struggling in this world but moving through it anyway. And whatever needs doing to make moving through possible, well then that's what needs doing. I've seen some folks from Valda or elsewhere that can't see too well, so they wear glasses to help. I've seen folks who chew on herbs every day to help them just get through living." She nodded toward the crutch. "There's nothing wrong with using a tool to get through the day. To function and to do what you need to do."

The knot around Drystan's stomach loosened. She was right. He was here helping Verity do just that. She wanted prosthetic arms to help her be more independent. It was just another version of what Addie was talking about, wasn't it? It was a tool to help her so she could live the life she wanted. It wasn't a sign of weakness, but strength. She could have given up, but she was fighting instead. Working hard and moving through.

And Drystan was about to fall into a panic over having to use a crutch for a while?

"Thanks," he said, running his hands over his face. "I, uh, I needed to hear that."

"Don't mention it."

"Does this kind of wisdom come from running an inn?"

Addie laughed softly. "No, definitely not. I feel like I'm losing my mind here most days. But about things like this, I speak from experience." She lifted the edge of her skirt, raising it to her knee. Between her boot and her knee was a narrow piece of metal. It wasn't complex like Verity's designs for her arms—it was simple, but functional.

Drystan's face burned. Not only had he been throwing a tantrum over a crutch, but he'd been doing it to someone who'd been through worse. He closed his eyes. "I'm so sorry."

"Don't be," she said. "It takes time to learn your way around big changes. But just remember that there's no shame in doing what you need to do to keep living your life. It's only when you stop trying that they win."

Drystan looked at Addie. "*They*?"

"Whoever tried to hurt you. Whoever tried to tell you that you can't, or that you're not good enough, strong enough. That you're not *enough*." She dropped the hem of her skirt as she shrugged. "If you give up, they win."

Chapter 26

Verity worked with the mechanist nearly every day. As soon as Drystan was able, he went with her, the crutch under his left shoulder and Verity's bag slung over his right. He only needed the crutch for a couple weeks, but while he did, Verity made sure he had a comfortable spot just outside of Noel's cabin. Each day, they stopped at the little library a few buildings down from the inn so Drystan could pick out a book. Sometimes it was an adventure story, sometimes it was a romance, and sometimes he selected something more informational.

Even this far north, the late spring days were mild, and while Verity and Noel spent their time in his workshop, Drystan lounged beneath a massive willow tree and read. If it rained, Noel's cabin had a cozy reading nook set against a large window, which was almost as good. Most days, Verity spent so long working that Drystan was able to finish whatever book he'd borrowed, giving him the opportunity for something new almost every day.

One afternoon, as he neared the end of his current read about cold-weather survival, a shadow appeared over him. He angled his head up toward Verity. "Finished for the day already?" he asked.

She beamed down at him, her smile broader and more genuine than he'd ever seen it. "Look what Noel made for me," she said. "It's just temporary," she added quickly before Drystan even had a moment to register what he was looking at. As he squinted to make out what she was showing him, she crouched down out of the sun.

On Verity's right arm was a prosthesis. It was much simpler than her designs, with only a hinged sleeve that fit above her elbow, and metal rods that ended in a two-pronged hook with blunt, rounded ends tipped in leather. Leather straps stretched over Verity's shoulders and across her chest. She reached for Drystan's book, and the two prongs pinched together, closing over the pages. With the book thus secured in her grip, she lifted it out of Drystan's hands.

He laughed. "That's fantastic!"

"It's just for now," she reiterated. "But this way I can finally do a few things on my own!" Her eyes shimmered as she spoke—at the simple idea of not being fully dependent on another person for every single aspect of her life. Drystan could only imagine how that must feel for her.

"It looks a hell of a lot sturdier than those damned porcelain ones," he said with a chuckle. He rose to his knees and pulled her into a fierce hug. "I'm so happy for you, Vee!"

She leaned back slightly, lifting her head to look up at him. "Vee?" One eyebrow arched.

"Sorry—I . . ." Drystan grimaced. Why did he say that? He hoped his face wasn't flushing too red. "Sorry," he mumbled again.

"No, it's alright," Verity said. "It's just, no one's ever shortened my name before."

"Oh." He ran his hand across the back of his neck. "You don't mind?"

She shook her head. "I like it." She smiled at him, soft and genuine. "It's nice."

As Verity got used to her temporary prosthetic arm, she became more accustomed to doing things on her own and was more willing to try something before calling Drystan in to help. It wasn't long before she was slinging her bag over one shoulder and trekking to Noel's workshop alone, leaving Drystan at the inn with little to occupy his time.

Verity's increasing confidence was wonderful, but a quiet voice began to nag at the back of his mind. If her ideas worked—if she and Noel were able to make arms that functioned the way she wanted them to—would she still want Drystan around? What use would he be to her if she were capable of doing things for herself? But he pushed the thought aside whenever it popped up. She was his friend, and this was important to her. He would help her no matter what.

While Verity was out most days, Drystan spent a lot of time at the bar downstairs, drinking and chatting with Isaiah, if he was working, or Addie, who seemed to always be around. She lived in one of the rooms upstairs, she explained. She liked to make sure she was always close by.

As the weeks went on, Drystan looked forward to his chats with Addie more than nearly anything else. He learned a lot about her—her favorite color was green, she preferred a mild herb tea to coffee, and she had a terrible sweet tooth, especially for anything chocolate—and Drystan found himself in awe of her brilliance and strength more and more.

It was late one evening, and Drystan was still at the bar as it was closing up for the night. Verity had come back earlier but told Drystan to take his time—she'd gotten quite adept at getting herself ready for bed and said she was going to turn in early. As a result, he was the last patron still downstairs when Addie started to extinguish the lanterns around the room.

"I should let you finish up," he said before downing the rest of his beer. A pleasant warmth hummed through him and the room swayed gently as he stood.

"I was hoping you might stay," Addie said. "Keep me company while I lock up for the night?"

Drystan's stomach tightened. "I'd be delighted to," he said.

She smiled, the room growing dimmer and dimmer with each light that went out. With each lantern she moved to, the flames danced and reflected off her fair skin, and her black hair rivaled the darkness beyond the little spheres of light.

She was stunning.

"What?" she asked, tucking a strand of hair behind her ear. "You're staring."

Drystan's cheeks warmed and he was grateful that most of the lights were already out. "Sorry," he mumbled. "It's so easy to forget myself around you."

"Now, Drystan." Her voice took on a dangerously mischievous tone. "Are you flirting with me?"

Drystan was no stranger to the idea of flirting with beautiful women. He'd always had good luck, both back home in Alton and while he'd been staying in Halcyn. Even though he often hadn't been concerned with the specifics of whose bed he shared—so long as they proved a distraction—he'd always thought he was rather *good* at flirting.

But now that Addie had called him out so quickly after his opening gambit, he wondered whether he had any skill at all.

"If I'm not?" he asked, his curiosity getting the better of him.

Addie shrugged. "Then I'd guess my read on you is off, though I'd be slightly disappointed."

His mouth quirked. "Only slightly?"

"Well, you're very young." With most of the lanterns extinguished, she moved back to the bar where the last one sat near Drystan. "And there is something to be said for not having to give too many instructions." She leaned on the bar, setting her chin in her hand.

"I see," he said softly. The curve of her lips pulled his attention. "And if I am?"

"Then I'd tell you that I enjoy your company, and I'd like to enjoy it a while longer. And I'd also tell you that my room's the one at the top of the stairs."

Drystan was grateful he'd already finished his drink, because he might have choked on it otherwise. "I enjoy your company as well," he said, and was happy to hear his voice didn't crack. "May I walk you home?"

Addie leaned toward Drystan and placed a gentle kiss on his cheek. "I'd be delighted if you would."

She extinguished the final lantern, and they mostly made it to Addie's door before their hands and lips started roaming one another.

Once she latched the door behind her, Addie stepped further into the room, putting some space between them. "Just to be clear," she said, her voice a little breathy, "I'm not looking for anything long-lasting. You're a nice person, and I meant what I said about enjoying your company. But I like my life the way it is, and I'm not looking to change anything about it."

"Of course," he said, stopping himself from rushing to her. "We'll be leaving here once Verity's done anyway. It can't be anything more than here and now."

"Great." Addie moved toward him slowly, wrapping her arms around his neck and threading her fingers through his hair. "To the *here and now*."

As the weeks turned into months, Drystan settled into this new, quiet life. Things in Snowfeld were simple–peaceful in a way he'd never known. Vee and Addie made him a small cake to celebrate his birthday, and Isaiah bought him a drink—somehow, Vee remembered him mentioning that it was on the summer solstice. Vee apologized that she didn't have anything more to give him, but in that very moment, there wasn't anything else he wanted.

Verity continued working with Noel on her designs, and Drystan spent most of his free time with Addie. Sometimes he just talked with her while she was working, silently marveling at how kind and thoughtful and bold she was. Sometimes they stole private moments together in the middle of the day. And other times, when the sky darkened and the tavern fell quiet, they took pleasure in one another. It had been a while since Drystan had considered himself *inexperienced*, but Addie—gods above and below! She taught him things that she liked, and she showed him things that he didn't know *he* liked.

One afternoon, as the weather turned colder and the first early snow of the year fell outside, Drystan was enjoying a drink at the bar and chatting with Addie between customers when Verity stormed through the door. She didn't say a word to him as she headed straight for the stairs, her face crimson.

"Vee, what's wrong?" he called after her, but she didn't even slow down as she marched upstairs.

"You'd better go make sure she's alright," Addie said, wiping down the bar.

Drystan was already spinning on his stool to follow her.

When Drystan entered their room, Verity was pacing, fury twisting her face. "What's wrong?" he asked again.

"It won't work!" She caught her knapsack strap with the hook of her prosthetic arm and swung it across the room. It struck the wall with a loud *thud*. "We've tried everything. It won't work!"

Drystan hung by the door, hesitant to get in her way. "What won't work?"

"My designs!" she cried. "All this time—months of work. For nothing!" Tears streamed down her cheeks as she paced. She caught the edge of one of the chairs with her arm and flipped it toward the bed. Drystan was grateful he'd chosen to stay by the door.

"What can I do to help?" he asked.

"Nothing! There's nothing anyone can do." She collapsed onto the bed, sobbing quietly.

Drystan waited a moment, unsure what to do. "Do you want me to stay?"

She lifted her head enough to nod.

He crossed to sit beside her. "I'm here for whatever you need," he said softly. He set his hand on her shoulder and squeezed. "I'm here, Vee."

Verity curled up with her head on his lap and cried. And Drystan stayed. He undid the tie at the end of her braid and unwove the strands. He couldn't reach her comb, and there was no way in hells he was getting up, so he ran his fingers slowly through her hair, smoothing it out where it splayed across his lap and onto the bed.

After a long time, her sobs slowed to quiet sniffles, but still Drystan didn't move. He would be there for her, for whatever comfort he could offer. Finally, she pushed herself up, her eyes red and her face still streaked with tears.

"Do you want to explain what happened, maybe try to work through possible solutions? Or do you just want to rage at the world for a while?"

"I don't know," she said, her voice tired and thin. "I don't think there are any solutions. We've been working on how to get the arms to work all week. I thought I'd be able to use magic to move them." She drew a breath that shuddered with the aftereffects of her sobbing. "I thought as long as all the pieces fit together and moved the way they should, that my magic would be enough." Another tear slipped down her cheek. "But it doesn't work."

Drystan brushed the tear away with his thumb, then tucked some of her hair behind her ear. "What part about using magic to make them move doesn't work?"

"It requires too much constant concentration and energy," she said. "And there's a lack of precision in the movements. I *might* be able to adjust for that over time, but it's still a constant, active use of magic for every single movement I would need. Picking up a glass, for example. It wouldn't just be one use of magic to pick up the glass. It's one application of force to open the fingers, another to close the fingers around the glass, and a third to bend the elbow and lift it. If rotation of the wrist is needed, that's a fourth use. It's too much. It's impossible!"

"When you worked on the designs earlier, you thought it would be simpler?" he asked.

"Well, yes. I didn't consider how complex the movements actually are. I'm such an idiot."

Drystan couldn't help the laugh that burst from his throat. "I can't think of anything that's further from the truth."

"It's not funny," she groaned. "I don't know why I thought I could do this."

"Probably because you can." When she glared at him, he continued, "Keep going. What would you need to make it work?"

"What do you mean? I *can't* make it work."

"But if you could. If it's impossible, fine, but what would you need to do to *make* it possible?"

Verity shrugged, tossing her head back. "I don't know! Infinite magic? Infinite ability to split my concentration on casting?"

"Alright, what else?"

She groaned, flopping over so her head was resting on his shoulder. He wrapped his arm around her. "Honestly, I would need them to work the way real arms do, moving with a thought, and not a series of complex magical incantations."

"How would that work?"

Verity scoffed. "It wouldn't."

"Humor me. How *could* it work?"

"They'd have to be a real part of my body, not just attached to me." She nodded toward her prosthetic arm. "Logistics of *that* aside, I still don't know how I could power them."

Drystan didn't know enough about how magic worked to ask any helpful questions, so he sat in silence.

"You'd need a periapt just to hold enough magic," she continued, almost mumbling to herself.

"Periapt?"

"There's only so much magic that someone can cast at a time before it starts to wear you down. A periapt holds magical energy for use whenever it's needed."

"Oh. Do you have one of those?"

"No, they're pretty rare. Only powerful mages tend to have them."

"Hm, so the peri-thing is out. What else could do it?"

Verity lifted her head and quirked a smile. "Periapt," she corrected. "And I don't know. Nothing else that I've ever learned about."

Drystan tapped his finger to his chin. "Alright, so far we've got that you need a peri-thing—"

"*Periapt.*"

"—That you could attach to arms that would be a part of you. That definitely sounds like a challenge."

"Exactly!" Verity leaned against him again. "I mean, the only way to even get close to something like that would be . . ."

He assumed she was just lost in thought, but when she didn't say anything more, Drystan leaned away from her, looking down at her face. "Verity?"

She launched herself off the bed with such force that Drystan almost fell backward. "Paper!" she cried. "I need paper. And ink. Now!"

Drystan grabbed the supplies from her bag where it'd landed against the wall and sat himself at the table. He knew she could write a little with her prosthesis, but it was a slow, arduous process, and there was no way she'd have the patience for it right now. Not with that gleam in her eye. That fire. She could work through whatever thoughts were swirling in that incredible mind of hers, and he would be her hands.

"Alright, I'm listening," he said, dipping a quill in the small pot of ink. "Go."

Chapter 27

Drystan sat with Verity for hours, taking notes as she talked through her ideas and sketching as best he could when she needed him to. She paced the room, occasionally looking over his shoulder and making corrections or clarifying points.

A knock sounded at the door, and Drystan hurried to open it while Vee continued pacing. Addie stood on the other side with a tray of food.

"I was worried when neither of you came back downstairs," she said.

Drystan's heart squeezed in his chest as he waved her inside. He cleared space enough at the table for Addie to set the tray down, then picked up the quill as another thought struck Verity and she rattled off something else for him to write down without checking to see if he was ready. Had she even noticed Addie come in?

Addie moved to stand behind Drystan, her arms gliding over his shoulders as she peered down at the notes he was hurriedly scribbling. She nestled a kiss in the little spot below his ear, sending a shiver through his whole body. "I'll let you two focus," she said. When she straightened though, she spent a minute rubbing at the knots in his shoulders before she gave him another soft kiss and let herself out of the room.

By the time they were done, they'd added another eleven pages to Verity's notebook, and Drystan nearly had to restrain her from rushing back over to Noel's house that night.

The next day, when Vee returned from Noel's workshop, she was still excited, which was a welcome sight.

"How'd it go?" Drystan asked. He was sitting at his usual spot at the bar, enjoying a book and his usual beer while chatting with Addie, when Verity slid into the seat beside him. "What did Noel have to say about your ideas?"

Verity could hardly sit still. "He thinks it might work." She beamed. "We're going to have to find someone who can do the technical parts, and probably someone else to help work the magic needed. But the best part is, he thinks he knows someone who might be able to help! He sent them a letter today to ask about it." She made a high-pitched noise in her throat, kicking her feet a little where she sat on the bar stool.

Drystan chuckled. "That's great!"

"Happy to hear it, my dear," Addie said, sliding a water over to Verity. Addie always poured her drinks in this one wooden mug that had a thicker handle than most. It was easier for Verity to grip with the hook on her prosthetic arm.

"Thank you! It'll take a couple of weeks for us to make the modifications to the current build, but by then hopefully we'll have heard something back." She inhaled deeply, her breath shaking a little. "I hope this works."

"It'll work," Drystan said, slinging his arm around her shoulder. "And if it doesn't, you'll figure something else out. I know it."

After three weeks, Verity declared that the newly redesigned arms Noel was building for her were complete and functioned as well as they could test in his workshop. Also, Noel had heard back from his contact—an old friend, he'd said—who seemed intrigued by the problem and was willing to take a chance on Verity. And they knew a mage who might be able to help with the magic part as well. Vee was bouncing around their room as she filled Drystan in on all the details.

"I can't believe this is coming together," she said as Drystan combed out her hair that night. "When do you think we'll be ready to leave?"

Drystan paused, his fingers tightening on the comb. Leaving had always been part of the plan. Snowfeld was a temporary stop for the work Vee needed to do. But if they left, he'd have to say goodbye to Addie. That thought alone made his chest tighten, but he forced his hand to move, bringing the comb through Verity's thick hair. "Where are we headed?" he asked.

There was a suspiciously long pause, and when Verity spoke, her voice sounded almost apologetic. "Kyleria."

He nearly dropped the comb. "Kyleria? In Bremmaran? Vee, that's halfway across the damn continent. More than halfway!" His mind reeled. The journey from Halcyn to Snowfeld had nearly broken him, and she was talking about doing even more than that, and in winter this time. Although it was still early in the season, snow already covered the ground this far north.

"I know, but I can do more on my own now." She turned to face him, and the words poured out of her, like she'd had all her arguments prepared for this moment. "It won't be as hard on you as it was before. You won't have to take care of me as much, and I can help out when we set up camp, and—"

"It's not about having to help you," he said. He set his hands on her shoulders. "It's never been about that. It's just . . ."

The words stalled.

He had a responsibility to Verity. And more than that, he still wanted to help her. He just wasn't ready to leave Addie behind. His breath snagged for a moment as a new realization slotted into place.

I'm in love with Addie.

But how could he say all that to Vee? So instead, he squeezed her shoulders and said, "It's nothing. I'm surprised, is all. I wasn't expecting things to happen so fast. But yeah, we can be ready soon. I'll get everything prepared. Give me a few days?"

"Of course," Verity said quickly. She hesitated for a moment before she seemed to relax. "Thank you, Drystan. You're the best friend I've ever had. I don't know what I would do without you. Thank you!"

Drystan pulled her into a hug, closing his eyes as he wrapped his arms around her as tightly as her words wrapped around his heart. He held her close. "You're welcome, Vee."

Later that night, after Verity fell asleep, Drystan knocked on the door to Addie's room. She opened it and grabbed him by the front of his shirt, tugging him into the room before he could speak. One hand snaked around his neck to pull him down to her, but she stopped, searching his eyes.

"What's wrong?"

"We're leaving for Kyleria," he blurted out. He set his hands on the curve of her hips.

"Oh, Drystan." She still pulled him down to meet her, though the kiss she set on his lips was far gentler than the one it looked like she'd been intending. "When?"

"Soon. A few days maybe." He blew out a long breath. The thought stuck inside his head was a betrayal of his friendship with Verity, but he spoke it aloud anyway, solidifying it in the world. "I don't want to go."

Addie took his hand and pulled him gently to the bed, sitting beside him. "Why not?" she asked.

"Because I don't want to leave you," he admitted. "Addie, I love you."

She angled her head, frowning. "Drystan . . ."

But he pressed on before he could think better of it. "Would you consider . . . coming with me?" He held his breath as she bowed her head, squeezing his hands in hers.

Addie was silent for a long time. "I care about you very deeply," she said at last. "But I have a life here. It's a life I worked hard to build, and it's a life I'm happy with. We said at the beginning that this—what we have between us—wasn't going to last forever. *Here and now*, remember?"

"I know, but—"

"Drystan." Her voice was far more sorrowful than he'd hoped. "I'll be sad to see you leave here. I've enjoyed our time together more than I can say. But I can't go with you."

His heart ached, but he knew it had to be this way. Why did he think it could have gone any differently? His father's voice echoed in his mind.

You understand that she would have to give up her entire life for you, don't you? Do you really think you're worth that?

He wasn't. He wasn't anything special, certainly no one worth rearranging one's whole life for. "I'm sorry," he said. "I shouldn't have asked that of you. I just . . . I don't want this to end."

"All stories end," Addie said. "Drystan, you are a beautiful person. You're kind in a way that's rare in this world. And you love with your whole heart. But I can see the pain you carry with you." She set her palm against his chest. "And I can see you trying not to let it eat at you. The way you hide from it and numb yourself against it . . ."

"I don't—"

"Drystan, no one drinks or fucks the way you do without trying to hide from something."

Heat rushed up his ears.

"But listen to me—your worth as a person is not tied to who you love. And it's not tied to who loves you. You don't need me, and you don't need anyone else to be happy. Somewhere you're going to find someone who loves you the way you deserve to be loved. But I truly believe that before that can happen, you need to love *yourself* the way you deserve to be loved. I wish you could see yourself the way I see you. Or the way Verity sees you."

Drystan paused in his slow, wilting retreat toward the door. "Verity?"

"She loves you, Drystan. And the love you have for her in return is beautiful."

"She doesn't . . . I'm not . . ." His mind snagged but he brought his hands up as though to ward off both Addie and her words. What did any of it matter?

All he knew for sure was that his heart was breaking in half, and he could hear Cora's words echoed in Addie's rejection. *You have a huge heart . . . But if you keep giving it to people who haven't earned it yet, it's going to keep getting broken.*

"I should go." Drystan wasn't sure he could look at her without losing the small amount of composure he had.

She didn't try to stop him. "I understand. And I understand if you don't want to spend any more time with me before you go. But if you do, whether it's just our usual talks downstairs, or being together for a while longer, I'll be here. Alright?"

Drystan left in silence. He didn't have an answer for her. He didn't know if he'd be able to look at her tomorrow. Or even before they left for Kyleria.

She didn't love him.

He'd given away his heart—*again*—and all he'd gotten for his troubles was pain. Cora had tried to warn him. Hells, even Addie had tried to warn him. But he hadn't listened. He'd had nothing to offer her, just like Genevieve, but like an idiot, he'd launched himself in headfirst anyway. Why had he thought things could be different?

Drystan descended the darkened stairs. He crossed carefully to the bar and lifted a full bottle of whiskey from its place in one of the cabinets before he headed outside into the cold night.

CHAPTER 28

DRYSTAN AND VERITY'S REMAINING days in Snowfeld trudged by. Verity had a few lingering tasks to take care of with Noel, and although Drystan had offered to go with her, she'd declined. It was well enough. Each morning brought with it a pounding headache and hangover from the drinking he did each night, and during the days he procured supplies for their journey and mapped their course to Kyleria.

Saying goodbye to Addie was hard, but Drystan had done his best to numb his heart so that he could leave without breaking down. He bid her farewell and hugged her. She planted a kiss on his cheek and told him to take care of himself.

All stories end, she'd told him. And that's all it had been. Another bit of fiction. Another fairytale.

The journey started smooth enough. Verity had become more independent while they were in Snowfeld, and it took a few days for them to find their new rhythm. They retraced the path they'd taken all those months ago, crossing the plains to Valda and then on to Whitehollow again before continuing east into the kingdom of Bremmaran. The northern snows seemed to follow on their heels, stretching the journey out even longer.

It was nearly a month before Drystan and Verity arrived in Kyleria. Drystan had never been to the kingdom of Bremmaran before, and the capital city was more impressive than he'd expected. Sprawling along the banks of the Kylerian River, the city was full of grand, sweeping architecture that had him staring in wonder more than once. Kyleria was also colder than he'd expected, considering they were farther south than Snowfeld, but with the Moontide Sea to the north, the wind that blew through the city was biting and carried with it a bitter chill.

Drystan pulled his fur-lined coat more tightly closed, fastening one of the upper buttons as they walked their horses through the streets. Despite taking it easier on himself this trip, his limp had returned full force, the cold seeping into the joint until it seemed perpetually stiff and achy.

The further into town they got, the more people Drystan caught casting glances their way, some more subtle than others. A few were curious—raised eyebrows and hushed voices—while others were furrowed brows and quiet scoffs.

Drystan risked a quick look over his shoulder at Verity. Her traveling cloak was around her shoulders but wasn't pinned closed as she'd often worn it before. Now that she'd gotten more comfortable with using her prosthesis, her cloak was hanging open. Her prosthetic arm was much more visible this way, as was the smooth side of her left shoulder, which had her shirt sleeve pinned to keep it out of the way.

"Aren't you cold?" Drystan asked. Maybe he could get her to cover up without calling attention to the looks coming her way.

But Verity seemed to notice the more overt ones. Regardless, she shook her head. "I'm Aethirian," she said with a hint of pride. "Between the mountains and the wind that sweeps across the basin, we don't get cold."

Drystan smiled, even as he blew on his fingers in the hopes of regaining a bit of feeling. He needed to remember she was tougher than she looked. Still, he kept an eye on their surroundings. On their journey to Snowfeld, they'd received their fair share of wary and uncertain looks. Though once they'd arrived, there were enough people who'd experienced hunting or trapping accidents that someone missing a digit or a limb—while far from the norm—hardly caused more than a second glance.

But here? Nearly everyone they passed seemed to have some opinion or silent judgment about the two of them. Drystan's hand tightened around his horse's reins, but he kept quiet.

Verity had all the details she needed, so they set to work finding a place to stay that wouldn't be too far from the hospital where Noel's contact did their work.

Verity spent the first week mostly on her own, making preparations and handling a few last-minute details, leaving Drystan alone throughout the days and into the evenings. He tried to take the time to rest after the long journey, not wanting to push himself too hard as he'd done on the trek to Snowfeld, but that didn't leave him with much to occupy his mind. His thoughts circled around and around as he tried to figure out whether he could have done anything differently with Addie.

Having spent so much time away from his father, Drystan had thought maybe he'd changed—and in some ways, perhaps he had. But in the end, he was still too soft. *Too eager*, as his father had said. Addie had made it clear at the beginning that she enjoyed Drystan's company, but she didn't need him around. She didn't *need* him for anything. He'd been a pleasurable distraction, but that was all. He wasn't someone she was going to fall in love with. And yet he'd still thrown himself in without thinking. Like a fool.

Again.

Drystan was desperately in need of something else to think about, and much to his relief, Kyleria had a sizable library, though it was several miles away and on the other side of the river. Drystan borrowed as many books as they would allow to ensure he didn't need to make the hike there every day.

Early in their second week in the city, Drystan was reclining on his bed, reading—the prince was finally about to confess his love to the mercenary he'd been pining over for two hundred pages—when Verity burst in.

"Tomorrow!" she cried.

Drystan jerked up, dropping the book onto the bed. "What's tomorrow?"

"Everything!" She gestured toward the table where the metal arms she'd built with Noel were wrapped in soft, black fabric. They sat near the broken sword she still brought with her everywhere they went.

"Wait, it's *tomorrow*?" He stood and hurried to her. "Vee, that's incredible!"

"I know." She took a deep breath, her exuberance melting into thinly veiled anxiety. "I don't know if I can do this, Drystan."

"Of course you can! You're so much stronger than you think you are. You can do this." He knew it as surely as he knew how to breathe.

Verity drew her bottom lip between her teeth. "Will you come with me?" she asked.

Drystan smiled, his heart squeezing in his chest. "I wouldn't miss it."

❊

Verity was up and pacing the room when Drystan awoke the next morning.

"This is going to work, right?" she asked before he'd even sat up fully.

"It's going to work," Drystan said. He drew one leg up, slowly stretching it. He rested his arm across his knee as he rubbed the sleep from his eyes.

"How do you know?" She paused in her pacing, crossing to the bed.

He smiled, broad and genuine, hoping she could feel the confidence he had in her. "Because you're brilliant," he said. "And because you've worked so hard for this. It's going to work." He tucked a strand of hair behind her ear before his hand came to rest on her shoulder. "You've got this, Vee."

They dressed and walked the few blocks to the hospital where the procedure was to be done. Verity led him down several long halls to a small, secluded room. A bed lay on one side, with a couple of stools positioned a short distance away. The center of the room had two tables side by side, each covered with a crisp, white linen cloth. One table was bare, but the other held a collection of tools and instruments that turned Drystan's blood to ice.

"Bring the arms over here," a woman called out a moment before she strode into the room. "We'll need to disinfect them before we can begin."

The woman was about the same age as Drystan's mother, he guessed, with ivory skin and golden blond hair pulled back in a tight bun. She wore dark blue robes over a white skirt. She smiled warmly.

"Drystan, this is Madeline. She's the friend of Noel's who'll be performing the medical parts of the procedure," Verity said.

Madeline's perfect brows rose slightly. "*Friend*? Is that what he told you?" She laughed, though there was something else hidden behind it. "I suppose we were that once as well. Please"—she gestured to another table along the back wall—"place them over here."

Drystan did as she instructed, unwrapping the bundled cloth for her. "It's nice to meet you," he said. "I'm Drystan."

"I know," Madeline said. "Verity's talked much about you."

"Oh!" Another voice cut through the room. Drystan turned as a man sauntered in. He wore crimson robes of a different style than Madeline's, and he looked younger than her by a decade or so, his olive skin smooth and unblemished. His dark, wavy hair was loose about his shoulders. He gave Drystan an appraising look. "Is this him? At long last we get to meet the *brother-in-arms*." He chuckled at his own joke.

Verity rolled her eyes, though the whole thing caught Drystan so off guard that he had to press his lips together to try not to laugh.

"That's not funny, El," Madeline drawled.

The man gave a shortened bow. "Apologies, dear. You know how I am before I have my coffee." He turned his attention to Verity. "And apologies to you, darling. I meant no offense."

Verity smiled, though it was tight-lipped. "Drystan, this is Eloquent. He's the mage who'll help me with the magic piece."

Drystan tried not to look too confused by the man's name, but he must not have hidden it well because Eloquent waved a hand as though shooing away something distasteful. "Yes, yes, I know," he said, his voice droning. "Aethirians and their virtue names, am I right? Just call me El. Everyone does."

Drystan took in these two new people who were about to help Verity attempt such an incredible feat. "It's a pleasure to meet you both," he said earnestly. "Have you ever done anything like this before? Either of you?"

Madeline smiled softly at Drystan. "From the medical standpoint, I've performed similar procedures, though nothing so intricate as this. But I have no doubts it can be done."

Drystan nodded solemnly, though when El didn't add anything, Drystan glanced at him.

"Magically, I don't think *anyone's* done anything like this before," he said with a wry grin. "But her theorem's sound. Just because it hasn't been done before doesn't mean it *can't* be. Isn't that right, Verity?"

Verity smiled at El again, though it was more genuine this time.

"Are you ready?" Madeline asked, looking at Verity. "We've got a lot to do, so we should get started."

Verity took a deep, shaking breath. Drystan couldn't imagine how nerve-wracking it must be for her to be so close to accomplishing the thing she'd set out to do months ago.

This thing that no one had ever done before.

She looked at Drystan. No words passed between them. None were needed. She nodded once and stepped forward, crossing toward Madeline. "I'm ready."

CHAPTER 29

DRYSTAN HADN'T REALIZED HOW difficult the waiting part would be. The procedure would take several hours, Madeline had said as she ushered Drystan to a common area just off the building's main foyer. He paced, read, and tried to think about anything other than how slowly time was passing, but nothing eased the uncertainty that tied his stomach in knots.

The sun was beginning to set when Madeline finally emerged. "The first part was successful," she said immediately, prompting a huge sigh of relief from Drystan. "I gave her a number of herbs to keep her sedated and for the pain, but she's starting to wake up. We need to wait until the morning for El to work with her on the magic ritual. I'll do my best to keep her comfortable in the meantime, but she'll need to be more alert so she can assist with the Binding spell. You can come in and see her, if you'd like."

"Yes," Drystan said quickly, jumping to his feet. "Yes, please."

Madeline led him down the hall, back to the room where he'd left Verity so many hours ago. El was already there, the sleeves of his robes rolled up as he worked over a metal basin on one side of the room.

Drystan's throat tightened as he spotted Verity. She was laid out on the bed, a linen sheet pulled up to her chest. Crimson blood stained her pale skin and the edges of the sheet, and bandages were wrapped tightly around her elbow and shoulder. It hurt his heart to see her bandaged again after she'd come so far. Yet where once the bandages had ended in nothing, these gave way to shining steel in curved, overlapping plates that formed arms, hands, and fingers.

Blood seeped through the linen bandages. Verity's face was pale, and sweat coated her forehead, matting down her hair. Drystan crossed to her, smoothing some of her hair out of her face.

Her brows knit, her lips twisting in pain. "Drystan?" she whispered. It was a dry, strangled sound, and his heart clenched.

"Yeah, it's me." He tried to sound cheery despite the fear and worry tugging at him, but his voice cracked as he said, "I'm here."

"It hurts."

"I know. I'm sorry." He swallowed around the lump in his throat. "Do you want me to read to you?"

Verity nodded as a tear slipped from beneath her closed eyelids.

Drystan grabbed a stool and pulled his book out of his bag. "I think you'll like this one," he said. "I've read it twice already."

He read to her for hours. Even after she drifted off to sleep, Drystan kept reading. When his knee got too stiff to sit anymore, he stood, pacing slowly while he read. And each time she awoke, and Madeline had to give her an herb to chew on for the pain, he was there.

She'd been alone for so long at the Wardens' camp. He wouldn't let her be alone like that again—not if he had anything to say about it.

"Drystan?" Verity's voice startled him awake. She sounded weak, and he practically jumped off the stool where he'd nodded off some hours ago. The book he'd been reading lay discarded on the floor, a few of the pages bent from the awkward landing.

His neck, back, and leg were all sore in equal measure, but he supposed that's what he got for falling asleep on a damned stool. At least there had been a wall to lean against.

But none of that mattered right now. Verity was awake, and she was looking at him.

"I'm here, Vee," he said, leaning in. "How do you feel?"

Verity's eyes seemed far less clouded than yesterday, though she was still pale, and her lips were drawn tight. "Everything hurts," she groaned.

"I'm sure," he said. He mustered a reassuring smile. "But you're tough. You're going to be alright."

"I know." The corner of her mouth curled just slightly. The small, secret smile that used to only be for him. "This is hardly the worst I've been through."

A laugh escaped Drystan's throat. Shit, she was tough. "That's fair." His eyes were stinging, and he wiped at them quickly with the heel of his hand.

"Are you ready for the Binding ritual?" El called as he entered the room. His demeanor was much more subdued—almost reverent. Madeline was right behind him, a bundle of fresh linens in her arms.

Drystan stepped back to give her space to work. "Can't we give her some more time?" he asked. "She's in a lot of pain."

"We need her mind clear for the ritual," El said, his voice somber. "Anything Maddie gives her for the pain will numb her faculties. The sooner we get this done, the sooner she can rest and get some relief."

Drystan sighed, his eyes darting to Verity.

"It's alright," she said, her jaw set. "I'm ready."

"The ritual," Drystan said, turning back to El. "Is it going to hurt her?"

"It shouldn't. There are no nerve connections in the arms. Only pressure plates."

"Pressure plates?"

"They'll help her with spatial awareness, and regulating how much force to use when picking up objects and the like."

"Drystan?" Verity pulled his attention before he could ask anything more. "Do you want to stay?"

He did, but he couldn't help but feel like he was asking too many questions. Was he being too protective of her? He didn't want to overstep his place. This was hers—she'd been working toward it for so long. He hated the thought of ruining it for her with his worry.

"Would you want me to?" he asked.

"You seem uncomfortable . . ."

"No," he said quickly. "It's not that. I . . ." How did he put into words that he wanted to support her, but didn't want to be a bother? He'd always been so good at talking to people back home. Why did he feel at a loss for words now?

Because back home, everything he'd ever spoken had been lies. Outright lies or lies built from truths. Whether he was lying to others or, as it had been with Genevieve and Addie, lying to himself, they were lies all the same. Sometimes hastily cobbled, sometimes beautifully crafted. But they were lies.

All damned lies.

Looking at Verity, something solidified in his chest. A resolve. He couldn't move away from his past—from all the lies and the history in which he did nothing but hurt people—if he kept hiding from the truth. So he leveled his gaze at her, making sure to meet her eyes so she could see the truth in his as he said, "It's your decision, but if you want me here, I would love to stay. I want to be here for you through"—*everything*—"all this."

Baby steps.

Verity smiled again. "Stay with me, Drystan," she said. "Please."

Of course he would stay. He would stay for as long as she'd have him.

He pulled the stool a little closer to her bed and sat. El and Verity briefly reviewed what each of them would need to do during the ritual—apparently it was too big a job for just one mage, and they needed to work in tandem to have a chance at making it work. Drystan couldn't follow everything they were saying, but he understood enough to know that if they couldn't make it work now, they'd have to wait at least a day to try again.

"Are you ready?" El asked.

Verity drew a steadying breath and nodded.

Then she closed her eyes, her breathing slowing further. After a moment, she began to recite words in a language Drystan couldn't understand.

El pulled a chair to the other side of Verity's bed and did the same, though his words were different, but no more comprehensible than Verity's.

Drystan wasn't sure how long it would take, or what to expect at all. But he wanted to be here for her.

He was sitting on Verity's left, the steel arm stretching all the way to her shoulder. Slowly, carefully, he slipped his hand into her metal one, clasping it firmly.

Verity and El continued their recitations. Minutes went by. By the time it had been nearly a quarter of an hour, Drystan risked a glance at Madeline. She'd been busying herself with other tasks—quietly folding some linens and the like—but soon she moved closer to El, watching the ritual in silence, as Drystan was.

Another several minutes passed until their words abruptly stopped, both at the same time. Verity's eyes snapped open as she looked to Drystan. Tears welled in her eyes.

Had it not worked?

Verity stared at him as she began to cry. Before he could say anything or offer any words of comfort, a faint movement caught his attention.

The metal hand—*her* hand—shifted just slightly in his grip. He squeezed on instinct, and a sob tore from Verity as she closed her eyes again.

"I can feel it," she choked out. The metal fingers flexed against his hand. "I can feel it."

Drystan's own vision blurred as he set his other hand on top of hers. "You did it, Vee." He looked to El, but he was slumped in his chair. Madeline held on to his shoulders to keep him steady. She didn't look concerned, but . . .

"Are you alright?" Drystan asked.

"He'll be fine," Madeline answered for him as she helped El to his feet. "They used an incredible amount of magic to pull that off. They'll need to rest to recover their energy. Both of them."

Drystan turned back to Verity as her face relaxed. She blinked slowly, almost lazily.

". . . Drystan . . . I can't . . ."

"It's alright," he said. "You did it. Just rest now. I'll be here when you wake up."

Her eyes were already closing. "Promise?"

Drystan squeezed her hand between both of his. "Yeah. I promise."

CHAPTER 30

WHILE DRYSTAN SAT AND waited, Madeline helped El out of the room. She came back periodically to check on Vee.

"She's doing great," Madeline told Drystan after a few hours. "Why don't you go for a walk? Grab something to eat?"

Drystan shook his head. "I promised her I would be here when she woke up."

"But that could be hours yet."

"I don't care," he said. "I promised her."

Madeline smiled a knowing smile as she turned to leave. "Young love is one of the sweetest things there is."

Drystan had plenty of time to turn that thought over in his mind. *Young love.* Cora had suggested something similar, as had Addie.

Was he *in love* with Verity? Did she love him?

It didn't feel like when he'd been with Addie. He didn't want Verity in the same way. He thought she was beautiful and smart and strong, but he'd never thought of being with her the way he was with other women. Whether that lack of desire was because of how much physical pain they'd both been in when they met or for some other reason, Drystan couldn't say, but the thought had simply never occurred to him.

And yet he cared deeply for her, that was certain. The idea of causing her any kind of distress or pain turned his stomach. The thought of being anywhere other than where she was hurt his heart almost as much as the thought of leaving Addie or Genevieve had. It was the same, and yet not at all.

Was that love?

Vee clearly cared about Drystan too, though she'd never seemed to think about him in a physical way either. At least not as far as Drystan had been able to tell, and he'd always been good at reading people. Or at least, he thought he had.

Memories of Genevieve's pitying smile and Addie's gentle rejection quickly absolved him of *that* notion. But regardless, why did Cora, Addie, and now Madeline all think he was in love with Verity?

Whatever this feeling was, it was strong enough to pull him across the continent with her, to have him sleeping on stools and spending days on end by her bedside.

As he tried to put a name to what he felt for Verity, another word struck him. *Sister.*

When they first met Addie, she'd asked if Verity was Drystan's sister, and had suggested the care he showed toward Vee fit within that context. Drystan didn't have a real sister, but he had brothers, and he'd certainly never felt that way with any of them. Then again, he supposed his family was far from a positive example. Or even a typical one.

He thought back to growing up in Alton—to the few friends he'd had as a child. Some of them had had much more normal lives and better—healthier, Drystan was sure—relationships with their families. He'd heard his friends tell their parents or their siblings they loved them. It hadn't meant much to him at the time; he'd thought perhaps it had been something unique to their families. But now . . .

Were there different kinds of love? More than just the desire to share someone's bed? Could he love Verity without ever wanting to sleep with her? Did he love her as one might family—a family he chose for himself, rather than the one he was born into?

Madeline came by every couple hours to check on Verity, and she brought a tray of food for Drystan a few times. Eventually El wandered back into the room, plodding slowly over to Verity's bedside.

He gave Drystan a tired smile. "She hasn't woken yet?"

"Not yet." Drystan took in El's haggard appearance. "How are you feeling?"

El angled his head as though surprised at the question, but he favored Drystan with a smirk. "No need to worry after me, dear. Magic doesn't come for free, but it's nothing another twenty hours of sleep won't fix." His face sobered as he surveyed Verity's sleeping form. "Though I've got to admit, that was one of the crazier things I've ever tried."

"What made you want to do it?"

Silence lingered between them. "I've always liked a challenge," El said at last. "It was an interesting problem. I've known Maddie for years, and when she told me about the letter from Noel . . . the way he'd described her ideas . . . I knew I had to be the one to try."

"Thank you, El. I don't know much about magic, but I know it wouldn't have worked without your help."

A small half smile graced El's lips as he glanced at Drystan. "She did the hard part," he said. "Honestly, you should be really damn proud of her."

"I am." Drystan set his hand on top of Vee's. "I really am."

"I had a dream." Verity's shaky voice cut through the silence of the room.

Drystan startled from where he'd been reading by her bedside. "Vee," he breathed. "You're awake." He didn't care that he was stating the obvious. He was just so grateful to see her open her eyes.

"I dreamt we tried the ritual," she said, her voice a dry rasp. "And it worked."

Drystan couldn't help but smile. "That wasn't a dream."

Verity looked down at her right arm. Her brow furrowed and one of the fingers moved. A startled cry escaped her. "Gods above," she muttered. She raised her hand off the bed, the wrist rotating slightly. Her movements were slow, jerky, but she was *moving*.

"You did it, Vee. How do you feel?"

"Honestly? The connection points hurt like hell." Her words were slow and sluggish.

"Let me call Madeline in. I'm sure she'll want to know you're awake."

"How long was I out?" she asked as Drystan crossed to the door.

"About a day." He stuck his head into the hall and shouted for Madeline.

When he returned to Verity's side, she was crying. Silent tears slid down her temples.

"Vee—" He smoothed her hair back and wiped the tears away with his thumb. "What's wrong?" Was her pain that severe? "Madeline's on her way, just—"

But Verity's small smile halted his words. "You stayed here that whole time?"

He grinned down at her. "Of course. You asked me. I'm here."

❋

Over the next several hours, Madeline busied herself in Verity's room, examining her, giving her some medicine for the pain, and changing the dressing around her elbow and shoulder. Drystan stayed by Vee's bedside, at her request, and so got a look at the *connection points*, as Verity had called them.

On her right side, just below her elbow, shiny steel met her skin, which was red and angry with flecks of blood rising up her arm. On her left side, where there'd been nothing but the flat side of her torso, there was now a metal shoulder. The steel spread partway across her chest, including her collarbone, and almost seemed to meld with her skin. In fact, her flesh, equally raw and aggravated on this side, appeared stretched over the metal plates, like the steel merged into her body.

That had been the idea, he supposed. Listening to Verity explain the theory of it was one thing. But seeing it for real—seeing the way her skin was torn and stitched to accommodate the metal arms—made his stomach turn.

"The grafts are healing nicely," Madeline said to Verity as she wrapped fresh linen around her elbow. "Though it will take some time for the limbs to be fully engrafted. And we'll need to be vigilant for any signs of infection. We couldn't give you time to heal before the Binding ritual, so there is still a chance that your body could reject the prostheses."

"I understand," Verity said, chewing on one of the herbs Madeline had given her.

"And I'm sure you're eager to begin practicing moving your new limbs, but—listen to me, now—it's very important that you take it easy until the connection points have fully engrafted and we see how your body reacts. Understand? If you try to do too much too quickly, you could cause yourself a lot of pain and could do lasting damage. This is new territory for all of us. You need to take it slow."

"I'll be careful," she said. Even through the haze that was settling over her from the herbs, it was clear she wasn't thrilled with the idea.

"It'll take you time to acclimate to moving your arms, especially your hands and fingers," Madeline went on. "It'll likely feel strange at first, and you may have trouble with things like fine motor coordination or regulating your grip strength. I'll let you rest for now, but we'll talk more about this soon, alright?"

Verity nodded, her body beginning to relax. Her sleepy gaze landed on Drystan. "Go," she said softly. "Get some sleep." He opened his mouth to argue, but she pushed on. "I'm fine."

He couldn't deny that lying in a bed sounded much better than dozing on the stool again. And he needed to make sure their room was paid up for the next week.

"El and I will be in and out," Madeline said to Drystan, "and my apprentice will be here in an hour to give me a hand. She won't be alone."

"Alright," he conceded. He squeezed Verity's hand gently. "I'll be back in a few hours."

She smiled, even as her eyes closed. "I'm not going anywhere."

It was weeks before Verity was cleared to leave Madeline's care. She was still learning her way around her new limbs, and her fine motor skills, as Madeline had suggested, were indeed posing a challenge. But Verity was determined to get it, and Drystan had no doubts that she'd succeed.

Verity sat on her bed in their shared inn room, now that she only had to check in with Madeline every few days. She had her hair pulled over her shoulder, and her face was twisted in concentration as she focused on weaving the three strands held between her fingers. The movements were stilted and a little clumsy, and she lost her grip on the segments more than once.

"Dammit," she muttered. "Why can't I get this?"

Drystan set down his book, leaning forward from where he'd been lounging on his own bed. "You'll get there," he said. "It's going to take time."

"Everyone keeps saying that." Vee's hands tightened into fists. "I should be able to do this by now. It's been a month."

"Exactly," Drystan said, earning himself a sharp look from Vee. "It's *only* been a month. It's going to take time to—"

"You have no idea how long it should take," she snapped.

"And neither do you."

She blinked at him, silent.

Drystan rose and moved to sit beside her. "Vee, this is all new. You've never done this before—hells, probably no one's ever done this before. You accomplished something amazing. And I know you must feel like you should be done by now, but I think . . . I think this might be when the real work starts."

Verity blew out a long breath, her shoulders relaxing slightly.

"We should go out to celebrate," Drystan said after a moment. "You've earned at least a little bit of a break!"

Verity's face flushed pink as she glanced down at her arms. "I don't know . . ."

"You deserve to take a moment to breathe. And besides, we've been cooped up inside since we got here. Come on, it'll be fun."

The corner of her lips lifted into that small, half smile. "Alright."

Drystan indicated her hair that still lay unbraided over her shoulder. "Do you want my help?"

Determination settled on her face as she took up the strands of her hair again. "No, I want to try again."

Drystan smiled, nudging her arm with his elbow. "I'll be here if you need me."

CHAPTER 31

DRYSTAN FOUND A NICE, upscale tavern right on the river. A section of the dining area overlooked the water through massive windows along one wall. It was still the dead of winter, but the snow drifting slowly down to disappear against the river's surface added a bit of beauty to the bitterly cold evening.

"What do you think you want to do?" Vee asked as they waited for their meals. She'd succeeded in braiding her hair, and now she fiddled with the end of it as it hung over her shoulder. "Once all this is done, that is."

"What do you mean *once all this is done*?" Drystan took a drink of his beer.

"I mean"—she gave him a wave of her fingers—"the thing we set out to do is nearly done. I don't think it'll be much longer before I can leave Kyleria. What do you want to do after? Where are you planning to go?"

Drystan's chest tightened at the question, at the realization of what she was really saying. Their time together was coming to an end. She'd been needing his help less and less, but soon she wouldn't need him for anything. His daydreams of adventure notwithstanding, he hadn't really considered what he would do once he was on his own again.

"Are you so ready to be rid of me?" he asked, masking his unease with a lighthearted question.

"Definitely not." Her face was more serious than Drystan had expected. "I was actually hoping our paths might continue to align."

"I'd like that," he said softly. "Troubles aside, I've enjoyed traveling with you, Vee."

She looked up at the nickname he'd given her, a smile on her lips. "Me too." Her eyes darted down to the table as she said, "Have you ever given any thought to joining the Wardens?"

Drystan nearly choked on his beer. "The Wardens?"

"As I understand it, they often take recruits from people who they've helped," Verity went on. "It wouldn't be that unusual."

While he'd dreamt about it more than once, imagining the adventures he might have, that's all they were—dreams. Could he imagine actually joining? Swearing their oath? Taking orders? He wanted to toss out another easy evasion, but he'd also told himself he wanted to be more honest with Verity.

His voice tightened a little as he said, "I've thought about it. Why?"

Vee shrugged one shoulder, leaving the metal one still. "I'd just been thinking, you've been so good at helping me. And you really care about others. I could picture you being a pretty incredible Warden."

Drystan's heart squeezed. She really thought so highly of him?

Cora's words the day they left the camp in Weryn echoed in his mind. *I still think you'd make a hell of a Warden.*

It was a nice thought, but it wasn't possible.

. . . Was it?

No, people like him didn't become Wardens. Wardens were protectors, defenders. Heroes.

"They say most Wardens have some kind of life they'd rather leave behind them," Verity continued. "It's a chance to start fresh. To become a version of yourself that you want to be."

If that was true, then could he be a Warden just because he *wanted* to? Just because he wanted to be something other than the brute his father had made him into?

Drystan shook his head, pushing the thought away for now. "What about you?" he asked. "You've done this incredible thing. Something that's never been done. What do you want to do? Are you planning to go back home? Back to your life in Aethir?"

Vee's face fell as she stared down at her new hands. "I don't know if that's really my home anymore. I know my parents only wanted to help me, but they wanted to lock me up, shut me inside the manor and keep me on display like some kind of delicate, broken doll. I don't know if I can go back to that. Broken or not." Her fingers clenched and flexed. "Broken things can still serve their purpose."

The resolve that had solidified within him a month ago resurfaced. Drystan set his hand on the table, palm up. An invitation. "Alright then, so we stick together." He grinned. "A couple of broken things."

She looked up at that, returning his smile, and set her hand in his. The cold metal of her grip tightened around his fingers. "A couple of broken things," she echoed.

"So if you don't want to head back home, what *do* you want to do?"

"It sounds silly." She pulled her hand back, hiding it beneath the edge of the table as her chin dipped. "I don't think I'm strong enough."

"You're stronger than you realize," Drystan said without thinking.

"I-I don't even know if I could do it." She breathed deep, steeling herself. "I . . . I thought maybe I could . . ."

Drystan sat up straighter, the realization hitting him all at once. "You want to join the Wardens."

Her face flushed. "It's stupid," she muttered.

"It's not," Drystan breathed.

She searched his eyes. "You really think I could?"

"Vee, I don't have a single doubt that you can do *literally* anything you decide to." As Vee's gaze drifted down to her hands, Drystan added, "You'll get there. I believe in you."

Their food arrived and the two of them ate for a while in silence. Drystan kept an eye on the room, as he often had a habit of doing. Patrons at more than one table were glancing their way, whispered words passing among them. The longer they sat, the more blatant the looks grew, and the more agitated the whispers became. Even their server looked more annoyed each time Verity struggled to do something with her new metal hands. Drystan caught an eye roll from him as he walked away after refilling their drinks.

Verity didn't seem to notice. She was focused on closing her fingers around her cup. She must have misjudged the strength needed to hold it, because the clay mug shattered in her hand, sending her drink splattering everywhere, including on the man who'd been walking by their table.

He stopped dead and turned toward Verity, his face scarlet. "What in the fucking hells, girl?!" he bellowed. All conversation stopped as every person there turned to stare.

"It was an accident," Verity snapped, clearly as annoyed with herself as the man was with her.

The man angled his head toward Drystan. "Maybe keep your pet freak at home next time, eh?"

"What did you say?" Verity demanded.

But Drystan was already on his feet. "I suggest you go back to your table, friend," he said between clenched teeth.

The man, who was as tall as Drystan and wider across, stepped closer. "Not my fault she's not housebroken," he sneered.

Vee was on her feet now. "You have no right to talk to me like that!"

The man wheeled on her, practically towering over her. "I wasn't talking to you, freak." He shoved her. Verity stumbled backward into her chair and toppled over, a startled cry escaping her as she fell.

The man laughed, though it was cut short as Drystan's left hook connected with the man's jaw. A familiar but long-absent sting flared in his knuckles.

The man fell back against another table, spilling meals and drinks onto the floor. That got them on their feet, and the man's friends seemed to want in on it too. Several more men closed in.

"Drystan!" Verity called as she pulled herself to her feet. "Let's just go."

"Yeah," one of the man's friends said. "Listen to your pet and run along home."

Drystan crossed to him in two quick strides and sent a punch square into his gut. The man clearly hadn't been expecting such a swift attack and doubled over. Drystan brought his knee up into the man's nose. Blood sprayed as he staggered back, clutching his face.

Drystan thought he heard Verity calling his name, but he wasn't sure. He was lost in the fight, lost in every time he'd beaten someone to within an inch of their life, every time he'd split his knuckles open on someone's face.

The adrenaline rushed through him, pushing him forward even as a punch to the ribs caught him from behind. Drystan spun and grabbed the person responsible, pulling them down until his arm was wrapped around their neck. Drystan had a clear shot to their kidneys, throwing a few punches while also using their body as a shield from the others.

"Drystan!"

He turned to make sure Verity was alright, and the man who'd started every-thing got a lucky shot in, catching Drystan in the temple. Drystan spun as his vision grayed out, but he caught himself on the table before he fell. Though that put him directly in front of Verity as everything came back into focus.

Vee.

Her eyes were round, and she looked as though she was holding back tears. "Drystan, *please*," she begged.

Gods, she looked terrified. That brought him back to his senses. He never wanted her to be scared—least of all of him. Shit, what had he done? He was nothing more than an animal.

His father's attack dog.

Drystan gripped the empty table and slid it across the floor toward his remain-ing attackers. It wouldn't stop them, but it would give Drystan and Vee a chance to get through the front door.

"Come on!" Drystan grabbed her hand. "Run!"

They ran a few blocks before Drystan had them circle around toward the inn where they'd been staying. Verity was panting hard as Drystan pulled her along, but he didn't dare slow down, and he didn't let go of her hand until they were safely inside their room.

When he finally released her, Verity doubled over, trying to catch her breath.

Drystan's skin felt too hot, and his muscles buzzed. He shook his hands out. "I'm sorry, Vee." There was a tremor in his voice. "I-I didn't mean for any of that to happen."

"I know," she said, though she was clearly still holding back tears. "It's not your fault."

Drystan paced the room for a moment. But it was his fault. Not that asshole's comments of course, but everything else. Drystan was the one to drag Verity out in the first place. And he certainly hadn't done anything to deescalate the situation.

The room was stifling. The unspent adrenaline from the fight still surged through every part of him. He needed to move.

"Where are you going?" Vee asked as he charged toward the door.

"I don't know," he snapped.

"When will you be back?"

Drystan's fist struck the wall by the door. "I don't *know*, Verity!"

She was silent as he stormed into the hall and slammed the door.

Chapter 32

Drystan loitered by the bar just long enough to swipe a bottle of whiskey when the barkeep wasn't looking, then he ducked out into the cold. Wind whipped through the city from the Moontide Sea, its chill biting Drystan's skin. He wished, briefly, that he had his coat, but they'd left dinner in such a rush that he hadn't grabbed it—nor Verity's cloak—on the way out.

That was fine. He popped the cork on the bottle and took a long swallow. The whiskey would soon warm him.

He didn't know where he was going, and he honestly didn't care. He wanted only to outrun the voice inside his head—his father's voice—that told him he was only good for hurting people, for causing pain. That was his *talent*, after all.

Even Verity, who he'd grown to trust and who had somehow come to trust him in return, had stared at him in wide-eyed horror. She'd never seen that side of Drystan before. She'd never seen the people he'd beaten to get the coin they owed his father, or the ones he'd sniped from a rooftop because his father had said there couldn't be any witnesses.

What if Verity decided she couldn't trust him after this? Could he blame her if she did?

Drystan had thought—he'd *hoped*—that things had changed. That *he'd* changed. But he hadn't. Not a bit. If all it took to send his fists flying was an altercation at a tavern, then he wasn't a hero. He wasn't a Warden. He was just the same brute he'd always been, no good for anything but hurting people.

An attack dog doesn't stop being an attack dog just because you dress it up.

He wandered the darkened, snowy streets for a while, putting a significant dent in the whiskey. His aimless walking soon brought him to a gambling den, and the reckless anonymity he knew would be inside beckoned him. In there, he could forget about anything.

Drystan tried to shove everything out of his mind. Vire's hells, he tried. He gambled, he drank, he paid a woman for her company. But after a few hours, the money he'd had in his pocket was gone, and godsdammit, none of it had done a thing to dull the ache in his chest. So back into the streets he went, wandering through the night until he came to a bridge at the edge of the city that crossed the Kylerian River.

He stood on the bridge, leaning his elbows against the cold, rough stone, the bottle of liquor still hanging from his fingers. The cuts on his knuckles had started to scab over, though they would split in the cold if he clenched his fists too hard.

He balled his hand into a fist and the scabs broke open. Far beneath the bridge, the river rushed by, all whitecaps and foam.

Nothing had changed. Not really. He was still the same as he'd been back home. He couldn't run from it, no matter how hard he tried to fool himself. It was all there was to him.

All there ever would be.

Drystan took another swig from the bottle, the liquor burning all the way down. Everything he'd been doing—all this running across the damn continent with Verity—was for what? What was he trying to accomplish? Had he wanted to help her? Keep her safe? Or did he think that if he helped her, it would prove something? That if he played the part of the Warden, it might actually be true?

Drystan scoffed into the bottle as he brought it to his lips again. What a joke.

That's not how the stories went. The villain didn't get the girl. The villain didn't get a second chance. And that's all he was—the villain in some hero's story.

Even that was reaching. He was a henchman at best; some nameless thug slain by the hero with less than a sentence devoted to his death. Nothing special. Nothing to lose.

Drystan glanced at the bottle between his fingers. It was nearly empty. He drained what was left of it before hurling it over the side of the bridge. It shattered against the rocks below before being swept away by the current.

How simple it was for nature to erase problems. Mistakes. A short fall into the freezing, churning water, and that was it. Where something had once existed, there wasn't even a trace of it left. There and gone in an instant.

Nothing special.

His fingers tightened around the edge of the stone.

Nothing to lose.

"Drystan?"

He turned as Verity approached, her boots crunching in the snow along the bridge. The world tipped and swayed as he moved, so he left a hand on the stone rail to steady himself. "What are you doing out here?" he asked, his words running together.

"Looking for you." Verity's brow furrowed. "What are you doing?"

He glanced over the side of the bridge again, down to where there was no sign at all of the bottle he'd thrown. "Just thinking," he said.

Verity followed his gaze. She frowned. "It's freezing out here. Come back to the inn."

"The girl from the mountains is cold?" He let out a wry laugh. "That's new."

"I'm cold because I'm not dressed for it," she said sharply, "and neither are you."

Drystan still watched the rushing water below. "What does it matter?" he muttered.

"It matters." Verity's voice was firm as she leaned against the side of the bridge, her metal elbow clunking softly against the stone. "It matters to me."

Cold metal against his skin startled him out of his thoughts as Verity took his hand in hers. She tugged him away from the edge of the bridge. "Come back to the inn, Drystan. Please."

He let her pull him off the bridge. As they walked in silence, the ground roiled, making him stumble.

Verity paused, a hand moving to his chest to steady him. "You good?"

"Never better," he mumbled.

"I need you to make it back," she said, moving to keep herself centered in his vision. "I can't carry you, and I can't leave you out here all night. You'll freeze to death."

"I'll make it." But the world refused to hold still, and it wasn't more than a few minutes later that the cobblestones tripped him up again, dropping him to his hands and knees.

Vee grabbed him by the elbow, trying to haul him up. He staggered to his feet, and she ducked her head under his arm, draping it across her shoulders. "Come on," she said. "Let's go home."

Home. The word nestled against his heart and stayed there.

The rest of the walk to the inn was a blur, though Drystan focused on keeping his feet under him. If he went down again, he'd take Verity with him.

And that was something he couldn't ever let happen.

✸

Drystan rolled over and immediately regretted it. Every heartbeat slammed a hammer blow into his head, and sunlight streamed in through the window, slanting its jarringly bright rays across his bed. How had he gotten into bed?

How had he gotten back to the inn?

His mouth tasted like the ass end of a horse. Or, at least, what he imagined the ass end of a horse might taste like. Before he could do much more than slowly push himself onto his elbows, the door to the room opened. Verity stepped inside, a large bowl in her hands. She moved slowly, like she was concentrating very hard on not dropping it. She didn't look up until she managed to set the bowl down on the table.

"Good, you're awake." She took a cloth from the table and dipped it into the bowl before carefully wringing it out. "Were you sick again?"

"Again?" he croaked.

Verity crossed to the bed and gently—but not *too* gently—tossed the damp cloth at his face. The cool water felt amazing, despite the nature in which it reached him. "Yes. It was a long night."

Drystan winced. "I'm sorry." He sat up the rest of the way, holding the cloth in his hands.

She took it from him and set it on the back of his neck. "I don't understand why you did that to yourself."

His face heated. He wanted to hide, but there was nowhere to go in the small room, and he realized, as he shifted uncomfortably beneath the blankets, that he apparently wasn't wearing anything. The warmth in his face spread to his ears.

He didn't know how to answer her. He didn't know how to explain.

Verity sat on the edge of the bed, letting the silence stretch between them. "You asked me last night what it mattered," she said after a long time. She stared at her metal hands. "I didn't have a good answer for you. But not because there isn't one. It was because I couldn't articulate it in the moment."

Drystan rubbed his face, trying to wipe away the haze that still clung to his mind. Lanara's tears, his head was pounding.

"It matters because you're a good person," Verity pushed on. "Whatever happened in your past, the things you've done . . . they're behind you."

"Apparently they're not." Drystan picked at the cuts along his knuckles.

"You did what you had to do."

"Did I? Or was that just the only thing I know how to do?"

Verity considered his question, drawing her lower lip between her teeth before she answered. "It's not the only thing you know how to do. You know how to be kind. You know how to care about other people. You know how to talk so people will listen. But besides all of that, even with the skills that your father taught you . . ."

She hesitated long enough that Drystan looked up at her. He'd nearly forgotten that he'd told her so much about his life, about growing up in the family that he did. That had all been before she started responding to him, when he'd thought she couldn't hear him or couldn't understand.

He'd nearly forgotten that she'd heard it all. Every secret of his heart that he'd been brave enough to admit to himself at the time, he'd shared with her. Verity knew more about him than anyone else on the continent.

"The things he made you learn . . . Those things aren't inherently bad," she continued. "It's what you choose to do with those skills that matters."

It was like what Cora had told him when he hadn't wanted to take the bow. *You can waste your skill to spite your father, or you can use it despite him.*

Could it be that simple?

"But I *chose* to hurt those men last night," he said, the ache in his chest returning full force.

"That wasn't your choice," Verity said.

"Wasn't it? No one forced me to—"

"That's not what I mean," she interrupted. "You made a choice last night, but the choice wasn't to hurt those men. The choice you made was to help me."

Drystan swallowed, trying to ease some of the dryness in his throat. "I don't like hurting people." The words slipped out of his mouth before he had a chance to second-guess the thought. He'd never given voice to it before—never even allowed it to fully form—but it was true. It was the truth of him, at his core. Causing pain nauseated him. It twisted his stomach upside down and left an emptiness in his chest.

He'd tried hard to fill that void, had tried to drown it in ale or bury it in the bodies of women whose names he couldn't remember or had never known. Nothing had worked, and that emptiness had grown until he was certain that was all that was left of him.

Then he'd met Genevieve, and she'd given him something that he hadn't thought was possible.

Hope.

Hope that he was more than emptiness and a thug with a talent for hurting people. Hope that he could escape the life he despised. But his hope had only ended in disaster.

And now, traveling with Verity these past months had done something to fill that void. That glimmer of hope had returned. He hadn't realized it until now, but he'd actually started to believe he could do something—that he *was* doing something—to make the second chance he'd been given worthwhile.

But after last night, had it all been a fever dream? A fool's hope?

"Sometimes," Vee said slowly, "it can't be helped. In my class on military strategy, we learned that sometimes you have to go to war not because you want to hurt people, but because something worse might happen if you don't." She gestured down at her thin, delicate frame. "Not everyone can defend themselves." She swallowed hard, as though pushing down a memory. "But using your strength to help people—to protect people who can't protect themselves . . . Like you did last night . . . Sometimes that's worth it."

Was that possible? Could he use his strength to help those weaker than him? Could that somehow make up for all the harm he'd done? His mind was far too clouded to give the thought the focus it needed. Despite his stabbing headache, he was pretty sure he was still drunk from last night, so he filed it away to mull over later, once he was finally sober and his hangover had abated.

But regardless, he still owed Vee an apology. "I'm sorry I scared you."

"You didn't scare me," she said. "I'm just glad I found you before you did anything too stupid."

His eyes darted to the floor. "I don't mean that. I mean before, when I . . . During the fight. You looked so afraid of me."

"I wasn't scared of you, Drystan." Her voice shook as she said, "I was scared *for* you. I was terrified you were going to get hurt, or—"

When he looked up at her again, her eyes were shut tight.

"You were standing there, surrounded by those men, and I thought . . . It was just like . . . He . . ." Her breathing quickened as a tear slipped from beneath her lashes.

"Your knight," he murmured. Drystan leaned forward and wrapped his arms around Verity in a tight hug, ignoring the pain sharpening in his temples at the movement. He held her close. "Vee, I'm so sorry. I didn't think—"

The cold metal of her arms pressed against his back, and Drystan's shoulders shook with his own tears as Vee hugged him for the first time.

When they finally parted, Drystan wiped his eyes with the back of his hand before brushing Verity's tears from her cheek with his thumb. "I'm sorry," he muttered again. "I'm sorry I'm such a broken mess."

Verity's lips curved as she sniffled. "But we're going to stick together, remember? A couple of broken things."

Drystan couldn't help but smile. "Yeah," he said. "We're in it together. Always."

"Always," she agreed. She studied his face for a moment. It looked like she might start to cry again, but then she blinked rapidly and shoved him in the chest as she stood from the bed. "Get yourself cleaned up," she said. It was stern, but he could still hear the smile in her voice, even as she said, "You reek."

Drystan chuckled, though it did nothing to help his headache, or the nausea that was slowly creeping back in. "That's fair."

Verity threw some clothes at him and gestured toward the large bowl of water she'd brought in before she turned to leave.

"Thanks, Vee," he called as she closed the door behind her.

He hoped she knew how much he was thanking her for.

CHAPTER 33

WINTER IN KYLERIA WAS no joke, but Drystan soon learned that early spring was even worse. Tempests from the north and the warmer weather made for massive storms that surged through, drenching the city and surrounding hills with rain for days at a time. A torrential downpour just two nights previous had caused the Kylerian River to rise nearly to its banks, and yesterday Drystan had joined a group of volunteers stacking sandbags at specific points along the river to stave off any potential flooding.

Lounging on his bed in the rented room he shared with Verity, Drystan looked up from his book as heavy rain battered the window. They'd been in the city for another two months while Verity continued working with Madeline and had begun training with El on . . . something that had to do with magic—Vee had tried to explain it to him, but it went right over his head. Vee was at one of her practice sessions with El now, so at least she should be safely indoors. Hopefully the weather would ease by the time they were done.

Drystan returned to his book, but a few hours later, shouts from outside startled him. He peered out the window. It was hard to see through the sheets of rain, but it looked as though the street below the window was moving.

No, that was water rushing between the buildings, carrying debris and even slowly pushing packing crates with the strength of its current. Across the street from the inn, a small group of people were huddled under the awning of another building, shouting something toward the inn.

Drystan rushed downstairs.

The water surging through the street didn't look deep—maybe only six inches at most, and it hadn't cleared the front porch of the inn yet—but the water roiled and eddied. Waters like that, shallow though they were, would be a powerful force.

Other people had gathered, shouting across the street to those stuck on the other side.

"Just wait it out over there," someone called.

"Are you kidding?" another yelled. "That rickety shack will never hold. Come across before it gets worse. Otherwise, you'll be swept away!"

"Stop!" Drystan shouted, just as one of the men set his foot into the edge of the flood waters. "It's too dangerous—wait a second!" Drystan dashed back inside. "Do you have rope?" he shouted at the innkeeper. He didn't wait for an answer before he ran up the stairs, taking them two at a time, and charged into his room. In the corner where he always left them were the bow and quiver from Cora. He hadn't touched them except to drag them across the continent and back, but he didn't hesitate as he grabbed them both. When he got downstairs, the innkeeper held out a coil of thin rope that looked as though it might serve as a clothesline. Drystan snatched it and hurried outside.

He was too late. As he burst out into the storm, the man who'd been testing the waters had started across the street. The water surged around him, battering his legs as he fought to keep his balance. Drystan rushed to tie the rope to one of his arrows, struggling to find a knot that would hold.

A cry rang out as the man fell onto his back in the water. The current dragged him down the street faster than even Drystan had expected. In moments, he was gone.

The four others on the far side of the road screamed and resumed their shouts for help. Drystan shoved through the crowd on the inn porch. He nocked his arrow and drew back the bowstring. The draw felt wrong—he'd left it strung for too long, but it was all he had. He'd have to make it work. He pulled harder, drawing the string back as far as he could to adjust for the loss of power from the warped bow. The muscles in his back burned as he searched for a target on the opposite building that would hold as long as he needed it to.

"Step back!" he shouted. He crouched, turning the bow sideways, and loosed the arrow. It flew, rope in tow, and embedded itself in the door frame of the other building. He then tied his end of the rope low and tight around one of the porch's support beams. The resulting line stretched across the street at about chest height, given the inn's front steps.

On the other side of the road, one of the trapped people grabbed the rope and waded into the flooded road. The others soon followed, all making their way slowly across, bracing themselves against the rope.

The water was rising steadily, lapping now at the edge of the inn's porch, and many of the other onlookers made their way inside. Drystan stayed, eyes darting between the rope tied on his end, the arrow still holding tight on the far side, and the three people in the middle of the road trying to get to safety.

Three? But no, there'd been four.

Searching the far side of the street, Drystan spotted them. A figure hung back in the doorway, hands braced against the frame, the water swirling around their legs.

Drystan dropped the bow and dashed into the downpour. Even though he gripped the rope, his first step into the water nearly knocked him off his feet. And it was cold. Aetherann's breath, it was freezing.

Drystan passed over the people crossing toward him, his long arms able to reach around them while the broad expanse of his body blocked some of the flood water from pressing into them for a brief moment. His arms were shaking by the time he made it across. A boy, probably a few years younger than Drystan but close to half his size, stood frozen as the water surged higher.

"We need to go!" Drystan shouted over the roar of the rain and the rising river.

The boy shook his head, eyes round. "I can't swim!"

Drystan couldn't tell him that, with water raging like this, swimming was irrelevant. He took the boy by the arm. "I've got you, alright? I won't let you fall."

They started back toward the inn. Drystan went first, lifting one arm so that he could shield the smaller boy from the worst of the flood waters as the boy stepped into the box formed by Drystan's arms. The water had been steadily rising and was up to Drystan's waist. Surges crashed as high as his shoulders.

Drystan didn't know how much longer he could remain standing against the force of the river. He tore his focus away from inching through the rushing water long enough to look up. The inn porch was only a few feet ahead. Two men, one of whom had made the crossing himself, were holding on to the porch railing, arms extended toward Drystan and the boy.

Drystan let go with one hand and shoved the boy toward them. The men grabbed him and hauled him onto the porch, which was already covered with a few inches of water.

The boy turned back to him as Drystan struggled to maintain his footing.

"Get him inside!" Drystan shouted. "Go!"

The boy hesitated, but one of the men took him by the shoulders and waded into the inn. The building was three stories high—it should be safe in there.

The other man stayed on the porch, his hand still stretched toward Drystan. "Come on!"

Drystan's fingers were numb from the cold; the only reason he knew he was still holding on to the rope was the fact that he wasn't being dragged down the street by the river. But the muscles in his arms shook as he tried to pull himself the last few feet. The rope was pressed against his chest, and the water was flowing up and over his shoulders now, pushing him down, trying to carry him away.

A loud *crack* sounded above the roaring river, and the rope shifted like it was trying to shake Drystan loose.

"Hurry!" the man shouted.

Drystan risked a look behind him. The flood waters had shifted the front of the building where his arrow was lodged. If the building came down . . .

Gods above, he didn't want to die.

Drystan dug deep and gripped the rope with every ounce of strength he had. He tried to pull himself the last of the distance to the inn, to the man's outstretched hand, but it was taking everything he had left just to keep the river from washing him away.

As the water began to hit the back of his head, Drystan found that his muscles were *less* strained, less exhausted than they'd been. He pulled against the rope and was amazed he could move the remaining distance. The man grabbed Drystan and hauled him onto the porch. He was out of the current, but as he fell onto his hands and knees, chest heaving with every breath, his face nearly hit the water.

A second set of hands joined the first, and together they lifted him to his feet. "Drystan!"

With another gasping breath, he straightened and found himself staring into Verity's brown eyes. Her metal hands gripped his arm. The man who'd helped him was beside her, as was El.

"Come inside," Vee said, tugging him toward the door. "You need to sit down before my magic wears off."

He followed them into the inn. The whole first floor was covered in frigid water. They hurried toward the stairs, the man heading up first while El and Verity pulled Drystan along behind.

"Magic?" he asked.

"I used magic to increase the amount of force your muscles produced for the energy you expended," she explained. "But your reserves are critically low and it's likely you're about to experience extreme lethargy."

At Drystan's blank stare, El said flatly, "She made it easier for you to move, but it'll wear off soon and you're going to crash from exhaustion."

That he understood.

At the top of the stairs, many of the rooms had their doors open as the patrons and staff gathered in the hallway.

"That's him," someone said. Drystan lifted his head as the boy he'd helped across the flood waters pointed his way. He had a blanket wrapped tight around his shoulders. "He saved my life."

As Drystan took the last step, his knee buckled, dropping him. He tried to catch himself on the wall, but all his limbs felt weighed down with lead and he collapsed onto the landing.

The crowd in the hallway rushed over, and a few of the men hefted Drystan up again.

"This way, please," Verity said quickly as she pointed to their room. The men followed her, half dragging Drystan down the hall.

"Thank you for saving my boy," one of the men said. "I didn't realize he wasn't with us until you went back for him. You saved his life. You saved all our lives."

Drystan tried to tell him that he was glad he could help, but his teeth were chattering so badly he couldn't manage to get the words out.

Verity directed the men to help Drystan to her bed before she ushered them quickly from the room.

El turned to leave with them. "I'm going to make sure this building is structurally sound," he said to Vee. His eyes darted to Drystan as he added, "It'd be a shame to get washed away after the heroics you just pulled."

"Go," Vee said. "I've got him." The door slammed shut as she hurried to Drystan. "We need to get those clothes off you and bring your core temperature back up."

He tried to peel his soaked clothes from his body, but his muscles were stiff, and his hands were shaking. He could barely move, so Verity did most of the work. Then she wrapped him in the blankets from both beds.

She looked down at him, frowning. "I . . . I could use magic to warm you, but . . . I . . ." Her eyes fell to her metal hands, and Drystan knew what horror she must be imagining.

"N-no need," he managed, pulling the blankets in tighter around himself. It already felt a little better, the warmth starting to seep into his muscles. "I'm g-good."

"I don't want to let you die because I'm too scared to use heat magic to help you."

"I'm n-not going to d-die," he said. A small smile tugged on his lips. "B-besides, you're n-not supposed to use m-magical heat to warm someone when their c-core temperature is t-too low. Indirect heat only."

Verity's jaw fell open. "Vire's hells, you're right. Gods, I . . . How did you know that?"

"I d-do read, you kn-know."

"Lie down," Verity instructed, even as she tried to suppress her own grin. "You've shown off enough. I'm going to find you some more blankets. Your lips are blue."

Drystan nodded and lay back, tucking his legs under the blankets as best he could. He wanted to stay awake, but his eyes were closing on their own. He drifted in and out, though the last sensations to reach his awareness were the heavy weight of more blankets covering him, and cold metal smoothing his hair out of his face.

"Rest, Drystan," Vee said.

He was asleep before he could answer.

When Drystan awoke the next day, the sun was already high in the sky. Verity wasn't in the room, so Drystan rose and found some dry clothes. Every muscle in his body ached and his knee was sore, but aside from that and some rope burns on his palms, he seemed no worse for wear.

Downstairs, the inn was a disaster. Dirt and silt, puddles of water, tree branches, and other debris littered the main floor. Several of the inn's patrons were pitching in to clean the place the best they could: one man pushed a heavy broom, shoving some of the residual water back outside; a woman collected some of the sticks and broken pieces of wood and piled them near the darkened hearth; someone else straightened chairs and tables that had been knocked over, wiping the surfaces down with a cloth.

Drystan moved into the room and grabbed another broom that leaned against the far wall. He swept some of the river silt toward the door.

"You don't have to do that!"

Drystan looked up to see the innkeeper headed his way.

"Shouldn't you be resting or something?" he asked Drystan. By now some of the others had paused in their work to look over.

With so many people watching him, his ears grew warm. "I'm alright," he said, shaking out one of his arms. "I'd like to be useful, if I can. Besides, my joints will get stiff if I don't move."

The man nodded, stepping back to allow Drystan to keep working. "In that case, don't let me stop you," he said. "We're just appreciative of everything you did yesterday. Can I get you a drink? On the house, o' course."

Drystan smiled and resumed his work with the broom. "Just some coffee, please."

As the man hurried off, the front door swung open, and Verity barely avoided getting a broom-full of river silt all over her boots.

"Drystan!" she shouted, hardly noticing the dirt. She threw her arms around his neck in a huge hug, and the force of it knocked him back a step. "You'll never guess who's here!"

The question stalled on his lips as the figure of a woman clad in storm gray stepped through the door.

Warden Cora Sylus set her hands on her hips. "Hello, Drystan."

Chapter 34

Coffee in hand, Drystan led Cora and Vee upstairs. The flood waters had receded overnight, Vee explained, leaving behind a hell of a lot of damage to the city. The Wardens were being called in to help people who'd been displaced by the rising waters, as well as repairing some of the structural damage.

"How'd you get here so fast?" Drystan asked. The warm mug between his hands soothed the ache in his fingers, as well as the pain in his palms.

"I happened to be up this way," Cora said. "I was actually supposed to be heading for Embercliff, but when we heard about the storm, I was redirected here."

As Drystan set his mug on the small table, Verity shot him a startled look. "What happened to your hands?" she demanded.

He glanced down at his scraped palms, red and scabbed over. "I think it was from the rope," he said.

"What are you doing pushing a damn broom and leaving that unbandaged? You could've ripped those wounds open again!"

Drystan turned a pleading look at Cora, but so did Vee.

Cora only laughed. "He hasn't changed a bit, has he?" she said to Verity.

Drystan chuckled, taking another sip of coffee as he waited for the accompanying jab from Vee, but instead she regarded him seriously.

"I don't know," she said, her tone softening. "I think he's actually changed quite a bit."

A warmth that had nothing to do with the coffee filled his chest.

The three of them worked through the rest of the day, pitching in on the cleanup efforts wherever they could. By the time the sun was setting, Verity bid them goodnight, opting to turn in early.

Cora gestured to the now-reopened bar. "Join me for a drink?"

Drystan was beyond exhausted, but he didn't want to pass up this opportunity to spend time with Cora, and he didn't think his mind would let him sleep just yet anyway. She ordered a dark beer from the innkeeper while Drystan asked for tea.

"Verity filled me in on a lot of what you two have been up to since you left the camp," she said as she took a seat at a nearby table. "It sounds like you both had a hell of a year."

Drystan sat beside her and sipped his tea, letting it soothe his parched throat. "Yeah," he said. "It was something."

Cora leaned one elbow on the table, studying him. "You've really grown up, Drystan."

His face heated as he rubbed the back of his neck. "I haven't . . ."

"You have. When I met you, you were this sad, scared kid. But I knew you were wasted in Alton. I told you as much, didn't I?" She nudged his arm, smiling for only a moment before her face grew serious again, almost as though a shadow had drifted over it. "I'm glad I was there that day," she said softly. "In Sevrun. I'm glad I got to you before it was too late."

Drystan inhaled a sharp breath. The feeling of the rough noose around his throat wasn't something he thought he'd ever forget. "Thank you," he said, though his voice cracked, "for saving my life that day. For giving me a second chance. I hope . . . I hope one day I can make it worth it."

Cora angled her head. "Worth it?"

"You know. I hope I can make it matter. Make it count for something."

She laughed before taking a swig of her beer. One hand gestured to encompass the inn and everything around them. "All this—not to mention everything you've done for Verity—and you don't think you've made it count for something yet?"

Drystan took a long, slow sip of his tea as he considered his next words carefully. If there was one thing he'd learned about himself, it was that he appreciated having a goal to focus on. More than that, he needed it. The times over the last year that he'd been the most lost were when he'd felt as though he had no purpose, that he was just drifting—cut loose to wander on his own, with nowhere to focus his energy or attention.

After these past months, Drystan finally understood what Addie had been trying to tell him. He loved Verity. She'd become his best friend, his sister, the only person who knew who he was at the deepest, most raw parts of his soul.

And he loved Cora, who'd been the first person to see something in him that was worth taking a chance on. But he needed to take a chance on himself. He needed to learn to see himself the way they saw him.

Addie was right—his worth wasn't tied to who he loved or who loved him. But maybe, if he committed himself to the idea of truly being something other than his father's son—if he took a chance on himself—maybe he could find it.

"Oh, come on!" Cora jostled his arm again. "You can't just sit there in a daydream and not answer me. Do you really think you haven't made your second chance count?"

"Not yet." He could already feel the smile tugging across his lips as he said, "But I have an idea for a way I can try."

Drystan smoothed the fabric of his cloud gray tunic. The darker gray pants he'd been given were a little too short, but you couldn't tell once he got the black, calf-high boots on. He fidgeted with the hem as he studied himself in the long mirror. He wasn't sure he recognized the man standing there: his blond hair shorter now and sticking up a little in the front, apprehension etched into the lines of his face. But there was something else beneath it all. Determination.

As unfamiliar as his reflection was, Drystan had to admit that he liked what he saw.

His heart drummed in his chest, picking up speed with each passing moment. Pyrannis's flames, was he really doing this?

In the two months since the Kylerian River had flooded, Drystan had gone over the idea so many times, he'd worn all the rough edges away. But now that he was *here*, was he ready?

Could he do this?

He wished Verity were here.

A knock on the door startled him. "Come in," he called, tearing himself away from his own reflection.

Cora pushed open the heavy door. "Hey," she called as she stepped into the room. She gave him an appraising look. "Damn, that really suits you, you know that? You ready to go?"

He blew out a shaking breath. "I don't know," he said truthfully. "I don't know if I can do this."

"You *can* do this." She crossed to him in a few quick strides and took both of his hands in hers, squeezing tightly. "Drystan, I knew you could do this when I met you on the road to Alton. The only thing that's changed between then and now is I've gotten to see even more reasons why I was right."

He turned toward the mirror again. She followed his gaze to the two of them standing together in shades of stormy gray.

"I don't know what you see," she said, her voice softening. "But I see a man who wears his heart out in the open for all to see. Who's seen what cruelty can do and is brave enough to choose to be kind instead. Who's brave enough to choose his own path."

Drystan breathed deep.

"What are you thinking about right now?" she asked.

"I'm thinking that before everything went to hell in Sevrun, my mother told me I should try to run away; she told me if I disappeared, she'd know I got out, and she'd be proud of me. I don't think I'd earned it before . . ." The corners of his eyes burned. "But I think maybe now I have."

"You never talked much about her," Cora said, still watching Drystan's reflection. "What's her name?"

"Serah. Serah Kalon."

"I think she'd be damn proud of you, Drystan." Cora wiped hurriedly at her eyes. "I know I am. Now, come on. We shouldn't keep everyone waiting."

The sun shone brilliantly as Drystan walked with Cora across the Wardens' base. The courtyard and training rings scattered across the space were empty, but ahead, dozens of Wardens gathered in a semicircle around a large brazier surrounded by a stone wall about waist high. The orange flames burned and flickered, shining bright even in the morning sun. Several long iron poles stuck out from the base of the fire, their ends glowing orange from where they were nestled among the coals. Cora led Drystan straight past the gathered Wardens, stopping directly in front of the burning brazier.

A man with broad shoulders and short, dark hair was standing near the wall. Beside him was a young woman with deep golden skin and half-moon glasses that perched on the end of her nose. As Drystan approached, they both smiled warmly.

"Good morning, Drystan," the man said. "I'm Joseph Cairn, High Commander of the Wardens of the Flame here in Whitehollow." He gestured to the woman. "And this is our lorekeeper, Ardyn Harrow."

"Nice to meet you both," Drystan said as steadily as he could manage.

The lorekeeper leaned a little closer. "You're going to do great," she whispered. "Just don't forget to breathe, alright? You'd be amazed at how many people forget to breathe."

A nervous chuckle slipped out of Drystan as Cora came to stand on his other side.

As Drystan turned toward the assembled Wardens, sunlight glinted off a pair of metal arms in the front row. Verity was there, beaming up at him.

"Vee," he breathed. "I didn't know you were allowed to be here." He'd been told no one outside the Wardens could attend.

"Are you kidding?" Her smile lit up her whole face. "I wouldn't miss it."

"I pulled a few strings," Cora whispered to Drystan. "Besides, I'm honestly not sure we would have been able to keep her out."

Drystan let out another soft laugh.

"Ready?" Cora asked.

He darted a look from Cora to Verity. His friends were here—his family. Of course he was ready. Drystan faced Cora and nodded.

Cora's voice boomed as she addressed the small crowd. "As you know, new Wardens are allowed to choose the name by which they will be known." She turned to Drystan. "State your name and let all gathered here bear witness."

He swallowed hard. "Drystan Serah."

Cora's lips curved into a smile. "Kneel, Drystan Serah." Her dark eyes were shining as she held her closed fist over her heart.

Drystan knelt and copied her motion.

"Now . . . Repeat after me."

ACKNOWLEDGEMENTS

I will keep this very brief. THANK YOU! Yes, you. If you're reading this, *thank you*.

Thank you for reading Drystan's story. Writing this book has been so different and special, getting it into the world felt both like an imperative and also like the most vulnerable thing I've done. Watching Drystan and Verity's friendship develop soothed something in my heart, and I hope it did the same for you.

Thank you to everyone who's been supporting my writing and publishing journey: my husband, my son, my parents, my best friend, my editor, my beta readers, my ARC readers, my street team, the people who scream at me in the most loving way on Instagram, and the people who cheer me on quietly from the sidelines. Thank you.

About the Author

Lindsey Brounstein worked in the publishing industry for fifteen years and now spends her days as a freelance editor and author in New Hampshire. For as long as she can remember, Lindsey has had a crazy cast of characters kicking around inside her head. Sometimes, she likes to put two of them in the same room to see what happens. When Lindsey's not writing, she loves immersing herself in both board and video games, knitting and — of course — reading.

You can follow Lindsey on Instagram or Threads as @writerlindsey or you can email her at lins@lindseybrounstein.com. You can also sign up for her newsletter at www.lindseybrounstein.com.

THANK YOU FOR READING

Thank you for reading *Broken Things*.
If you enjoyed it, please consider leaving a review. Your ratings and comments help indie authors like me reach wider audiences, and they help other readers find books they might love.
Scan the QR code below to connect to various reviewing platforms.